THE DOCTRINES OF FIRE

ALSO BY CL JARVIS

The Edinburgh Doctrines series
The Doctrines of Fire
A Treatise of Air

THE DOCTRINES OF FIRE

THE EDINBURGH DOCTRINES SERIES
BOOK ONE

CL JARVIS

PEWTER LYNX PRESS

First published in 2023 by Pewter Lynx Press

ISBN 978-1-7392644-0-6

For everyone who tried again.

I

9 NOVEMBER 1779

Professor Joseph Black considered himself thirteen years too old for sneaking around cellars investigating rumours of slain medical students.

"Did you check under that chair, Joe?"

Yet here he was. Black sighed. "Not yet."

His companion and fellow faculty member, William Cullen, paused his rummaging through a cobweb-choked dispensary cabinet. The meagre light from scrounged together candle stubs made it impossible to read his expression.

"Did you hear something?" Black asked. Cullen had the advantage of better hearing; Black had better eyesight. Not that either counted for much at their age.

Amused, Cullen shook his head. "I told you, no one's summoning the Town Guard in response to our presence." He patted his coat pocket, which gave a satisfying *clink*. "And if they do, it's a quick misunderstanding to rectify."

Black couldn't argue with that. The Edinburgh Town Guard weren't known for their zeal apprehending criminals, excluding those misfortunate enough to murder a man outside the Guardhouse the day they left their purse at home.

The two professors had simply stridden into the College of Surgeons and descended into the cellars, talking softly as if preoccupied with cerebral affairs. No one questioned their business, and it was unlikely anyone could overhear them through these thick walls.

"See if there's any traces of blood on that dissecting table, Joe. Fresh blood, I mean."

"I already inspected that table. It's impossible to tell." The air here was stale and thick with mildew. While there were signs this storage space was recently occupied—the presence of fresh candles and an order to the row of lidless leech jars— unless a large group of individuals came in regularly, it would be impossible for their activities to replace the scent of disuse. They would need to spill a lot of bodily fluids.

"Well, perhaps one of them dropped written notes?"

That seemed improbable.

"How much do you know about the victim this time, William?" Cullen had hurried him from the college grounds ten minutes ago, his whispers struggling to keep pace. Before that, Black was ignorant of anything amiss.

"Next to nothing, Joe. Ha! I learned the boy was dead only an hour before you did. Questioned a few students on my way to you, but no one knew who attended to him in the Infirmary yesterday, and I'm stuck visiting patients across town all afternoon. Since my next visit is just along Nicolson Street and she's recuperating well, I thought we'd use what little time I had to search the suspects' domain before your morning class began. Before they return and remove all evidence." Cullen cocked his head, listening for unwelcome footsteps in the corridor.

If someone from the College of Surgeons did deign to enquire what the venerable professors were doing down here it would—as usual—fall to Black to come up with a convincing explanation. If the individuals responsible for the dead student returned and found the duo poking around in their secret quarters...

Well, he hadn't thought that far ahead.

Black rubbed his lower back. "I doubt we'll find proof they conducted any procedure here." Was it a medical procedure? Or was "ritual" a more apt descriptor? He'd heard enough of Cullen's theorising on the distinction these past months, but nothing in this cramped space brought clarity. If the student died because of what happened to him here yesterday—still conjecture on Cullen's part—those responsible would have scrubbed the place clean before their victim reached the Infirmary.

Right now, they were clutching a handful of truths and rumours.

"Once my ten o'clock lecture is over, I'm engaged most of the afternoon too," Black admitted. There was a row of brown glass bottles on the shelving in the corner. He shook them in turn. All empty. This was useless. "How sure are you of the culprit, William? There's been a nasty fever spreading through town these past weeks."

"Oh, it *has* to be him and his associates. The student in question was sympathetic to his views."

Black preferred simple solutions to problems. There was an elegance in simplicity. One or two students always fell to fever in the winter months: the consequence of dwelling in a crowded city. Of course, Cullen tended towards the classical in his outlook. That's why he favoured ornate solutions.

"I don't dispute your rationale for searching the Surgeons' buildings," Black began, "since we know the suspects congregate on the premises, but uncovering a half-empty poison bottle won't help us. The intent behind the deaths is no clearer than it was in August, and the other faculty aren't going to believe us unless we can convince them these deaths were deliberate."

"Any fool can see they're deliberate," Cullen said, almost knocking over a candle as he raised his hand. "The faculty are choosing wilful blindness."

"Well, if we prove intent and a compelling motivation, they'll find your suspicions harder to dispute." Black realised he should have said "our suspicions", but Cullen didn't seem to notice so he ploughed on. "Right now we're chasing day-old echoes. Our best hope is to get wind of the next casualty before it becomes a fatality. Catch the culprits before they destroy the ephemera."

It wasn't that Black disbelieved his colleague: it was more that he possessed an absence of fixed belief on the matter. But he didn't like seeing Cullen this agitated.

Cullen took a step closer. "You really want to bring the students into this, Joe? That's what you're suggesting, isn't it? No professor will cooperate with us; neither of us has the time to maintain the necessary levels of vigilance."

"We might not need more than one student," Black mused. His colleague's posture indicated the inspection was abandoned. Just as well—he'd finish prepping that jug of aqua regia before class began. "One student we can put the time in to train might be more useful than a squabbling crowd of them anyway."

"I barely have the time to hunt and train students either. But yes, securing a good one could be worth the effort..."

2

"Stephens—for God's sake, make the fire more lively."

Hiding his displeasure at being ordered about by someone younger than him, George Stephens slipped off the sofa and crouched by the parlour fireplace, flicking his coat out from under his feet and moving a cracked oil lamp to one side. He jabbed the fire—more ashy smoulder than blaze—with a crooked poker. With the venerable professors almost at the door, preparing the parlour fell on the lodger easiest to order around.

Behind him, the remaining student lodgers filed into the room. It seemed he wouldn't have a choice about being present at this social call. He'd first worried it'd be presumptuous to stay when the professors—who were, strictly speaking, calling upon fellow lodger Edward—arrived, since Edward was months away from completing his medical dissertation and had known the two men for years, and George didn't know them at all. Then he worried that retiring to his room or contriving an errand would be a greater snub to such eminent guests.

"You said Doctors Cullen and Black were almost here?" he

asked Edward, prodding the fire. The flames edged higher, and George was rewarded with their warm touch on his cheek and brow.

He wanted to tell Edward that if he was so concerned with the state of the hearth he should administer to it himself. He'd seen Edward take such remarks from his friends in stride, but would George come across as rude?

"They're waylaid four doors down," Edward said. "A group of bairns were playing with too much spirit on the street corner: Dr Cullen's admonishing them for their carelessness." He shrugged, smoothing his curly brown hair. "At least there's now a warm room waiting for them."

It would have been nice to know I had several minutes' leeway before I rushed to fix the hearth, George thought. Shame Edward didn't view such helpful information as necessary for him to complete the task.

There was a time, strictly speaking only a few months prior, but it belonged to an age of innocence, when George believed his military experience would garnish cachet with other Edinburgh medical students. Instead, he was greeted by awkward silences when the students he spoke to realised he never held officer status. After learning that, most deposited him in the same category as "manservant" or "costermonger".

The lodgings owner shuffled into the parlour. She was a small, white-haired woman who subsisted, as most Edinburgh landladies did, on overcooked vegetables and other people's private business. George was surprised at the liveliness in her posture, like a blackbird hopping along the ground.

"The tea is ready for the gentlemen when they arrive," she told Edward eagerly. George hadn't expected her to care about the visiting professors.

A knock at the front door, though genteel, carried over the now-crackling hearth.

The parlour door opened to reveal the two men, garbed in

traditional physician black. A rush of wind from the street sent flames jumping into the chimney.

William Cullen, professor of the practice of physic, who strode in with a welcoming beam, was the older and stockier of the two, with a genial, expressive countenance. He wore an oversized horsehair wig in a style several decades out of fashion. Cullen's greetings towards those he knew seemed derived from genuine delight and affection the recipient could not help but match.

Following just a step behind, like a cool draught on a humid summer afternoon, was Joseph Black, professor of chemistry. Where Cullen was stocky and lively, Black was tall, thin and graceful. Where Cullen's complexion was hearty, Black's was pale as milk. Although delicate, he looked younger than his fifty years, powdering his mostly brown hair in a more modern, understated style. Black's eyes moved with simple economy of movement around the room as he greeted those he recognised with a short but respectful nod. Despite his unnatural stillness and quiet, George found himself glancing at Black time and time again. What was he thinking? Was he displeased or indifferent by the company?

Cups of piping-hot tea were passed around, and the lodgers settled into an awkward circle as the visiting professors —now seated—moved through the appropriate social motions.

This stilted scene reminded George of the feral puppies he encountered as a child at his aunt's farmhouse. A stray bitch that roamed the nearby woodland gave birth to a litter one summer, hidden away from humans in a makeshift den. When the puppies were older, George and his cousins tracked them down, bringing scraps of cold meats to the den every evening. The puppies flinched and cowered with every movement the boys made, backing two steps into the undergrowth, then edging forward towards the scraps tossed their way, bobbing their heads as far away from their tensed bodies as possible. The puppies were simultaneously enthralled and terrified by George and his cousins, and the nervous energy of the medical students in the presence of their professors reminded him of them.

Not that I'm any braver than the other students, he thought ruefully. He'd been in Edinburgh scarcely a few weeks, and this was the first time encountering Cullen and Black outside the college grounds. He'd had about as much exposure to medical faculty before now as those feral puppies had to humans. He turned his head away to recompose his expression.

"Your background is very interesting, Mr Stephens."

The voice made George start, for it sounded like someone had spoken into his ear. He turned. From his seated position several metres away, Black watched him with a look of mild amusement. The kindling let out a few satisfied crackles.

"It occurred to me that your background is very interesting, Mr Stephens," Black repeated, leaning forward with what George believed a genuine smile. "Your military conduct in New York was superb, so my sources tell me. I hear you are already adept in many fields of learning, and a keen study." Without strain, his low voice carried across the room. Black spoke in a melodious tone, with an accent that shifted as the listener concentrated: the product of a youth transposed between France, Ireland and Scotland.

"Thank you, sir," George responded. This sudden attention was daunting, but he knew he should keep the conversation going, though he worried any remark he made would sound foolish. Wetting his lips, George ventured, "I understand Mr Pearson was a former student of yours?"

Black nodded.

"The very same. A delightful correspondent; he speaks highly of you."

"Neil's still an army surgeon?" Cullen asked. "When I spoke to him several years ago, he wanted to set up a school in London."

George was sure Cullen had directed the question at Black, but Black held George in his gaze. A slight nod gave George permission to answer.

"I got the impression Mr Pearson likes army life more than he expected," George hazarded. He could have added that Mr Pearson was often disparaging of the medical school community and what he called its insular, conservative nature—but that seemed improper to mention in polite conversation. It was why Pearson never studied beyond the minimum necessary to qualify as a surgeon.

Another nod from Black as George struggled to add something intelligent to his reply. "That is the sentiment I gathered from reading his letters."

Cullen made complimentary remarks about Mr Pearson before moving the conversation back across the room. The lodgers were relaxing, curiosity triumphing over caution. George leant back in his chair and let others carry the discourse. A short but positive interaction with two giants of medical science wasn't a bad start, and he dared not contribute more, for fear of ruining his success. Black didn't say much else, though George noticed that when the other lodgers turned their heads away he would sometimes study them with a thoughtful expression.

A few tolerable hours passed, and the professors readied to leave. George rose to bid them farewell. As Black stood in the doorway George noticed he'd left his walking cane leaning against the chair, so he picked it up and handed it over. As he did so he was momentarily confused—Black's slender cane was heavier than it looked.

"I'm glad to meet you, Mr Stephens," Cullen said,

grasping his hand. "I'm excited to see where your medical studies take you—your abilities are certainly promising."

"Indeed, sir." George cursed himself for agreeing so readily with this assessment. "I know Mr Pearson finds great fulfilment in his work. I owe much credit to him for setting me on this path, but I suspect my medical studies won't take me back to the battlefields."

"No," said Black, with more of a smile than George had seen all afternoon. "I don't imagine they will."

* * *

The encounter weighed on George's mind in the days that followed. As he went to lectures and ran errands around the town, he spotted Black and Cullen from afar on several occasions. Sometimes together, sometimes drawn in carriages alone. He never got close enough for a greeting or acknowledgement, though he suspected both men recognised him as surely as he did them.

Black's remarks were the first time anyone in the medical school had said something complimentary about his background.

George remembered the reverence for former soldiers gathered in the dusty taverns around his hamlet, how willing the other tavern-dwellers were to listen to their exploits and saucy tales. He wasn't proud to admit it, but sometimes as he lay awake in his tent he wished he'd depart New York with a gruesome injury, because those ex-soldiers commanded the most attention.

As it transpired, he came home intact, but his interest in martial glory was severed. The British Army was subject to the same incompetent leadership that dogged every honourable profession, and George resented the snakes among his ranks who ingratiated themselves to gain promotion.

Neil Pearson had sensed George's disillusion with the army and urged him to consider a medical education whenever George took to loitering around the field hospital.

"You have the head of a physician," he told George. "I can recommend you to the faculty at Edinburgh."

George had no reason to doubt the advice of the army surgeon he so admired.

* * *

A rude banging at his door disrupted George's belated attempt at composing a letter home.

"Yes?" George asked, feigning politeness.

His fellow lodger James shoved the door open. Noticing the boy's sour expression, George prepared himself for an argument. James was several years younger than him, with hair that couldn't be bothered deciding if it was blond or brown and a childlike dearth of lived experience. He was the type of wealthy boy who could afford to be coddled by his parents, and for whom life as a medical student in Edinburgh would be his first time navigating the world alone. When animated, he brought George to mind of a screaming American possum.

Mrs Collins' lodgings was the third boarding-house James had occupied this term. According to him, the first place was "too dirty"; the second landlady made what he considered unreasonable demands regarding use of her kitchen; and here James had already quarrelled with George and other lodgers over the kind of minor, almost non-existent slights he was yet to realise were a fact of life.

"A messenger delivered these for you, from Dr Cullen."

So the handful of books James clutched were for him. George moved to stand, but James dropped the books on his bed and slammed the door shut. A folded note slid off the stack. James hadn't appeared too curious about the delivery, but George knew he'd probably inspected the contents as thoroughly as he could while ascending the stairs and deemed them of no interest.

George unfolded the note.

Drs Black and Cullen humbly request Mr George Stephens' company for dinner tomorrow night at Dr Black's, 5 o'clock. Have you the time, you may find the following reading useful. Respectfully, your humble and obedient servant, WC.

Turning his attention to the books, George saw they included translations of scientific treatises by Georg Ernst Stahl and Cullen's own work, *First Lines of the Practice of Physic*.

An invitation to dinner wasn't unusual in itself. The medical faculty hosted many students, even those not yet enrolled in their classes. George wasn't even the first of his cohort to receive such an invitation. However, although these evenings often turned to discussions of medical and educational matters, George wasn't aware of any friends receiving reading material in advance of a dinner.

Instead of soaring with triumph, George was crushed under anxiety. No one noticed if he was lost in class: at the professor's dinner table no one could miss it. Reluctantly, he pushed his incomplete letter aside.

The hours ticked towards evening, but first came George's college classes. Dr Alexander Monro's anatomy theatre was located down a winding staircase in the college basement. Thin windows near the ceiling were so meagre with illumination that Monro usually boarded them up and resorted to candles.

As George entered, Monro was in the centre of the room, bent over the dissecting table. A body lay concealed under a black sheet, though in the dim lights its outline didn't bear much resemblance to a human. Spreading out from the central table were circular platforms for students to stand on and peer over the dissecting table, and raised tiered seating at the back of the room for everyone else. Beeswax candles were set around the table and along the first row of seating.

George was often the first student to arrive to Monro's one o'clock lectures, given most students came direct from clinical rounds at the Infirmary. Seating in the old anatomy theatre was a careful art: sit on a high row at the back and you may experience a blessed breeze through the boarded window, carrying away the stench of decomposing matter. Sit or stand nearer the front and you'd have enough light to see what was going on.

The dais creaked as he crossed it. Monro looked up. He was the kind of oversized, naturally humourless figure who always performed a poor impression of joviality, as if unsure what true happiness looked like. "Ah, it's Mr Stevenson, isn't it?"

"Stephens, but yes, sir."

"Of course! Forgive me, Mr Stephens. I'm terrible with names."

This was after multiple conversations at the start of term, and Dr Monro agreeing to waive George's course fee on account of his reduced means.

From this angle, George saw Monro was preparing a pig's body for dissection. He could hear a knife snipping through gristle.

"There's talk of that murderer from Prestonpans hanging soon, but no definitive date as far as I can tell. Anyway, this early in the term we'd be wasting the body on students still in the habit of vomiting and swooning when they see a corpse. A pig or dog illustrates the anatomical principles well enough for now." Monro eyed George, his fleshy face concealed in shadow. "I imagine with your military adventures we won't have to worry about you taking ill?"

"It's unlikely, sir," George admitted. A skeleton hung from the ceiling beams, left twisting idly by footfalls in the old wing above. Behind Monro, he could make out a web of blood vessels displayed by the door, preserved in red wax. Next to it were several jars containing pale and delicate fronds of human tissue; George couldn't decide what they were.

It was true he'd seen the dead and dying, but none of the deceased things in here bore much resemblance to humans.

"How are you finding the lecture material?" Monro asked. "I don't hear much from you during class. Or after." His reproach was undeniable.

George had assumed his professor would be annoyed by his questions, some of which he feared laughable, and would not want to deal with another lost soul after his lecturing duty ended. He bit his lip.

"You know, of course, that there is still space in the evening demonstration course," Monro continued, turning his attention back to the carcass. "Run at the College of Surgeons by my colleague Mr Fyfe. He's a tolerable lecturer, if I say so myself—huh-huh—and the students who attend find his smaller class size conducive to deepened understanding of anatomy."

Which is another thing that costs money, George thought. Another guinea that I don't possess. His family saved what they could, but hadn't appreciated that every step of his medical education involved separating coin from purse: course fees, books, evening remedial lectures, private tutors. Seeing how they struggled after parting with the funds that covered his boarding, George couldn't bring himself to ask for more.

Asking his fellow students for assistance yielded mixed

results. All but one of them acted like George wasn't there, and he didn't like dwelling on the anomaly.

"I tell my students I don't expect them to know everything on the first day of class," Monro went on. "Or else they wouldn't need to be here. Nor do I expect them to agree with me on every theoretical point. If you scrutinise Professor Cullen's theories"—here George's heart rate spiked—"you'll see our thinking diverges considerably on matters relating to the nervous system. But this kind of healthy disagreement among academics is important to advance the field towards true understanding of the human condition."

Monro spoke in such a flat tone, preoccupied with snipping through tendons, that George couldn't tell if he was sincere. Nothing the anatomy professor had said in class so far implied friendship with Cullen. Had Monro become aware of his dinner invitation? Was he delivering some kind of warning?

A soft chirbling noise from across the room startled him.

A small child, no older than five, was perched on the front row of seats. George hadn't noticed it was there. The child was waving its fingers in front of its face and making little noises to amuse itself.

"That's my oldest, Alex," Monro said, with a careless wave of his hand. "He's a bit young, but I reckoned getting him used to the smells and sights in here now would only help him later. I must have been the same age when my father first brought me to watch his dissections. I was eighteen when I started assisting him in the demonstration of anatomy; I don't know if I told you that."

"No, sir."

George had heard some of the older faculty refer to Monro with the epithet "junior", since he shared the name Alexander with his father.

"He usually settles when I get to speaking," Monro

continued, still observing his son. "If not, I think I've got some kidney stones he can play with." Another set of creaks broke his attention. "Well, look—if it isn't Misters Sinclair and Campbell. Good of you to join us, boys!"

When George arrived to dinner at Black's that evening, the two professors were conferring in the elegant dining room. The teal wallpaper with its intricate floral patterns was the most vibrant internal decor George had ever seen.

Black rose and walked over, with more liveliness than he displayed in public.

"A pleasure to see you again, Mr Stephens."

"I appreciate your invitation, sir." George wasn't used to being in houses with dining rooms.

Cullen waved from across the room. "I trust a studious scholar such as yourself will have found the time to read all those books?"

"Correct. I was familiar with your work, of course, and knew a little of Stahl's theories before settling down to read his essays."

Black motioned George to join him at the table. His dark mahogany furniture gleamed in the fading evening light. George noticed the furthest end of Black's dining room was occupied by a large cabinet filled with what appeared to be rock specimens. Aside from that, there was no other indication he was in the house of a natural philosopher. Dinner consisted of a respectable green pea soup, roasted sturgeon, mutton pie and apple dumplings. The conversation wound through trivial, light-hearted topics as they began to eat, though George sensed both men, but Cullen in particular, wanted to get to the real reason for their invitation as soon as it was polite to do so.

When he decided that point was reached, Black leant

forward. He'd given George enough time to relax into the surroundings, but not so long his imagination carried him away debating the possible nature of his visit.

"How familiar are you with the theories of John Brown?" Black asked.

George looked at both men. Neither Cullen nor Black gave indication as to how they hoped he'd respond.

"I heard his medical theories are considered...radical," George admitted. "But I know little of their nature."

"His extramural lectures are very popular with students," Cullen pressed. "Have you considered attending them?"

George's heart began to accelerate. The professors were shepherding him towards a potential trap, that was clear, but he didn't know what the trap was.

George knew a little of Brown. James, the querulous fellow, spoke glowingly of Brown's private lecture courses and of the man himself. Brown had reputedly been so close to Cullen he'd named his infant son William Cullen Brown in honour of his former teacher. Rumours suggested the two men had fallen out, that Brown was recently denied a faculty position, despite a long career lecturing outwit the university. For all George knew, the two men were now reconciled, though if so it was strange the professors were querying him about Brown.

Whatever the answer Black and Cullen were looking for, George realised he couldn't guess it. He also suspected Black had a keen sense for lies.

"I certainly considered attending Dr Brown's lectures," George admitted. "For the reason Dr Cullen stated. But then I decided against overtaxing my schedule." He also worried that if James was a typical adherent of Brown's, he'd struggle to enjoy their company. His consideration period was shortened by the knowledge Brown charged three guineas, like the university professors.

"Do not feel ashamed, Mr Stephens!" Cullen laughed. "Youths and their natural curiosity bring so much into the world."

George allowed himself to believe he'd answered the professor's question satisfactorily. The meal almost concluded, Black offered him a glass of wine.

"What do you know of phlogiston, Mr Stephens?" Black then asked.

This was at least a clearly defined trap, George noted, because the books Cullen had sent pertained to this topic.

"It is the element of fire," George replied. "The driver of combustion and calcination, in the words of Stahl. Burning is the release of phlogiston from metal, wood or a match. Once burned, a metal can be returned to its pure state by reacting it with a phlogiston-rich substance, which replenishes the metal's deficiency." He knew he was giving the professors a simplistic answer, but they appeared satisfied with the information he had obtained from a few hours' study. After a pause, he added, "Stahl hypothesised phlogiston could be harnessed for uses beyond these simple chemical transformations, but he didn't elucidate further."

"Yes, it's a wonder, isn't it?" Cullen mused, slipping into the tone of the lecture halls. "Phlogiston exists in all matter, living and inanimate, and simple experiments show it can be transmitted from one substance to another. We see what destructive and restorative power it is capable of. But maybe you can think of some uses for phlogiston?"

"Phlogiston exists within man, as well as nature?" George asked after an uncomfortable pause. He knew Cullen loved to draw students through this type of Socratic dialogue to the truth, but he had no idea where he was stepping.

"Indeed. Knowing that, now what do you think?"

"Well, I'd assume man has the power to generate fire, though losing phlogiston would surely come at a terrible cost to his body." George thought of wood in the hearth turned to blackened, crumbling charcoal.

"A wise assumption. But man is more complex than a lump of metal?"

George had been wondering how the evening's lines of questioning were linked, but now he thought he knew. From James' rants on the subject, he was aware that a key point of theoretical contention between Brown and Cullen was their understanding of the nervous system. "Well, Dr Cullen, you yourself write extensively of man's nervous system and its capacity for excitement and depression, which in the healthy individual can regulate itself but otherwise requires the attention of doctors." He paused. "You think the innate balance of man's nervous system can protect him from a sudden loss of phlogiston?"

The two professors were looking at each other. Cullen's hand was resting on his chin, but now he leant an elbow on the table and lightly clenched his fist in front of George's plate.

"After a fashion," he said with a chuckle.

Cullen's fingers began to glow.

3

Standing poised in the college library, Black awaited the morning's first set of chemistry students. The college was composed of three quadrangles: the smaller Printing House Yards and Low College, and the expansive High College. Behind the old library building stretched the college and principal's gardens to the east. There was a freshness to the air here not found in the squares down the hill towards the Cowgate: the faintest hint of ocean salt from the Firth blended with the warm, earthy scent of rolling pastures just south of the old city walls.

Black lectured at a table in an unobtrusive corner of the room behind the bookshelves, surrounded by a semi-circle of still-empty chairs and desks. In front of him were several large glass beakers and distillation apparatus already filled with water. On the floor a box of ice nudged his shins. Black busied himself lighting candles and rearranging his equipment for ease of access.

He thought only briefly of their conversation with the boy last night.

George Stephens knew almost nothing of phlogiston. This

wasn't a huge surprise, though Black had assumed knowledge of it had become more commonplace in recent years. Maybe only among the more affluent and landed students: they would learn about phlogiston in family libraries or from a private tutor. The boy came from farming stock, so no libraries to speak of.

"This is...secret?" the boy had asked, fumbling for words to articulate the thoughts rushing into his head.

Black noted the boy's ill-fitting waistcoat and his discoloured linen sleeves. Most students contrived to look dishevelled, but the boy seemed uncomfortable in his worn clothes, aware of their inadequacy but powerless to conceal them.

"More ignored than suppressed!" Cullen had cheerfully replied, snuffing out the dark red flames curled around his knuckles. Although it darted and crackled like normal fire, there was an insubstantial quality to its appearance. "Phlogiston is very hard to master, and not all that useful for the effort taken."

"Phlogiston can be accumulated and discharged from the body," Black had added, "but its energy quickly diffuses out into nothing upon contact with the air. Many great men have sought to understand and harness it, but its applications remain limited so far."

"There are a few manifestations of phlogistonic energy. Fire is the most common and easily mastered one. It can also be dispelled from the body as a kind of kinetic force." Here Cullen took a folded sheet of paper from his pocket and held it in the palm of his hand. Black saw the telltale flickers in the muscles of Cullen's arm and face that preceded the sheet of paper jolting into the air out of his hands. If the boy's eyes popped any wider, they were in danger of joining the letter on the floor.

"That said, it's little more than a party trick, except in the hands of men like Dr Black," Cullen added as an afterthought.

Black wished Cullen hadn't told the boy that. It was an oversimplification bordering on misrepresentation. The boy kept glancing at Black as they finished the wine and apple dumplings.

Still, Cullen had his reasons, and he'd agreed not to overload the boy with information. Just a basic explanation of what the two men needed from him right now.

"Near the end of August, a medical student was found dead in his lodgings," Black began. "Reported as a sudden onset of fatal sickness, despite the fact his friends saw him the day before, a picture of vitality. In mid-September another student stumbled into a High Street tavern, delirious and scalding to the touch. He died the next day. Last week, a third student is said to have fallen sick and passed away from a similar affliction.

"The symptoms these last two students suffered—delirium, weak pulse, elevated temperature, possible internal bleeding—present as fever but for a few crucial differences. Without going too deep into the specifics, we suspect an artificial, rather than natural, source of illness. But we aren't sure who is responsible or why."

Cullen registered subtle disapproval with Black for omitting Brown's name.

"We don't know that Brown is responsible," Black protested later. "We don't want the boy to rush off on too narrow a search."

Cullen found it suspicious that three student supporters of Brown all died of perplexing, fever-related symptoms. Especially when internal bleeding and fevers were also brought about by improper phlogiston-wielding.

"There's no rest for Dr Black and I," Cullen continued,

acting as if he were in perfect concert with Black. "And it always seems like the students learn of these tragedies before we do. Up until now we've only found out about these deaths after the fact: we've been unable to reach the students in time to treat them. Would you be able to keep an eye out for us, lad? Let us know if any of your classmates are struck ill in this manner?"

Black thought about his trip to the Surgeons' cellar with Cullen. Brown's supporters congregated in the Surgeons' College; others observed them making trips to the cellars. But in a vexing development, after the latest fatality they appeared to have moved elsewhere; Cullen's sources didn't know exactly.

The boy made some panicked protestation about other students—senior students—more friendly with Cullen than he was.

"We're casting a broad net," Cullen replied. "I speak to Edward and the others most days anyway. The more eyes the better, I say."

That was true enough, Black knew. But of course it didn't address why George Stephens was the candidate they'd plucked from the medical student body. If the boy wanted to protest or probe their motivations further, he didn't have the courage to do so. The two professors bade him goodnight shortly after.

Black didn't spend long thinking about the boy, because it wouldn't do for him to get his hopes up. Maybe Mr Stephens would come back to them with vital information, but it was just as likely he'd hear rumours of the next casualty *after* word reached Cullen. Or maybe the professor's final tempting proposition wasn't all that tempting.

"If you're interested," Black had told the boy as they walked him from the dining table to the front door, "Dr Cullen and I can teach you how to wield phlogiston. It's very time-consuming and difficult, requiring several months of dedicated study, but I see no reason why you can't learn."

"There's no rush to make a decision. If you feel your studies are too demanding then we can always come back to this next semester. Give it a week and see how you feel," Cullen said. Seeing the boy debate with himself, he hastened to add, "We wouldn't charge you for the lessons." George blushed.

Black could tell the boy was trying to pretend he wasn't as interested as he was. But too much curiosity brokered risks, too: he might approach Brown instead. Black only hoped he'd learn about Brown's true nature before such temptation presented itself.

As he heated his water beakers, Black thought about the latest deceased student. Pierre, the name was. He'd attended Black's chemistry course last year. Black could just about fit names to faces, though it got harder each year as his class sizes grew. Not a bad youth. A little too self-assured, too easily distracted, but that was often the case with youths. He hadn't deserved to die. Could someone really have betrayed his trust and brought him to harm?

A rumble of deep voices came from the staircase behind him. Black laid his hands on the table and turned.

"Excellent November weather, aye?" one of them called out in greeting. "Made getting out of bed this morning all the easier."

Almost all the twenty men Black expected had arrived in this group as the college bells rang out. They ranged in age from thirty to infirmity, with none of the leanness or furtiveness associated with true medical students. These men made their leisurely way into the library, safe in the knowledge that Black, as all other gentlemen in this city, wouldn't start business without them. Their glossy powdered wigs and embroidered coats marked them for what they were: lawyers.

The youngest of the pack, Lord Ross, smiled at Black as he took his customary seat in the front middle. "Good morning, Dr Black."

"Good morning, your lordship," Black replied evenly. While some aspects of Ross' smile and expressions could be classified as "boyish" or "delicate", his poise conveyed steeliness.

It was true his eleven o'clock chemistry lectures were open to anyone. Medical students took and retook the class as their aptitude for the material dictated, but gentlemen engaged in natural philosophy and visitors from across Europe also graced Black's lectures, eager to watch one of the university's most popular professors work his chemical magic. This year his class had even been graced by Russian royalty.

However, Black understood there was an opportunity to be had amongst the tier of Edinburgh men greatly interested in natural philosophy, who didn't want to cram into a sweaty auditorium with several hundred teenage medical students to satisfy their curiosity because their money, as it always did, offered a more pleasant route to satisfaction. These men were willing to pay an extra few guineas to attend Black's smaller, early class in the warm library.

Black ran his gaze around the filling circle of lawyers and minor Scottish nobility. He didn't mind teaching a private course for the lawyers. Unlike the young medical students, who were keen but easily distracted, the lawyers came to class every morning with the unwavering focus of men who knew how to learn, and knew exactly what they wanted from Black. The medical students asked deceptively simple questions; the lawyers asked complex questions born from their lived experiences.

He knew most of the attendees through social encounters prior to enrolment, though he couldn't claim to be their equal. Ross and Sir Grey were closely connected to the Town

Council, and were rumoured to influence Council decisions concerning the university. Even the less affluent attendees were well connected: Buchanan, for instance, had business dealings in Jamaica that overlapped with those of the wealthiest men in Edinburgh.

"I trust you're all settled, gentlemen. Today we'll cover latent heat and, if we have time, begin discussing the heat properties of mixtures."

Black's two lecture courses were almost identical, though at times he wished he'd changed their content. The lawyers was that they were serious men who trained their flinty eyes to reveal nothing. There was something unguarded about the young medical students that led them to gasp and cheer as they watched Black's experimental demonstrations. The temperature change of boiling water had no capacity to excite the lawyers, and it disappointed him.

The class sat and watched the temperature of two beakers—one filled with ice slurry, the other the same volume of water—continue to rise. It was apparent that despite being heated by candles to the same degree, the temperature of the beaker filled with ice was barely rising.

"And there we have it, gentlemen," Black said, smiling. "The energy from the external heat source is consumed by the melting of the ice, and thus the thermometer registers no change in temperature. The heat used to change water from solid to liquid is what we call latent heat."

An elderly lawyer, his meagre frame beaten down by a voluptuous horsehair wig, coughed out a chuckle. "In my student days, chemistry was little more than the preparation of medical compounds. Did you know Professors Crawford and St Clair, who first taught chemistry at Tounis College? They charged students to sit and watch them prepare their pharmaceuticals, then sold what they prepared to sick customers that very afternoon! A tidy business arrangement, it must be said. You're certainly a genius, Dr Black, no doubt about that, but it's hard to believe you are also a chemist."

Black smiled. "Chemistry has changed a lot since Dr Cullen began teaching it over forty years ago. I'm merely following his visionary trail."

Another senior lawyer stirred and leant forward. "That's a question I've wondered myself. Your experiments with heat are very fine and clever—I doubt any other man in the country could have designed them...but what use do the physicians of tomorrow have for this modern chemistry? It seems to barely touch upon the preparation of pharmaceuticals or medical concepts."

Black paused, then straightened his back. "Truly, gentlemen, I believe only a fraction of chemistry's potential has been uncovered and harnessed. I agree with Cullen that our medical students deserve more than to sit through demonstrations of medical compound preparation—there is merit to understanding the whys and hows of these transformations." He knew better than to comment that his students often posed the same questions. The divide between students interested in chemistry for its own sake and students who viewed it as an obstacle between them and a doctorate of physic was only widening.

The elderly lawyer with the chestnut wig continued to cough and gurgle in amusement, his gaze wistful. Funny how as we get older we lose control of our memories, Black thought. Either our memories betray us and hide, or they flood us all at once. He could hear the ice creak in the beaker beside him. Finally, the lawyer spoke.

"Remember the fiery arguments those professors got into? Men would argue for hours at a time over the measliest differences in opinion. Correct Latin nomenclature, what have you.

At the time we thought our teachers were gods, clashing in the heavens. Of course, with time it now appears foolish. No one cares!" He gesticulated, cawed, then settled. "I imagine the likes of young Dr Black will never engage in such folly."

The other lawyers smiled indulgently, but Black's responding expression remained tight-lipped.

"He leaves the arguing to John Brown, I wager!" someone called out.

And there we have it, Black thought.

"Dr Brown's theories fall far outside conventional medical doctrine," he said with all the ease he could dispense. "We at the university have little cause to engage with him."

Under no circumstances would Black indulge these patrons with speculations pertaining to Brown. The faculty had done what they could to keep him at a distance from the university, but admitting how little control they had over him would be devastating. He wished with all his being none of these men had cause to notice the number of students with links to Brown who had sustained mortal injury. It was best he and Cullen worked quietly to sort out the mess; the fewer outsiders knew, the better.

His audience appeared satisfied, allowing Black to resume his lecture. He took great care not to pause long in the remaining portion of the hour, lest they take another opportunity to interrupt.

As the lawyers rose upon culmination of the class, Lord Ross tapped his signet ring on the desk to attract Black's attention.

"I was out hunting with Sir Henry and Major Gyle the other day. They told me you're petitioning the Town Council to construct a new chemistry laboratory on the university grounds. I was looking around the college as I came in today and wondered...where on earth is there room for it?"

Black made his way around the table so he was in front of Ross. The young lawyer was one of the chattier ones. Black leant back against the table and folded his arms.

"The laboratory and classroom will be constructed in Printing Yards." He nodded behind him to where the smaller quadrangle lay. "The university senate indicates they support my proposal. Fitting nearly three hundred chemistry students into the existing lecture rooms is getting ridiculous, and the senate understands splitting my class in two wouldn't be acceptable."

"Yes, I can see how tiring that would be for you," Ross agreed with good humour.

Besides, there was no way to fit a third chemistry class into the day without it clashing with another medical course, something the other faculty had good reason to fear.

Black estimated Monro stood to lose fifty-four guineas per year in course fees if that chemistry class was scheduled at the same time as anatomy.

Ross became serious. "Do you think the Town Council will approve your proposal?"

Black really wanted to turn the question back to Ross, who he suspected knew more than he did. University support didn't mean much, given the Town Council enjoyed stamping their own mark on university affairs. Maybe Ross was testing him.

He settled on a thoughtful pause. "Early word from the Council seems favourable. But I'm sure they have questions and wish to examine my proposals in depth."

Ross nodded, but that was more an acknowledgement that he'd heard what Black said than one of agreement or endorsement. "Your recommendations are always carefully crafted, Dr Black. I can't imagine they will find fault."

Black stared off into the middle distance. He thought of the dead student Pierre and the almost imperceptible threads linking him to Cullen and himself. Not of direct blame, but lawyers would understand all the minute tones that existed between "direct responsibility" and "entirely free of culpability". Especially when Cullen made stopping the deaths his personal responsibility.

"Thank you, my lord. I never like to assume in matters as complex as these."

4

George made it all the way home from dinner with Black before he put two and two together.

The professors suspected Pierre's death was deliberate.

For a few warm days in October, George had wondered if Pierre would become his first friend in Edinburgh. They'd met during anatomy: Pierre noticed George staring wistfully at his intricate lecture notes and slid them across the desk for him to copy.

Seeing George continue to glance at him and work his mouth, Pierre offered his name. In fact, George was working up the courage to ask the boy if he could translate several Latin terms Monro used in the first week of class that George still didn't know the meaning of, but he accepted Pierre's name as almost as useful.

George was able to sit near Pierre a few more times, though they didn't exchange many words. That said, those few exchanges were more polite and warm than any other conversation George had had since matriculating. In their last anatomy class together, Pierre mentioned the street he lodged on, and George spent that evening deciding on the politest way to invite him for afternoon tea.

But Pierre didn't appear in class the next day. Or the day after. Then rumour reached his lodgings that he had died of fever. His fellow lodgers were alarmed that a deadly illness was stalking the student population and cancelled their social plans. No one had a kind word for unfortunate Pierre.

The loss of a potential friend pained George, after he too worried about catching Pierre's fever from their classes together. In the days that followed, he realised it was only his own anxieties afflicting him. No one noticed George's sorrow, nor that he buried it under sullen resentment.

Pierre's sudden death was nothing more than bad luck dealt out to George.

But no other students had died of fever last week: the student rumour mill was clear on that.

Who committed such maliciousness against Pierre? George allowed his anger to reignite, stoked further by regret that he hadn't gleaned more about Pierre's acquaintances and habits.

He simmered for a week.

On Saturday morning, George was disturbed by a knock at his door. Edward poked his tawny head inside.

"Morning, Stephens. Me and some friends are heading up Calton Hill today. If the weather holds I think we might go down to Leith for a game of billiards. Sounds more entertaining than copying out lecture notes, right?"

"Indeed," George agreed.

He was clearly an afterthought, because Edward would have planned the weekend's activities during Friday classes—but it seemed churlish to point that out.

"Good man!" Edward retreated into the hallway, slapping the door frame as he went.

* * *

It was early afternoon by the time the party reached the top of the hill, by which point thick grey clouds were rolling in. Catching his breath, George pivoted to take in a city that trailed from the castle on the precarious outcrop down to the squat Holyrood Palace. Behind the palace the flat plate of Salisbury Crags jutted up towards the heavens. Between their vantage point on Calton Hill and the swarming High Street was a deep cleft of pastures, occupied by small flocks of livestock.

"Not bad, is it?" Edward asked with a grin.

George didn't know how Edward had attained such easy confidence. It grated that his fellow lodger was several years younger than him and effortlessly led him around. George wanted to resent Edward more than he did, but he couldn't avoid his charm. Edward was a man blessed with a strong chin, which to George was as clear an indication of divine favour as any.

Edward hailed from a wealthy Scottish family, though his childhood was spent in Jamaica on his father's sugar plantation. George heard that Edward's mother—his father's second wife—had died of a tropical fever some years ago. As his only surviving son, Edward's father shipped him back to Scotland to receive the education suitable for wealthy landowners.

The story of Edward's upbringing had the advantage of being such a blatant falsehood that no one bothered to confront him over it. Especially since everyone knew his father's "first" wife was alive and well in Aberdeenshire and that Edward's sallow complexion was atypical for a Scotsman. Despite these scandalous circumstances, Edward's father was publicly supportive of his sole heir and the two seemed close. Edward never acted anything less than the favoured son of a rich man.

Standing on the windswept vantage point above Edinburgh, George suspected word of his recent dinner with the two professors had got out, which explained why Edward added him to this social outing and was now entertaining a conversation.

"What is the business between Professor Cullen and John Brown?" George asked. He'd mulled over what Cullen and Black had told him over dinner. They'd asked him about his interest in Brown's teachings, and the suspicion George cultivated was that Brown was connected to the death of Pierre, even though the professors didn't spell it out.

Edward laughed. "You don't want to jump into that affair so rashly, George! You only arrived in Edinburgh a month ago."

George felt his cheeks sting.

With a twinkle in his eye, Edward continued, "I'm teasing you a bit, George. There isn't as much of a dispute as everyone says. Sure, there's a bit of ill will between the two men, but Dr Brown's theories aren't all that divergent from Dr Cullen's doctrines. In fact, most of the medical faculty disagree with aspects of Dr Cullen's medical theories."

The other students took this level of disagreement between faculty for granted. To George it was surprising. He must be very sheltered.

His companion turned away from the city to admire the shimmering Firth. Small enclaves and fishing villages studded the landscape as far as the eye could see, punctuated by smoke rising from the distant port of Leith and the forest of masts clustering around it.

"I thought you were close to Dr Cullen," George said, blinking rapidly. The northern wind stung his eyes and made it hard to see his companion.

"Good heavens, George! Dr Cullen is a dear friend of mine —I believe I'm at liberty to call him that. He's the one encouraging us to think for ourselves and never stop questioning prevailing dogmas. Dr Cullen overturned quite a few dogmatic apple carts when he first took up his teaching post in Edinburgh—I don't know if he told you that?"

George shook his head, annoyed at how much of his ignorance was being exposed on this blustery hilltop. Edward didn't seem interested in stopping, though.

"If you want my opinion, George, the real reason Dr Cullen dislikes Dr Brown is because Brown's doctrines are simpler for a lay audience to grasp. Fewer classifications, more unified rules. Dr Cullen hates the idea of fishwives—that's what he says—teaching themselves medicine and acting as equals of credentialled physicians."

"The doctrines of fishwives..." George affected nonchalance to hide his shame. The ease with which Edward laughed off Cullen's eccentricities made him feel like a dupe.

A cry carried across the mound. They turned to see another cohort of students approaching: more friends Edward had promised they'd meet up with.

"Well, look here! George, I wanted you to meet the good Thomas. I think you'll like him."

George looked over at the short, bluff man striding towards them. His dark curly hair and hearty complexion made George's heart sink before he even opened his mouth.

"How're ye doing?" asked Thomas, beaming.

They really think so little of me, George thought, that they'd herd me off with the Irish.

"Thomas told me he wanted to acquaint himself with gentlemen his own age," Edward continued. "George here served at New York for a few years—he's something of an old man in our lodgings."

Then Edward raised his head to the skies.

"That'll be the rains," Thomas commented. "Ye sure we

can't find ourselves a platter of oysters nearer than Leith, fellows?"

* * *

A few days later, on his way to class, George spotted Thomas passing through College Street.

George called out and waved, but it appeared Thomas was ignoring him. The rebuke stung, because they'd spent several hours in animated discourse about farming on Saturday, so he crossed the street. Now Thomas couldn't avoid the encounter.

"Oh, it's George, yes?"

"Everything alright?" Up close, Thomas looked distracted and irritable.

"Not really. One of the boys in my lodgings was taken ill this morning. My wife and I tried to tend to him, but we just ended up arguing with the others about how to help. They didn't want to catch his sickness. He's at the Public Dispensary now."

"It was a fever?" George hoped he didn't sound too eager, but Thomas was not in the mood to pay this casual acquaintance much heed.

"One of the nastier cases." He sidestepped George to continue on his way. "Good day, George."

"Who did you say was taken ill?" George called after him, belatedly realising how critical Thomas' remarks were.

"Doubt ye know Bennie," Thomas replied, without breaking stride or looking back.

For a few minutes George wasn't sure he'd act on the information. Edward had treated him warmly following their jaunt up Calton Hill, without even returning to the topic of Cullen or Brown, so George dared hope he wasn't yet an object of mockery. He'd allowed himself to believe his chances at friendship hadn't ended with Pierre.

Brown may or may not have been involved with Pierre's death. The causality was confusing, unless Pierre caught the illness from Brown. George wanted justice for the boy who'd helped him, but after Sunday's activities he wondered if it should come at the expense of future social connections.

However, George's mind was set as soon as he entered the quadrangle and spotted Cullen striking to his lecture surrounded by a flock of medical students. George felt a stab of disappointment, before realising the students couldn't be conveying news of Bennie's illness. They were laughing and shoving each other in jest. Cullen tapped a book one of them held out, saying something witty. Watching this tableau of exalted professor with favoured students, George yearned to be part of it.

"Professor!" George gasped, trying to catch his attention.

"Why, it's Mr Stephens," Cullen exclaimed with delight. George wondered if he was insincere, but none of his pack treated it as such, for they parted to let George into the fold.

"Sir, there's a student, Bennie—" George began.

Cullen shot him a look. He stopped abruptly.

George realised that, far from being prized information to flaunt, he should be careful letting on what he was doing. He didn't really know the students surrounding Cullen.

"Oh yes, thanks for reminding me about that," Cullen said, waving his hand with a knowledgeable murmur. "I'll send word to you later today."

George retreated with no small air of confusion. Did Cullen already know about this student? Or was the dismissal a ruse to hide their business?

After anatomy, George retreated to his lodgings for dinner. He didn't have long to wait before Mrs Collins was barging into his room and pressing a scrap of paper into his hand. He wished she knocked.

G.S.—Please call upon me this evening as soon after 4 as is convenient. Yrs, etc.

The letter was in Black's handwriting, using his particularly dark, expensive ink.

* * *

"George, my boy, you deserve the utmost gratitude," Cullen said as soon as George entered Black's parlour. Cullen was standing at the window, viewing the darkening street, while Black sat at his desk near the fireplace, working through correspondence. "What do you know of the sick student?"

Black's house servant handed George a glass of wine. George swallowed.

"Very little, I'm afraid. Only that his name is Bennie, and he shared a lodging-house with Thomas"—George inwardly cursed, because he'd forgotten the Irishman's surname—"and was taken ill this morning and brought to the Public Dispensary for treatment."

"The Public Dispensary is Andy Duncan's domain," Cullen said, crossing the room. "We should speak to the good doctor without delay."

Cullen started buttoning up his coat, ignoring George, who stood mutely in the corner, swallowing the rest of his glass, rushing to finish the nicest wine he'd ever drunk. The professors were readying to depart, and once they remembered George was still in the room they'd politely thank and dismiss him. And it was unlikely he'd hear anything more about the mysterious illness that claimed Pierre.

George tapped his wine glass, hoping to rouse insight from the remaining crimson drops.

"Err, my lodgings are a few streets over from Dr Duncan." The words tumbled out before the professors could silence him. "I can walk over there with you."

It was a stupid, blatant excuse to keep himself in the professors' affairs—but it had the merit of being true.

The older professor shrugged and readjusted his bicorne hat.

"He'll be hosting the Beggar's Benison tonight," Black commented without raising his eyes from his writing. "It might be a short encounter."

"I thought the Beggar's club met on Wednesday nights?" George asked without thinking. As soon as he spoke, he felt shame contradicting the eminent Dr Black.

"He's right, Joe." Cullen tapped his friend on the arm. "The Beggars meet on Wednesdays, don't they? I almost forgot."

Black's expression and posture remained the same. "Ah, that's the ordinary Benison meetings. They hold their...special gatherings on Tuesday nights."

"Oh." Cullen froze. "Yes, of course. I forgot about those too." His face began to flush. "You know, Joe, perhaps we should call upon Andy first thing in the morning. Well, maybe first thing tomorrow would not be productive, but you know..."

Black carefully laid down his quill. "No, I think given the severity of the unfolding situation, we best call on him tonight. Come the morning, events may have overtaken us."

"You're right, as always." Cullen wiped his brow.

As the three men covered the short distance to Duncan's lavish Adam Square dwelling, George reflected on what he knew of the man personally, and what rumours supplied to fill his gaps.

Dr Andrew Duncan was the object of deep professional respect within the community, despite being relatively youthful (at least compared to Black and Cullen). His primary reputation among the medical faculty and students, however, was that of the person you avoided talking to at parties. So desperate were some long-suffering Edinburgh citizens that money was whispered to have changed hands between dinner hosts and guests to ensure seating arrangements kept Duncan beyond arm's length. Once drawn into an evening conversation with him it could be hours before your ordeal ended. No one wanted to risk rescuing a friend, for fear Duncan would ensnare them instead. And once it began you couldn't just *leave* the conversation: Duncan was such a sweet and kindly soul no one wanted to hurt his feelings.

Yet, George also knew that during daylight hours Duncan was a principled physician, whose commitment to the public good had led to the creation of the Dispensary, the public hospital where poor Bennie had ended up. George had heard other medical students talking about Duncan and his groundbreaking medical jurisprudence theories: the students sounded very excited as they argued about them.

All in all, Duncan was a pioneer in many spheres of Edinburgh life. His leadership role in The Most Ancient and Most Puissant Order of the Beggar's Benison and Merryland, a secretive sex club, was almost a throwaway detail.

The dark square outside Duncan's house was deserted when the trio approached: only faint lighting through cracks in the shutters indicated his stately home was occupied. In Duncan's doorway leant a tall and broad-shouldered man. As they approached, his features emerged from the shadows to reveal a handsome, clean face with the faint trace of a polite smile. This man was of a finer calibre than most hired strength in this city, but his build and confident movements indicated he could quickly get forceful.

"Good evening, sirs. May I be of assistance?" He positioned himself in the centre of the doorway.

"Ah, yes, good evening to you too, sir," Cullen blustered, stepping forward. Black slipped a step behind his older colleague without a word. As George watched, Black's eyes took a slow sweep of the dark street. "We, erm, have urgent business with Dr Duncan—very, very urgent—and request the briefest of his time right away."

George had never seen Cullen so discomposed. Although it was too dark to see, he suspected the blush had returned. "It's, um, Doctors Cullen and Black. He knows who we are."

The guard bowed. "Yes, of course I recognise who you are, Doctors. And good evening to your young friend. I shall send word to Dr Duncan alerting him to your presence and the delicacy of the situation. However, you must understand my lord is entertaining guests this evening, and if he is unable to disengage you must respect that." The guard shifted his position slightly, enough to expand his chest and highlight the advantage of size and strength he held over the old professors.

"Yes, yes—of course." Cullen waved his hands in front of him. "We will depart quickly, very quickly in fact, should Dr Duncan be too deeply, too deeply..." He trailed off hopelessly. With another nod, the guard opened the front door and whispered a few words to whoever was stationed inside. Without taking his eyes off the trio, he nodded again and drew the door closed.

"This was a silly idea, Joe." Cullen turned to his friend. "We arrived too late. Duncan's not going to see us."

"It doesn't hurt to ask," Black replied calmly. "Given what is at stake."

"What if he invites us inside?" Cullen wailed. "Heaven have mercy on us!"

"I consider that unlikely," said Black in the same tone.

"Gentlemen!" came a guttural cry from the building. George looked over to see the doctor hobble down the steps towards them, his outline recognisable due to his uncurled, cropped brown hair. The wave of light from inside his house illuminated Duncan for a moment, and George realised with shock that the elder statesman was dressed only in an embroidered silk banyan, which he was tugging tight across his sunken, dilapidated chest. Cullen let out an audible gasp.

"An unexpected pleasure, but a pleasure nonetheless." Duncan ambled over to Cullen and Black, shaking their hands in turn. Cullen's blush retreated into white.

"Likewise, Andrew," Black said in smooth tones, seemingly covering for the struggling Cullen. "We are sorry to take up your valued time and call you outside so late, but I can assure you the urgency of the situation necessitated such measures."

"Oh, it's no problem!" exclaimed Duncan. "I was just taking a short rest from the evening's activities, a refractory period, as it were..."

George stared at him. How could he ever sit in medical lectures delivered by this man? What changes must he make to his studies to ensure he never came face to face with Duncan again?

"Andy!" Cullen cried, rushing back into the conversation. "We're so sorry, but you treated that wretched creature Bennie at the Dispensary just today, didn't you? The boy with a nasty fever?"

"Yes..." said Duncan, too confused by the sudden change in conversation to object or resist.

"Well, the lad, and many others, it turns out, are in grave danger. Or could be soon. Please, tell us everything you can remember about him. Was there anything queer or peculiar? What was he saying?"

Duncan blinked, then his professional physician instincts kicked in.

"Why yes, gentleman. Poor laddie. He came in covered in cuts: it's hard to say one way or the other, but there seemed to be patterns within them. Couldn't figure out how anyone could accidentally sustain such cuts. He was thrashing about; it was hard to perform a proper examination."

Cullen nodded. "Right, right, yes. Did he say anything that you could understand?"

Duncan shrugged. "Very little of it. The delirium was strong, I'm afraid. He kept apologising to someone, was crying out for air. I gave him the usual sedatives—wasn't much else we could do. Who knows how much that will help him in the long run, but sometimes that's what it is."

After his initial panic and fluster, George saw Cullen regaining his usual air of confidence and certainty. Duncan had evidently told them something of value. He thought Cullen or Black would try to press the matter, to tease out more vital details from Duncan while he was still cooperative and unfrozen by the night air. Instead, the two men pulled back and murmured.

"That's been very helpful, Dr Duncan. Perhaps we can take a look at the patient in the next few days."

"Of course." Duncan shuffled his feet. "If you think there's more insights to be uncovered."

"I have no doubt you've settled on the best treatment for the unfortunate, but it might help allay our own concerns. Anyway, we won't detain you any longer."

"Oh, well, happy to do what I can. Let me know if there's more I can assist you gentlemen with." Cloaked in his usual social oblivion, Duncan turned back towards the house, and his eyes fell upon George, seemingly for the first time in the encounter.

"Well, if it isn't the promising young Mr Stephens! I'm delighted to see you in the company of such esteemed figures as these. Studies going well then, they must be?"

"Yes, sir," stammered George. Behind Duncan, a sheen of horror returned to Cullen's eyes.

"Well listen here, young esquire, because what they won't teach you, even at this, the finest medical school in the world, is that regular and satisfactory *sexual activity* is the surest guarantor of long-lasting vitality and happiness. Ignore the priggish morality of church men—treat your prick as an object of veneration!"

George thought his face was about to melt off. He couldn't even look at Cullen, who was surely frozen in terror again.

"The venerable Professor Cullen is blessed with his magnificent filly of a wife, and undoubtedly partakes of her hidden caverns with deserved frequency. How old are you now, sir—seventy? You can see how regular amorous congress continues to benefit the man's intellect and constitution in his later years..."

George was going to pass out. He could no longer see anything.

"...while the honourable Professor Black here will know the importance of regular masturbation—"

"You have been most gracious with your time and medical insights this evening, Andrew," Black interrupted, his tone the same calm smoothness it had been all night. "But our urgent business cannot wait. We will be sure to call on you again shortly to explain everything. Thank you and good evening."

"Right, good evening," mumbled Duncan, again too confused by the rapid shifts in conversation to resist them. He spun back around and started up the stairs to his front door, groaning and stretching his limbs. The guard let him back inside with barely an acknowledgement.

With a gentle nudge to the shoulder, Black propelled the dumbstruck Cullen, and by extension George, away from Duncan's house into the darkness of the square.

George's dizziness of embarrassment finally wore off.

"Dr Black," George whispered, "I'm so sorry! I didn't mean—"

"Think nothing of it," Black said, reaching out to pat George's shoulder as they walked. "Dr Duncan is wise in many respects and misinformed in others."

Cullen's breathing sounded raggedy. Black was acting like they'd taken their leave from a conversation about the weather. Whatever George had thought the experience of investigating his friend's death would resemble, it wasn't this.

The cool night air on George's cheeks provided a pleasing distraction, easing away his hearty blush. Soon he would have to point out that his lodgings were in the opposite direction and he should flee home, since Black's preoccupation seemed to be getting them away from Duncan.

As George emerged further from his fog of mortification and noticed Black hadn't let go of either set of shoulders, a sudden, violent squeeze of Black's hands brought the two dazed men to a standstill.

"Unfortunately," Black continued in the same level tone, "we are not alone out here tonight, gentlemen."

5

The pressure on George's shoulder guided his gaze right. The men had almost left the illumination of the street light. In the dark recess between two nearby houses, a clump of figures were detaching themselves.

Despite Duncan's bizarre, humiliating behaviour, George found his instincts were clear and focussed as he viewed the threat. It was almost a relief: the academic world was full of inscrutable rules calculated to make a mockery of him, but he understood fighting. Beside him, Cullen tightened the grip on his walking cane.

"Remember, George, disable without inflicting mortal injury." The figures burst forward onto the square's paving and Black released his hand.

George counted four men approaching. He stepped in front of the two professors.

The first assailant swung a punch. George ducked under it. This one was an amateur fighter: wild swings like those took a long time to arrive and were easy to dodge. He punched straight down into the man's bladder. Most men didn't anticipate blows that low. His assailant grunted in shock. As George rose, he caught him under the chin with his elbow and the man folded into the dirt.

The second assailant had more skill and caution. By the time his comrade hit the earth he'd already grabbed George's lapel and was trying to knee him. George blocked with his hands and headbutted the attacker. He heard a satisfying crack as the man's nose gave way, but the brute didn't let go.

A third attacker slashed at George's arm with a dagger, but he was able to shift sideways when he sensed movement. Before the attacker could aim for a second stab, George peeled his other opponent's hand off his collar and twisted his wrist as sharply as he could. Another crunch of bone, this time raising a scream. He kicked the knife-wielder in the knee. As the man's leg buckled, George finished him with a strike to the neck.

George let go of the second attacker's mangled wrist and pushed him away. These men weren't professionals—if he gave them the space and didn't immediately re-engage, he wagered they'd flee. Sure enough, this assailant backed into the wall, clutching his wrist and glaring at George with fury.

He was still in the process of asking himself where the fourth man had gone when he saw a flash of movement out of the corner of his eye. The fourth assailant, also armed with a knife, charged round him at the two professors. Cullen, the closer of the pair, swiped at him with his cane. Black tried to push in front of his older colleague, but Cullen let out a roar and collided with the attacker before he had time to. For a moment the two were grappling, Cullen's cane clattering to the floor, but before George could cover the distance, an intense flash of light erupted between Cullen and his assailant and the attacker was hurled to the ground. Cullen took a step backwards, his hands outstretched in front of him.

George made eye contact with Black. Black nodded and beckoned him over. It wasn't worth finishing off these thugs or inflicting more violence than was necessary. Two of the assailants were lying unconscious, but the least experienced fighter had hauled himself upright. His nerve had evidently broken, however, and he took off down the street. The remaining fighter, the one with the broken wrist, continued to glare with murderous hatred at George, but without the protection of numbers he had no choice but to run after his friend towards the West Bow.

George's upper arm stung, and he remembered the dagger had caught him. He pressed down on his wound, though it didn't feel like a serious injury.

"Let's take this way home," Black was saying, pointing to the circuitous route around the college. It was also better lit, with wider streets. "We can attend to your arm, Mr Stephens. My guest bedrooms are set—it won't do for any of us to venture alone tonight."

Cullen was already moving. He flicked his middle finger across his palm, and his hand burst into flame. It evidently caused him no discomfort, for Cullen raised the phlogiston torch to shoulder level.

George nodded to Black and moved to close the gap with Cullen. The darkness of the streets stalked a wary distance around them.

* * *

Many hours later George was lying in one of Black's bedrooms, the one with peach walls and another mahogany cabinet lined with dull rocks. Cullen had briskly cleaned and dressed his flea bite of a wound, and now George could begin to process his feelings about the attack.

Although dismayed that the violence of his military life was no longer a distant memory, as far as fights went, this had been one of George's easiest. It wasn't a random purse theft—

no threats or demands were made—but it wasn't a murder attempt either. The men fled too readily for paid killers. It seemed apparent who had sent the warning, but neither Black nor Cullen was in the mood to talk once they were safe inside. Instead, they urged George to rest and assured him they'd convene in the morning.

Even though this bed was softer and warmer than the one in his lodging room, and the cotton quilt blemished with fewer holes and stains, George knew better than to pretend he would fall asleep. He stared at the ceiling.

Cullen was no fighter. The old professor trembled all the way home, and was eager to be distracted by ministering George's injury.

But Dr Black...he was something else. Up until now, George had made sense of the professor by viewing him as a cautious but calm figure, an enlightened man who kept the worst of his human impulses at bay. Now George saw him more like a military captain giving cool direction to his troops under heavy cannon fire. He had yet to see Black wield phlogiston. Up until tonight he had found this omission disappointing, but now he felt a frisson of anticipation. What skills was Black hiding?

George considered himself a prompt riser, but floorboard creaks and murmured conversation woke him up. Once he was dressed, he found Black and Cullen picking through a breakfast of bread and milk in the morning room.

"I do my best to avoid strong stimulants," Black remarked, gesturing for George to join them at the circular table, "but tea or coffee is available if you wish."

Neither man seemed the kind for leisurely morning rituals. Black hadn't donned his coat, but his hair was already powdered. How did a man who handled acids and hot glass-ware every day retain such bright linen shirts?

"Thank you, sir." George reached for the plate of butter.

"Unfortunately, last night confirms for Dr Cullen and myself that Brown played some involvement in Bennie's misfortune. Some of the students with Dr Cullen in the yards attend Brown's lectures, and we think they alerted him. Brown then sent men to follow us."

"You're sure Brown is responsible?" Reflecting on Edward's remarks, George wanted assurance he hadn't made a fool of himself for no reason.

Cullen finished chewing on his bread. "The other faculty aren't the type to utilise street thugs to intimidate us. Or more to the point, the likes of Monro Junior, Young and Gregory could afford to hire better thugs."

Thinking of the brief fight, and of the menacing sentry outside Duncan's residence, George had to agree.

"He's warning us, telling us not to dig further," Cullen said.

"Perhaps, or he's trying to attract our attention," Black mused. "A prelude to sending us a message, once he's sure we're taking him seriously."

Cullen shrugged and took another bite of bread.

"But why would he kill his own students?" George felt less fretful of propriety now men in dark closes were drawing knives on him. He hesitated to admit he was acquainted with Pierre, in case the professors thought he was motivated by revenge.

"I doubt it's intentional," Black remarked. "It's more likely a series of accidents Brown is trying to keep under wraps. Whether he's directly responsible for the accidents in some way or it's negligence on the part of the students themselves we still don't know."

Cullen studied George for a moment.

"How much do you know of John Brown's history? Really know?"

"Only vague rumours," George replied, relieved at this opportunity to perhaps find out what was going on. "Very little of substance."

Far from reluctant to rehash old enmity, Cullen appeared delighted to retell the story.

"Well, Brown really started to tread on dangerous ground after his last failed bid for a faculty position." Cullen took a sip of tea. "He learned nothing—same as before—sought to blame everyone for his misfortunate except himself. I ended up in the line of fire."

"I imagine your remarks to the Town Council didn't much calm his rancour," Black said. There was an edge in his voice.

Cullen's face tightened. "For God's sake, will you let that go? How many times do you need to hear me admit I know I was wrong to say what I did? With the wisdom of time, yes, I wouldn't have replied in such a flippant manner to the Town Council when they asked about Brown's suitability for that faculty position—of course private words would find a way out. I imagine, of course, you would have known better if placed in such a situation."

Black said nothing. His arms remained folded and his gaze pointedly fixed on a portrait above the fireplace.

Cullen rose and began to pace the room.

"Come on, Joe. That man is an excellent Latin scholar and a competent tutor—I've spoken of his literary genius a thousand times. But that doesn't make him medical faculty material. Brown couldn't muster a doctoral thesis in the ten years he attended classes in Edinburgh: he had to buy one from St Andrews, and even that was only after much prodding and needling from myself and others."

Black continued to avert his gaze, appearing almost as discomfited as his colleague.

"I encouraged Brown in many ways I considered appropriate to his talents: I gave him my lecture notes to build his own course with; countless friends of mine seeking Latin instruction for their children were sent his way. But I never once suggested he put his name forward for the medical theory chair, or promised my support for such a foolish endeavour."

The slightest shift in Black's crossed arms communicated his disagreement with the last point. Silence fell.

To George's surprise, it was Black who uncoiled himself and finally turned his gaze away from the wall.

"You don't need to tell me these things, William. I know all this already." His voice was low, but George sensed a lot of internal will mustered to produce Black's genuine conciliatory tone. "I don't want to quarrel with you."

Cullen let out a loud sigh and returned to his seat.

"I know you know. The whole business still upsets me."

"Perhaps you can tell Mr Stephens about Brown's phlogiston theories."

After pausing to gather his thoughts, Cullen continued, "A few years back, Brown started up with all sorts of notions about phlogiston and the nervous system's role in its genesis and replenishment. Some of them I considered a misinterpretation of experimental evidence—which I told him, don't worry about that. Then he gets it into his head he is qualified for the medical theory chair. When Dr Gregory Senior died suddenly, Brown told me he put his name forward for the role.

"Well, of course I tried to gently dissuade him. I pointed out candidates usually required a published body of work to secure academic appointments. His lack of a doctoral thesis was also going to count against him, though even I knew he was capable of rectifying that.

"To his credit he conceded some of my points. He buys that degree from St Andrews; I permit him the title of doctor since there are plenty of those St Andrean 'doctors' running around already. Next thing I know, Brown publishes his damnable heretical theories on phlogiston and calls *that* his contribution to the medical literature! The only mercy was he published the tract in Latin, so none of the students can read it. And that he failed to secure the chair, I suppose." Cullen let out a bitter laugh.

George tried to remove his confused expression.

"Sorry, Dr Cullen, does that mean Dr Brown can or cannot wield phlogiston?" From what the two professors had said, the way to harness phlogiston within your body was strongly prescriptive.

"Oh, he can wield phlogiston alright." Cullen shook his head. "He grossly oversimplifies the technique, is ill informed in most regards to its provenance and control, but the phlogiston comes out.

"The problem is what the rascal does once his so-called textbook is published. One early June morning I'm going about my business on the High Street when I run into one of my students from the winter term. I ask him what he's busy with this summer, and he tells me he's keeping occupied with some medical lectures.

"Now, the semester is well over by this point, so I ask him who is offering extramural summer courses. This was a sharp lad—I'm surprised because he was a competent student of mine; I didn't think he needed to spend his summer in remedial or repeated classes. He tells me, 'Why, Dr Brown is! He's expounding on his novel theories, and sir, I've never missed a class.'

"Good Lord, I could barely get my words out! Brown was teaching his phlogiston theories to unsuspecting students out of a tavern off the Cowgate. I tell this lad to come round for dinner, and I get him to show me what he's learned. It's absolutely shocking. The lad can dispense phlogiston half the time he tries, but there is no control. I brought a flagon of water into my living room in anticipation of this—I had to douse my curtains before they went completely up in flames. The boy gets an awful nosebleed doing it—one of the worst I've seen."

"You've got to relax as you discharge the phlogiston out of your body," Black explained. "It's easy to let it all out as fast as you can, but that disrupts the natural equilibrium of your nervous system. Internal bleeding is a serious risk if you don't know what you're doing."

Cullen nodded. "It doesn't end there though, Joe. I help the boy stem his nosebleed and he tells me Brown recommends strong stimulants to reduce such bleeding. He was back preaching the damnable benefits of laudanum and brandy on ailing bodies! That was too much for me. I had to warn the lad he'd be lucky such a regimen hadn't yet endangered his health and not to play with phlogiston in such a manner. He seemed to accept my advice."

Cullen paused and rubbed his forehead.

"That said, I never saw the lad again. Not that summer, and he withdrew from college classes come November. Even the brightest ones don't always persist in their studies. I know there's not much you can do about it, but I was disappointed to lose this one. It's likely the first thing Brown did was refill the lad's head with his ideas. I wouldn't know for sure, since it was at that point Brown and I severed all friendship."

It made sense to George. Curious medical students could wait until their education was almost over to maybe learn some of Cullen and Black's secrets, and then spend months more studying their craft in increments, or they could attend Brown's summer course and manifest phlogiston by the end of their first tavern lecture. Regular nosebleeds were a small price to pay.

George felt a cold grey dizziness wash over him.

"So how will we find out why Brown set men on us?" He didn't want to return to military life, to that state of constant watchfulness. Where every half-heard sound or motion out the corner of his eye could herald mortal danger.

Black and Cullen looked at each other. Cullen blew air from his mouth.

"Well, Brown frequents The Mermaid tavern on the High Street—my plan was you go and ask him."

George's dizziness vanished in a snap, replaced by disbelief.

"Ask him, Professor? Me?" This was the man who had hired thugs to attack him!

George looked over to Black for protection, but Black was nodding in thoughtful agreement.

"Yes, you see," Cullen explained, "there's a lot of dark sentiment between Doctors Black, myself and Brown—he's wont to quarrel whenever we meet. While he knows, no doubt, that you are working with us, that fact alone isn't enough to send him into a rage. It also helps that you have no developed phlogistonic talents. He won't regard you as a threat."

The rise of panic consumed George as Cullen's words sank in. Neither professor intended to accompany him into Brown's den. It seemed a perilous mission.

"Do not fear," Black assured him. "Brown is, in most regards, a charming and cheerful fellow. It's difficult to casually provoke him, nor is he seized by violent rashness. Besides, he and his fellows know you can handle yourself well in unpleasant situations."

"But he'll be angry I struck his friends!" George protested.

Cullen snorted. "Those weren't friends of Brown, young man. Mere accomplices, none with lasting harm."

Further discussion was futile. George wanted to trust the professors' faith in his safety and prove his loyalty, even as they dismissed his fears. He couldn't imagine Cullen asking Edward to carry out such a task, and tried to decide if that meant Cullen placed him in higher or lower esteem than his fellow student.

Black and Cullen had no reason to share what they learned with George. He was their extra set of eyes and fists, not a confidant. If George wanted to find out what happened to Pierre, he'd need to conduct his own inquiries.

He sighed. "If you think it will be fruitful, Professor, I can try."

6

It was a short distance from his house to the Public Dispensary, but Black elected to summon a carriage. He didn't have much time, and wanted to throw off any watchers in the pay of Brown.

Black felt a measure of guilt that he hadn't told the boy what he intended to do this afternoon while Brown was engaged with him in the tavern. Of course, it was implied from the conversation with Duncan in Adam Square that either Black or Cullen would visit Bennie in the coming days, and maybe George could deduce the probable timing, but Black knew it was unlikely he'd make the leap. It was better this way, he reminded himself. Since George didn't know of Black's plan, he couldn't let it slip to Brown and his associates. Black would happily explain his thinking to the boy once they regrouped—it would be an instructive lesson.

The carriage jolted as it passed the college, the road uneven from decades of heavy traffic. After a few minutes they passed into the wider boulevard of Nicolson Street and the road smoothed out. The carriage had the musty odour of dirt left to settle for years, the velvet curtains at the windows faded.

Enlisting the George Stephens' help proved a good idea. The events of last night showed he could follow instructions. In fact, Black sensed the boy's relief at being told what to do. He was obviously smart and observant, but seemed overwhelmed by the university and confused about how to conduct himself among students and faculty.

Black sensed a burning spirit under George's reticent, obsequious manner, but wasn't yet sure what motivated the boy.

His additional set of talents were undeniable, though. Plenty medical students possessed similar levels of talent—Black had cultivated those with a lot less—but George's felt particularly promising.

The noise of Edinburgh receded as the road continued half a mile south. Here there were fewer shops; the bakers, grocers and shoemakers maintained a steady queue of customers without the yelling and jostling associated with shops in the narrower, older parts of town. The new tenement buildings and mansions lining Nicolson Street had a uniform quality Black deemed pleasing on the eye.

The only disagreement between Cullen and Black was whether to be upfront with George about the true nature of their interest in him. Of course, Cullen wished to explain everything upfront. Black persuaded him it was a bad idea.

"We don't know anything about the boy," he'd argued. "We don't know how he'll react." Left unsaid was the concern they'd push a talented student towards Brown, who held no qualms about stoking a vulnerable ego.

Cullen wasn't going to argue too forcefully with his colleague, but he made his sentiments clear enough. "Well exactly, Joe. Let him react how he may, and then we won't waste any of our time." Black assured Cullen he didn't intend to withhold the truth long.

Unfortunately, their negotiations took place before the

events in Adam Square ripped Black's neat schedule out of his hands. Cullen didn't need to say anything in reproach.

The carriage pulled up outside Duncan's Public Dispensary, a modest two-storey building just off Nicolson Street, with a few columns built into the facade to convey a touch of respectability. Black slipped inside. He would have liked Cullen to have accompanied him on this trip, but the pair drew more attention together than alone.

Black thought of the letter draft on his study desk, abandoned this morning shortly after the words "Dear Madam". The recipient had enquired after Black's personal news, and he wished he was able to communicate how much Brown occupied his thoughts and time of late. Bringing George Stephens into their business at least meant Black felt less alone.

The head nurse he encountered in the entranceway was familiar, for she used to work at the Infirmary.

"Good day, Olivia. Dr Duncan has a patient he wished me to take a look at." Duncan wouldn't object to another physician examining his patients, as long as they didn't interfere with his treatment plan.

The nurse nodded and gestured for Black to follow her through the ward.

Bennie was sleeping when Black approached, an opium-infused rest. He was a sturdy lad with vivid ginger hair, though right now he looked pitiful, lying in the Dispensary coated in sweat. There were red ligature marks on his wrists. Faint groans and murmurs eased through the ward. Duncan did what he could with the place, but the Dispensary still stank of stale bodily fluids.

"The boy arrived with injuries?" Black asked.

The nurse pulled back the thin bedsheet. Scratches clustered near his heart, a dense network of lines. Black leant closer. Traces of dried blood dribbled from some of the wounds. Although the cuts were scabbing over, they had a redness about them Black wouldn't have expected from wounds several days old. Their appearance didn't point towards an infection, though.

Black sensed patterns and order within the random array of notches on Bennie's body. Many of the clusters resembled chemical affinity symbols, the kind Black taught to hundreds of students a year. Fire, salt, sun. Triangles divided with one or two lines, circles overlaid on crosses. Duncan was right—these cuts were deliberate. With the scabbing process beginning to blur the original shapes, Black wondered if he was just looking at simple symbols drawn sloppily or more complex emblems rendered on a challenging canvas.

Memories over twenty years old shuddered inside Black.

Don't rush to conclusions, he told himself. Conclusions interfere with further observations.

The nurse let the sheet fall and drew back, but she stayed close to the bed. Despite her delicate frame, Black's opinion of Olivia was that she was one of the more reliable nurses in this city. She wasn't going to leave a visiting physician alone with one of her patients, not without a direct order from Duncan. She bore responsibility if anything happened during her shift.

Black leafed through Bennie's medical notes, watching the patient more than the words. He could taste phlogiston in the air—the metallic scent of it had caught him before they reached the bed. At first he assumed it came from someone hidden nearby, because it couldn't be from the unconscious boy. Raising and discharging phlogiston was an active act. Yet as Black turned his head and drew his tongue across his lips, he knew the phlogiston emanated from Bennie.

"It's strange the patient is suffering from low nervous fever," Olivia commented. "All other cases I see this time of year are of the inflammatory variety."

"Indeed..." Black remarked, his mind racing. "Though several of my patients presented with low nervous fever last week. That's part of the reason I visited, as it happens. There's a small epidemic."

"Hmm," was Olivia's response. Black hoped his fabricated cases were enough to ease her general suspicion that something was unusual about Bennie. Physicians knew it wasn't worth their time teaching medical theory to the nurses tasked with looking after patients, but smart ones like Olivia picked up snippets from listening in during the teaching rounds.

"Dr Black? Do you think the scars of clinical interest?" Olivia asked after a pause.

"The injuries are no more than foolish student acts, perhaps brought upon himself in delirium. I was simply curious if disturbance caused by the fever hampered the body's wound healing. I observe it does not."

Black felt uneasy deceiving Olivia, but he knew how much the nurses gossiped. The last thing he wanted was for Bennie's case to generate speculation, or for others in the city to become aware of strange fevers amongst the student population.

Having finished flipping through the notes, Black pretended to re-read the second page in more detail.

Bennie shouldn't have that much phlogiston coursing through his nervous system. Aside from his lack of consciousness, bodies weren't designed to hold the levels Black could sense. While fevers and delirium were often associated with internal damage from a phlogiston build-up, any residual energy should have discharged...or killed him.

Black lowered the medical notes and reached for Bennie's wrist as if to check his pulse. It was bad form to treat another physician's patient without their knowledge or approval, and Black knew there was no such agreement between him and Duncan regarding Bennie—but right now he only had a hunch about what was wrong with the boy, and in the time it would take to send word to Duncan and secure permission,

Bennie would either have recovered or deteriorated and Black's theory would remain untested.

The delicate spot in Bennie's wrist was hot to the touch. The metallic taste of phlogiston spilled from Black's mouth into his nose. He could feel it vibrating against his fingertips. A noise or movement somewhere on the other side of the ward distracted the nurse's gaze for a second.

With an imperceptible motion, Black drew some of the phlogiston from Bennie into his body. Not all of the excess— Black knew that could be dangerous to the boy—but a significant quantity. Setting down the medical notes, Black flexed his fingers and let the excess energy slide out his other hand. Discharge it with too much force and the phlogiston would ignite. The air around his hand grew hot, but Olivia wouldn't be able to see that.

"What is Dr Duncan's treatment plan for the patient?" Black asked.

"We're continuing with the sedatives for a few more days, Dr Black. If his fever doesn't come down by then he'll move to a purgative regime."

"Very good," Black murmured. Duncan did not like to rush into risky treatments, especially not when he wasn't confident what ailed the patient. Duncan had no ability nor inclination for wielding phlogiston, and according to his medical theories it wasn't that central to health or illness. The heat around Black's hand was almost unbearable, but he did his best not to flinch or draw Olivia's attention towards it, in case the phlogiston sparked. "Does the patient appear to be stabilising?"

"His pulse and temperature haven't improved since he arrived. Though they don't seem to be getting worse."

Black kept his eye on Bennie. Drawing the phlogiston from him hadn't caused an immediate destabilisation of his condition. He was breathing normally. Black put two fingers on Bennie's neck. He pulled again. This time he drew in as much phlogiston as he could, letting it circulate within his body. The taste of metal grew stronger in Black's mouth, and his heart rate rose. Now his body was the one struggling to adapt to phlogiston overload.

The question was if the symbols cut onto Bennie were expressly for the purpose of trapping phlogiston in his body or if that was an unintended effect in pursuit of some other goal.

"Thank you, Olivia. I shall send word to Dr Duncan that I've examined the patient and will share my private thoughts once I've consulted some references at home." Black smiled at the nurse. "It's been good seeing you again—I trust the position is treating you well?"

"Yes, Dr Black," Olivia replied, sounding relieved. "How kind of you to enquire."

Black picked up his cane. He could feel the excess phlogiston burning within him, but he couldn't risk discharging it in front of Olivia. His hand, now concealed in a coat pocket, looked like he'd plunged it into scalding water. Black knew what his body could tolerate: he'd be able to hold the phlogiston in for a few more minutes before the pain descended. He felt flushed as he turned from Olivia.

Behind him, Bennie sighed and rolled over.

This was one of several possibilities he'd considered this morning, though not the most likely one. Black had consumed a sizeable breakfast of bread, prunes and a glass of milk in anticipation of his constitution being challenged like this.

Waiting outside the Dispensary for a carriage, a chill Edinburgh wind providing sweet relief to his burning skin, Black opened his hand and let the phlogiston slip out. The translucent flames danced down the street into nothingness.

.   .   .

Instead of returning home, Black directed his carriage to the college. His presence there would provide a basic alibi, concealing his afternoon business at the Dispensary. He would need to make a sketch of Bennie's markings while the memory was fresh.

Before he even entered the library wing, his journey was interrupted.

"Dr Black! I hope I'm not disturbing you; I wanted to seek your advice." A young man with sandy hair and mismatched waistcoat buttons hurried over. He was taking Black's lecture course for a second year running.

"Such advice will cost you," Black told him, with an amused expression. "For I need someone to help me unpack a delivery of Wedgewood jars taking up room in the cellar." He needed to do this anyway; an assistant would help him finish the job faster.

Rather than projecting discouragement at being roped into this menial task, the youth beamed. He trailed Black downstairs into the library cellar with undisguised delight.

"I was as fascinated by your latent heat theories as I am confounded by them, and hoped you could direct me to your original papers on the subject."

"There are no papers, so to speak."

"Ah, that would explain why I was having so much difficulty finding them."

Black lit several candles with the aid of matches, though the young man didn't seem to appreciate he could do it any other way, and motioned to the large wooden crate next to the door. He'd prised it open earlier, and together they removed the jars and set them on the table.

Behind him were several rows of laboratory equipment, some over forty years old and belonging to the previous chemistry chairs. The cellar was a low-ceilinged space underneath the library where Black stored his equipment and chemicals between lectures.

The Wedgewood jars were more elegant than Black expected. He'd had them custom made, and designed specifically for demonstrating in a large lecture hall.

"My students were the first to hear about my discovery of latent heat: I presented a full account of my experiments to them as soon as I was satisfied with my ideas. They became its most vocal heralds. Every natural philosopher knows the origin of latent heat, so I don't have to worry about setting my claims to print."

His assistant looked dubious. "If I had such a wonderful insight I would be terrified of others claiming credit for it. Truly you are an example to us all, Dr Black."

Black thought this was enough conversation to satisfy the youth, and he bade him to redirect his attention towards clearing space on the shelves for the new jars. However, to the youth, proximity to his teacher meant the opportunity to ask every single question fermenting in his mind.

"But what of your current philosophical enquiries? To be struck with a second seismic insight would seem like a blessing from heaven, but if any man of learning was favoured by God it would be you, Dr Black. What new questions are you investigating?" The young man regarded Black, his focus on the jars and glassware slipping away.

Black tried to recall the last time he'd conducted original research. Earlier this year he carried out those experiments to measure animal heat, did he not? Or maybe that was more than a year ago. Could it really have been that long, he wondered.

Black shook his head. "A few questions from manufacturers come in now and then: analysis of this material, an opinion requesting the viability of some new process. I wish I had time to devote to keeping ahead of the latest ideas, but other business demands my attention." He hoped he didn't sound too defensive.

It wasn't that he never managed to get into the laboratory and experiment—it was just that he never had the mental breathing room once he was done solving other people's problems. Analysis and opinions often came with compensation, coin or otherwise, while original discoveries were supposed to be their own reward.

This went some way to explain why Black remained eager to push his proposal through the Town Council. If he had the dedicated laboratory space, why, then he'd have no excuses not to get back into research.

"It's tiring for me just sitting through your lectures five days a week," the student admitted, unaware anyone could misconstrue his casual honesty for rudeness. "I can't imagine how tiring you must find lecturing."

"I've only ever presented a few scientific papers to my peers, and I much prefer teaching," Black said. The last time he attended a debate at the Medical Society, he was shocked at how charged the atmosphere was, as the students clashed over a paper from the French Academy.

The young man was caught up in his own imagination now, and only half listening. "To think how fast our understanding of nature is changing, how many questions each new discovery poses! You must have followed Dr Brown's theories on phlogiston—his insights are sure to change the face of medicine."

7

Despite their nocturnal adventures, the two professors insisted George attend anatomy as usual. He crossed the yards with a heightened awareness of his surroundings and the pockets of students conferring on the edges. How could he identify Brunonians? Was there any chance last night's street thugs included a fellow student?

The anatomy theatre was almost full when he arrived. In the grimy light George saw space next to James in the middle tier of seating. He was seated and fumbling for paper when it occurred to him that sitting next to a Brunonian sympathiser wasn't a smart decision.

Beyond a disdainful sniff, James barely reacted to his presence, which was a normal response from the boy. There was no indication he knew what had transpired in Adam Square last night.

George initially thought Black's invitation to stay in a guest bedroom was pure kindness. Now he wondered if Black had used it to delay word of the attack circulating. If he'd returned to his lodgings clutching a bleeding arm, it would've invited questions.

Helming the dissecting table, Monro remained in discussion with another student, neither appearing in any rush to end the conversation and commence the lecture.

Pierre and James must have known each other. Pierre was a Brunonian, was he not? James was in Mrs Collins' parlour when news of Pierre's death reached the lodgers—George couldn't remember how James greeted the news. The fact he couldn't remember meant there was nothing unusual to James' reaction. Neither too little nor too much emotion. George was desperate to ask him about Pierre but couldn't think of a naturalistic line of questioning.

Squinting at the papers on his knee, George plunged through his memories in search of clues as to what yesterday's lectures were about. Copying his lecture notes every evening after class was how he usually kept the content in his mind, but he had been too distracted by circumstance yesterday, and the street fight flushed every other recollection out.

There was a mocking quality to James' expression, ostensibly fixed on the front of the room. George feared he was still his target.

"Say..." George didn't want to engage his fellow lodger on coursework, but he feared if he didn't control the conversation, James would use the silence to question why George didn't come home last night. "Can you recall the matter with the superior oblique and the medial maxillary bone? I know Professor Monro spoke of it yesterday, but I failed to capture the specifics."

"The superior oblique and the medial maxillary?" James hooted. "Stephens, you scab! Your wit is slower than usual if you think that's what Monro spent half an hour lecturing us about."

Stung, George fumbled through his papers again. He was sure that was what Monro had spoken about—his messy notes implied it was so—and he couldn't understand why James suggested he was mistaken.

"Haha, Campbell—you can't really believe Stephens would make such a ridiculous mistake," came a voice behind them. Edward leant forward with a dramatic flourish, squeezing James' shoulder. "I rather imagine Mr Stephens here is jesting with you." He gave George a conspiratorial pat on the back and reclined.

For a moment James looked dubious, unwilling to concede he'd been duped. He frowned at George. "That's not possible."

George could be honest and admit his mistake, even if it gave weight to James' insults. Agreeing with Edward pushed the mockery onto James and gave him precious relief, though it wouldn't help him figure out what Monro had actually told them yesterday. Passing the mockery on didn't feel fair, but that was surely George's naivety thinking. The medical school was a harsh, competitive place. Success in this city only came to men like Edward.

"I'm afraid it is, James," he scoffed, as Monro cleared his throat in signal for the class to pay attention. "Fancy you not realising that."

* * *

By late afternoon The Mermaid was crowded, but it took George only a minute to identify a large group of individuals around the central table. George took a few cautious steps towards them.

After breakfast, once Cullen was in the other room, Black had pulled George aside.

"Before you depart, know that Dr Cullen and I are secure in our reputation and honour, and you don't need to defend us against every one of Dr Brown's crude slights. Focus on uncovering his goals, and stay your tongue."

George wasn't sure why Cullen might contradict what sounded like sensible advice from Black, but since it seemed Black wanted his words delivered in confidence, he made no further comment on it.

There was only one individual in the tavern who could be Brown. He was seated at the biggest table, and whenever he laughed or cracked a witticism, laughter rippled out across the room. Most men in the group had at least one eye on him, even when they were engaged with others.

Brown was a hefty man, with a bulbous nose and florid cheeks. The other reason the eye was drawn to him was because unlike every sombre physician George had encountered, he was dressed in a cinnamon-coloured suit—the brightest attire in the room.

George didn't know how he was going to attract Brown's attention, given how involved he seemed in everybody's conversations: he would jump into what the men behind him were saying, then direct a separate comment halfway across the room. As he stood there awkwardly, a lad George recognised from somewhere about the university pushed his way over to Brown and whispered in his ear.

"Wha'?" Brown bellowed. Then he caught sight of George.

"Well, if it isnae the man of the hour, Mister George Stephens! Wha' took ye so long, lad?"

It sounded like half the tavern let out a sarcastic cheer. George tried to back away, but someone draped a heavy arm over his shoulders.

"I'm jist joking, son," Brown said. George was familiar with plenty of rural accents, but he struggled to comprehend this Doric burr. The arm over his shoulders drew him up to

Brown's table. "The Old Spasm too busy cutting open patients' arms to come along too?"

George did his best to keep his expression neutral. According to James—who wasn't here, thank God—one of Brown's biggest contentions with current medical practices was its supposed over-reliance on bloodletting as the cure for all ills. He now appreciated Black's advice of stoicism might be difficult to adhere to.

"I cannot say, sir." It was true. Neither Black nor Cullen had told George what they were doing this afternoon.

His discomfort was enough sport for Brown, who laughed and slapped the table.

"Seat yerself down, that's a good lad. Wha'll yer drink be? Today the drinks are on Bruno!"

The tavern keeper, seemingly attuned to the group, set several cups of watery ale on the table and pushed one in George's direction. While unfazed by the unpleasant men crowding her, George saw no sympathy in her eyes towards him. He was on his own here.

Sitting in close proximity to Brown was one of yesterday's attackers, left arm bandaged and held close to his chest. The man glared at George with the same intense hatred he'd bestowed last night.

George decided not to say anything to him, because it was almost certain to deepen his ill will. His silence didn't make things better either, but the attacker was unlikely to want George's apologies. He settled on a brief nod.

In response the attacker pulled back his coat with his functioning arm, his eyes not once leaving George's. Tucked into his waistband was a pistol. He sneered. George looked away.

"Unfortunate incident the other night, eh?" Brown remarked. "Dinnae look so frightened, son! It's no' your fault the *guid* doctors chose to confront the men I asked tae keep an eye on them."

George blinked. That wasn't what he had expected to hear from Brown, and he wasn't sure if he should point out that his men were the ones confronting them. But as he debated, Brown moved the conversation along.

"Anyway, did ye hear about the uproar at the boxing match last week? I imagine an active young lad as yerself would be interested in the sport."

"Umm, I couldn't say, sir." George had no interest in boxing.

"Well, out with it! What's on yer mind then?"

"I heard about Bennie," George told him, feeling his heart race. Leaving aside the question of fire-wielding ability, a man as large as Brown couldn't move as fast as him. But if Brown practised boxing, he wouldn't have to.

Brown cocked his head. "Wha' did ye hear, son?"

Casual conversations bubbled down to a minimum. Now it felt like the whole tavern wanted to hear his answer.

"Very little," George hastily replied. He didn't want to provoke Brown. There were a lot of men standing behind him, out of his line of sight. "Only that he was a loyal student of yours."

Brown grunted. "Damn fine lad, our Bennie. I got word he was taken ill at the same time others heard. Woulda treated him myself had I known."

George took a sip from his ale in a bid to collect his thoughts. Should he imply he knew Pierre's death was connected to Brown?

"He was sick...or injured?"

Was it George's imagination, or did he hear someone scoff behind him?

"Whit are ye, my confessor? Nah, I know what fanciful thoughts the Old Spasms have about me. Why would I injure the fine fellows who drink to my health every night?" The loose congregation around the table roared again.

"I didn't mean to offend you," George added hastily. He had first thought ten or fifteen men in the tavern were Brunonians; now it seemed everyone kept an eye on Brown, mirroring his reactions. "But others who didn't know what transpired were growing concerned." Brown knew he was here at the behest of Cullen: he may as well admit it.

Something heavy collided with George's back. Shoved forward, he smacked into the table, causing everyone's drinks to wobble.

Winded, George struggled around to identify the source of the attack, but a large hand was already on his shoulder.

"Haha, apologies, young squire—that scoundrel over there jostled me. You want to call him out?" The heavyset man at George's back dug his hand deeper into George's shoulder, in a way that wasn't meant to be soothing. George couldn't see who he was pointing to. He shook his head and tried to refocus on Brown.

The hand lingered on George's shoulder for several more seconds before it trailed away. George clutched at his drink. His mouth was dry, but he wasn't thirsty.

"Come on, son," Brown murmured, not reacting to the exchange. "Yer no longer in the army, no more blindly following orders. Yer now a man of learning who asks questions and comes to his own conclusions."

How was George going to extricate himself from the tavern? His questions about Bennie were barely tolerated, and he dared not breathe Pierre's name.

"Respectfully, Dr Brown," George said, "I did give my word to Doctors Cullen and Black that I would come here on their behalf, and I wish to uphold that." He would do what he could to survive this encounter, but he couldn't let the ruffians assume he was an utter coward.

He thought Brown would slide back into mockery, but

the man merely smiled to himself and tapped the tavern floor with his cane.

"A man who keeps his word? My, they're in short supply these days. The Old Spasms havenae tried proculopathy on ye yet, I hope."

George had no clue what that meant, but Brown spoke with such assurance he didn't dare to admit it. No one else within earshot seemed confused.

"No, sir."

"Good. Nasty, underhand tricks, if ye ask me. Stay well clear of it." Brown heaved his body up from a slouch. "Tell ye wha', son. Come along to the Medical Society meeting this Saturday evening. I encourage the free spirit of debate among my students, and the Medical Society is where my brightest match wits. Howell over there is presenting a paper that'll no doubt promote an energetic discussion of Cullenite doctrine. I imagine yer scholarly journey being so new, ye'll be unfamiliar with certain aspects of Cullen's theories, and'll find our debates illuminating."

How could George refuse? Declining Brown's invitation would make him appear a slavish adherent to Cullen. The onlookers would interpret it as rudeness.

He bowed, his ribs complaining. "I'm honoured by the invitation, Dr Brown."

Brown slapped the table. "Intelligent fellow we have here, eh! Come on, less talking and more alcohol flowing through yer system."

George wasn't sure how much time passed. No one showed any interest in departing. The tavern keeper wordlessly distributed ale whenever she noticed the men's cups were empty, never bothering to engage them in conversation. George could tell she made good money of this crowd, though very few coins changed hands. Brown interspersed consumption of ale with generous portions of snuff, all with the rhythmic steadiness of a man trained for heavy drinking.

George hoped if he stayed long enough Brown would let slip an insight into why he'd hired men to follow the two professors. At this point he was too intimidated to ask directly.

Someone standing behind Brown made a comment George couldn't hear. Brown let out a particularly delighted roar.

"See, they dinnae even dispute the effectiveness of my methods. They know wha' the Brunonian doctrine can do, they're jist scared it'll eat into their patient practice." Then he looked straight at George. "Listen, son—I'll tell ye a tale that illustrates my point.

"Not so long ago I received an urgent letter from Sir John Campbell of Inverneil, telling me his son-in-law, Major Campbell, was seriously ill, and begging for my assistance. Naturally I prepared for an immediate departure from Edinburgh. Ye know where Inverneil is, son? It's almost as far to the west of Scotland as you can go without getting yer boots wet. It was winter when this happened, the weather much like it is now, and every brook was overflowing, every road mud-logged as a privy. Of course, that was only when there were roads to travel upon. Despite this I kept my carriage moving every waking hour: I just had to re-read that desperate, panicked note from a doting father in fear for his son-in-law's life to keep me going through all that shit.

"After the most miserable, filthy weeks, I got to Sir Campbell's country home, and before I had a chance to wipe my mud-stained arse, they brought me to see the poor major.

"'This man is dying,' I told the distressed family. 'There's nothing I can do.' It's no' like me to take one look at a patient and declare defeat, but if ye'd have seen Major Campbell as I saw him then, ye'd come to the same conclusion. Waxy grey skin. Barely a pulse. The major hadnae been able to keep fluids down for days. I couldnae rouse him.

"Well, Lady Campbell let out this awful wail and begged me to say it wasnae so. She loved that boy. She told me, 'Dr Brown, if anyone in Britain, or Europe even, can save Major Campbell, it's yerself.'

"I had tae try, seeing the family weep and plead with me. This was despite a death rattle shuddering in the patient's throat. Everyone who was there with me can tell ye they heard it.

"I couldnae open Major Campbell's mouth—it was locked shut. No chance I could get my medicines into him. So wha' I did was I dipped a quill in wine and put the wine, drop by drop, into the major's mouth.

"All the family and the servants were crowded into Major Campbell's bedchamber with me, yet as I worked I heard not a whisper. Blessed be our Creator, for finally the patient swallowed! After that, I couldnae hear mysel' think because of all the noise. Major Campbell took in more wine, one small sip after the other.

"All together I remained with the Campbells about three weeks. By the time I left, the major was eating and drinking wine with me, a lively dinner companion as ever I met! Oh, for those three weeks I wanted for nothing from the Campbells— I couldnae move from one side of the room to the other without them rushing over, tears in eyes, to heap gratitude upon me for saving the beloved major's life.

"That's the Brunonian doctrine in action, son. That's wha' it has the power to do."

8

Entering the senate room, Black made his way over to Cullen, who was watching the other professors. Black's gaze swept across the room, taking in the marble busts and portraits lining the walls. He understood a new portrait of the lord provost was to be hung, and amused himself predicting where its final location would be. Black then engaged John Hope, professor of botany, in polite conversation for a few minutes.

Black was still thinking about the conversation with Lord Ross regarding his laboratory proposal. After reflecting on Ross' line of questioning, he suspected there were hold-outs in the Town Council. It wasn't clear if their concern was lack of money, or whether Black's proposal intruded upon funds or land earmarked for someone else. Not that it mattered at this juncture—he needed to ascertain who the hold-outs were first.

At this point, Black had his list of Council members and associates he was intimately acquainted with, who would already have cast a favourable opinion on his proposal. The members objecting to his proposal were unlikely to be swayed by any further comments from him now.

Black ran through names, tapping them off with an invisible quill. He needed to focus his efforts at the faculty senate level, talking to those who had an ear to the elites whose support he was missing.

Black supposed he needed two new supporters in the Town Council. Or perhaps one very vocal one.

As he looked around the room at the medical faculty engaged in quiet discussion before the meeting was brought to order, Black marvelled at how harmonious they appeared. Cullen was laughing with Monro and Gregory.

In reality, the school of medicine was more like a loose confederation. They struggled the same way the disparate American colonies struggled to achieve unified action, which was why Black was cynical the colonists' rebellion would hold.

None of the professors subscribed to the same medical theories; in fact, they often diverged dramatically. Nor was there a rigid hierarchy beyond the agreement, often made through gritted teeth, that as chair of the practice of physic, Cullen sat at the top of the pile.

"I suppose we should commence this thing..."

The day's main order of business concerned a gentleman from France who wished to complete his medical education in Edinburgh. The problem was he'd accumulated a couple of years of study at a small French university, and no one in Edinburgh knew the first thing about the quality of instruction there. Although the gentleman's letters seemed satisfactory, at least according to Monro, to whom they were addressed, Doctors Young and Gregory didn't consider his two years of education in France to be equivalent to two years at Edinburgh and didn't want to waive any of the usual course requirements.

"Had he attended Montpellier, I agree we wouldn't be having this conversation..." one of them argued.

It didn't make much difference to Black whether the usual requirements were waived—he was sure the gentleman would want to attend his chemistry course. But his support for one side could be transformed into a bargaining chip for himself.

Monro was already firmly in support of Black's chemistry laboratory proposal, because a split chemistry course would dampen his own enrolment numbers. He'd even shared with Black some of the material he used to petition the Council for his new anatomy theatre.

After Monro it was probably Dr Young, the professor of midwifery, whose political influence Black could most benefit from. Regrettably, Dr Young was distracted by a power struggle with Dr Hamilton, who privately lectured on midwifery and sought Young's chair for himself.

Right now, Monro wanted to give this gentleman the same benefits he'd give a student who studied at Leiden, Reims or Montpellier. Black couldn't afford to take a strong opposing stance to Monro, but he decided there was space to come down closer to Dr Young's position.

Black leant forward in his chair.

"I agree with Dr Young that the gentlemen from Besançon should submit to the oral examination, even if he claims to have passed it. However, we should consider waiving the aphorism commentary requirement." Agreement murmured around the room. This was a compromise the faculty could tolerate.

Looking over at Monro, Black caught a flicker of annoyance in his expression. It was clear Monro wouldn't get this student matriculated without some remedial education—that was the consensus most faculty would agree upon—but perhaps he'd hoped for a stronger show of support from Black.

There would be no lasting harm to their relationship, but Black hoped an opportunity for him to support Monro would come up before he needed to call in any kind of favour. A professor like Monro always kept score.

Black chose four o'clock, when most students were on their way to dinner, to head into the college library. Given his own scholarly book collection at home, he didn't need to borrow many books from the university, though today he wanted to consult some old dissertations.

The library was warm without being stifling; high windows protected its manuscripts from the Edinburgh elements. The stained-wood furnishings and dark royal portraits from the previous century added respectability to the space.

Students were usually cowed by the austere, dimly lit hall, but today Black could hear raised voices from a table in the corner. Frowning, he strode towards the source of the noise. But before he was within admonishing distance, Black heard the name Dr Brown.

Shrinking behind a row of books, Black listened to the students. This was the first time in months he'd encountered a group of Brunonians, and it seemed they hadn't heard him enter.

A pale boy with dirty-blond hair dominated the conversation, the nasal edge of his voice rising above the rotunda.

"Getting into the Infirmary wards was the easiest part—how many pennies did it cost you, Alfie?"

A deeper voice chuckled. "Ten pennies between two nurses." The speaker settled deeper into his chair.

"The night-time nurses are cheaper than the daytime ones," the nasal boy continued. "All they want is an excuse to sit with their bottles for an hour."

Black's eyes darted around the library. No one was in his line of sight to witness his eavesdropping. It was just him and the gaggle of Brunonians, who didn't realise he was there.

"Remember that lass with puerperal fever?" another voice

piped up. "Terrified as anything! I've never seen James move as fast as he did to clamp her mouth shut."

"Right, right," the ringleader agreed. "Dr Brown told you, it's best to approach the insensible ones. Some of the patients in the Infirmary genuinely believe the traditional Cullenite approaches will save them. They won't listen to reason."

"It's not like the sick ones have the wits to understand," the deep-voiced student replied. "Once they see how our therapeutic regimen helps them, then they're our loyal friends."

"I suggested bringing a bowl of dripping pudding and offering them that first," the Scottish Brunonian said. "As soon as they ken Dr Brown recommends heavy fat and meat sustenance instead of culinary abstinence, then they become a lot keener on receiving our treatment."

"Best food some of those Infirmary patients have eaten in years," the deep-voiced student noted with a laugh. "And that's Mrs Collins' cooking we're talking about!"

"Hmm..." The nasal ringleader's tone took on an edge of resentment; Black imagined him folding his arms at the table. If his comrade hadn't already suggested his idea to Brown, Black suspected he'd claim credit for it. He was the sort who wanted attention on him at all times.

It was years since Black had supervised clinical rounds at the Infirmary, or attended to patients there. Every physician selected patients for their teaching ward; the patients had to endure an endless stream of gawping medical students and an attending physician who loudly shared their every humiliating medical detail so the stragglers at the back could hear too. Yet countless sick denizens of Edinburgh were turned away from the door every day, because treatment was free.

But here were Brunonians bragging about sneaking into the wards to experiment on patients, bribing nurses for access.

So why would the Brunonians experiment on their own

adherents? Especially when those procedures endangered lives?

"Mind that Flemish lass with the sickly wean? No' more than a bairn herself. How many of her sick weans did she bring to Dr Brown afterwards?"

"They weren't all her children, I don't think. I wager a few facts got lost in the Flemish-to-English translation."

From the Brunonians' injudicious conversation, Brown's nightly excursions into the Infirmary were more about advertising his medical approach and collecting clients from the lower rungs of society. Brown couldn't be making much money off those people—but he could brag about the successful charitable cases and cite them as evidence of his doctrine's superiority.

Removing his hands from the shelf and wiping the sweat off them, Black debated sneaking a glimpse at the Brunonians. He didn't recognise their voices, which unfortunately meant he was unlikely to know them by name.

Black retreated to the far end of the library, the bookshelf blocking his line of sight to the Brunonians. The door there was ajar, and he slipped through without making a noise. He didn't need identification or confrontation.

Especially since it was better all around if the Brunonians didn't know it was him who'd ratted them out.

As Black cut across the yards, a student of his nodded in greeting. He was a thin boy with a wisp of a mouth, freckles and an ungainly stride. The student reminded him of the circumstances under which Brown had first come into Cullen's orbit.

The best part of a decade ago—somewhen in the early 1770s—Black was waiting to receive the draft of a student's medical dissertation he'd been dreading for weeks. The dissertation belonged to a student of the name Horatio, he recalled: another genial but disorganised duke of limbs. Every stage of Horatio's dissertation from conception to delivery proved painful to Black as its supervisor and reluctant midwife. Horatio changed his mind about dissertation topics, ignored Black's advice and ran into all the difficulties Black predicted he would have avoided if he'd just listened the first time. A week before the agreed-upon submission date, Horatio had only read two of the ten medical books Black recommended he consult. He was one of Black's first dissertation students in Edinburgh, and Black feared Horatio had set the miserable standard for medical students to come.

In the most pertinent memory, Horatio crashed into the library where Black waited to receive his draft: the door banged against the wall; the librarian stormed over in uproar because apparently last term Horatio misplaced or damaged several books and had not got around to paying for them.

Black slipped between the librarian and Horatio, apologetically extracting the dissertation and exiting before the boy drew him into the dispute.

When Black was safe in the yards, he turned the bound thesis over in his hands and leafed through it, not doing any more than checking he had plucked the right object from Horatio's hands. He almost tripped, right there in the middle of the college. He had to retreat over to the wall so he could take in what he was reading.

Despite the switch to English as the language of instruction several decades past, medical students still delivered dissertations in Latin. Horatio had stuttered through his oral examinations with barely comprehensible dictation, and Black expected similarly dismal writing that would take him hours to correct.

Instead, Horatio's Latin prose was clean, elegant even. It had to be Horatio's dissertation because the topic was what they'd belatedly agreed upon, but his Latin flowed beautifully. The phraseology also made Horatio's clumsy interpretation of animal heat sound plausible.

"Who was the grinder that helped Horatio compose this dissertation?" Black asked Cullen sometime later.

"Probably John Brown." Cullen shrugged. "Last year he helped several medical students translate aphorism commentaries—word of his Latin fluency got around and he's now in high demand for dissertation translation. I heard he's studying theology, but picks up medical concepts incredibly fast."

"His talent is wasted on the theologians then." Black smiled, a quip he later came to regret.

9

George picked his way home. He left the tavern on a circuitous route to throw off anyone following him, but after a few turns he realised James could tell Brown where he lived. Fortunately, no one came out of the tavern after him.

George intended to return to his lodgings instead of directly meeting the professors. He needed some time to compose himself, for he was shaking with anger.

The professors were awfully quick to send him into such a dangerous situation. George hadn't realised Brown boasted that many supporters, and he'd assumed from the professors' remarks they would be less hostile than they were. To make matters worse, he'd gleaned nothing from the encounter.

He was two doors from his lodgings when he found his path blocked by Edward and a group of his friends.

"Tell me you're not back from Dr Cullen's dwellings again, Mr Stephens!" Edward called out, elbowing George in the ribs. "Old Mrs Cullen will be sick of the sight of you."

George winced. Edward meant to be jocular, but the pointy end of his elbow stung.

"Not in this instance, no." The fact he was going to

Black's house later, and that he'd yet to set foot inside Cullen's home, didn't seem worth mentioning. "I thought you called on Dr Cullen often?" he asked.

"Not as often as you do." Edward laughed, though it sounded forced for some reason. "He's a busy man and it seems ungracious to demand too much of his time."

What a blundering teuchter I am, George thought. Too little time engaging with the faculty in this town and I come across as ignorant; too much time spent with the faculty and I come across as entitled.

Since Edward had defended him against James in anatomy, George had thought he was in Edward's graces. Now the air of mockery blew back in his direction. Was this fickle treatment just the price of existing in Edward's orbit? Or had he inadvertently offended his chum?

Begging Edward to tell him what the matter was seemed like an invitation for more mockery, so George settled on giving him a stiff bow. "Likewise, Edward, I would not wish to impinge upon your time, as you are evidently called off somewhere."

Edward let out another laugh. "No exalted mission for me. I'm meeting Neville at the theatre. He promises me the Bard receives good treatment."

"Which play is it?" George asked, affecting more interest than he felt. He'd dared believe Edward would include him in his next social outing, and felt wounded that he hadn't.

"*The Tragedy of Julius Caesar*. Or is it the tragedy of Marcus Brutus? Anyway, don't drink Mrs Cullen's wine cellar dry!"

In the safety of his room, George let his anger coalesce. It was mostly directed at Black and Cullen, though a smaller quantity was aimed back at himself. He'd thought by helping the professors he would raise his social standing and the trajectory of his medical studies. Instead, he was pushed into humiliating situations: derided by the Brunonians and successful students like Edward for associating with the wrong crowds.

Whatever the truth in Cullen's paranoia, it wasn't George's problem. Brown knew George was little more than Cullen's messenger; he didn't see him as a threat. Or much of anything, if he was honest.

George considered refusing to call on Black. However, that seemed unduly spiteful. He would tell the professors what had transpired in the tavern, then politely excuse himself from rendering further assistance.

* * *

"Good evening, Mr Stephens. I was worried something happened. Can we set you up with some wine...or maybe just tea?" Cullen ushered George over to the parlour settee next to the hearth. Black was already seated on a chair across from him, staring pensively into the flames.

George wasn't sure what to say. It was true he'd arrived late, and that was only partially due to how long he was trapped with the Brunonians. He worried whatever came out of his mouth would sound accusatory. The fact that Cullen, unlike Brown, seemed so welcoming towards him added to his confusion.

"You engaged with our acquaintance at The Mermaid?" Cullen pressed when it was apparent George wouldn't start speaking of his own accord.

"Yes, sir," George started. "It was no use, I'm afraid. He said nothing of value."

Cullen passed George a teacup and remained standing. "But you asked him why his men followed then accosted us?"

"He claimed we accosted them." Though he accepted the tea, George didn't want to drink anything, not when he was on a mission to confront the professors.

Cullen raised his head to the ceiling and mouthed an exclamation.

"And his students? He had no answer to their fate?"

George shook his head. "Said they just fell to illness."

"It's not like our Bruno to avoid bragging about his wild schemes," Cullen said. "Circumspection was never his strong point."

Black barely engaged with the conversation. With Cullen in a constant of motion, Black kept his eyes on the fire, without indication of what was on his mind. Fluttering shadows concealed his expression.

"One of my attackers was there with him," George blurted out. "Waved his pistol at me. Most of them in the tavern weren't even medical students; it was a wholly unsavoury crowd of characters." He didn't want to admit outright how threatening it had felt. Black's parlour was uncomfortably hot.

"Yes," Cullen agreed. "Brown has a lot of acquaintances from boxing, wrestling and the Freemasons. Some of them even attend his lectures; it is indeed unsavoury."

The possibility that the men surrounding George in the tavern knew how to wield phlogiston hadn't even occurred to him.

George hadn't questioned the professors' claim it would take him months to master the art of phlogiston-wielding, but he felt a stab of annoyance knowing they'd sent him into a Brunonian lair without any means of defending himself from their powers. Surely they could have taught him one or two basic attacks?

"I don't think I'm of any use trying to get information out of Brown," George said, hoping he wouldn't have to resort to a direct snub of the professors. He rotated the delicate cup in his hands, even as hot liquid splashed onto his fingers.

"Not at all," said Black, finally turning to face him. "You did everything we expected of you. We can surmise that Brown is not ready to negotiate with us, because he would have been more cooperative with you. So perhaps his agenda remains ongoing. And obviously he didn't menace you in the tavern, so we can conclude assailing us further is not his immediate objective."

While Black was correct that Brown hadn't issued a direct warning, the implicit threats from his accomplices were very real to George. Maybe the danger didn't feel great to Black, but it was to him. Which is why he finally made an incautious reply in the hope his feelings would be acknowledged.

"Brown did threaten me, in a way," George admitted. He thought of the confrontation in Adam Square, and Black's words before he pushed George to attack. "And respectfully, sir, I don't think it was wise of you to declare that I shouldn't inflict mortal injury on those ruffians last night—they could have taken advantage of us."

A very queer expression played across Black's face. Cullen stopped pacing and looked pointedly at his colleague.

"Oh, really? I wasn't aware I said...

...anything at all."

George started. Black's last words leapt towards him, sounding as if they were muttered in his ear while Black remained in calm repose in front of the fire. He couldn't doubt auditory trickery was at play, but he was still struggling to make sense of what was going on.

"Not everybody has this natural ability as strongly as you, George," Black continued. *"It's why Dr Cullen and I were keen to make your acquaintance after our first meeting."*

Finally, George began to process what was so strange about this conversation, which was turning his stomach and clouding his brain. Black was talking to him and he could hear every word, but his lips weren't moving.

"Sir, I..."

"I apologise, George. I meant no malice by not explaining

sooner." Now Black's mouth moved in sync with his words, which dislodged some of George's queasiness but meant that other emotions were rushing in.

What was this cruel trick the professors were playing on him? They'd been toying with him for weeks! This was just another deception piled onto deception.

George wanted to hurl his china teacup at the man's face. Instead he set the half-empty cup down on the table, but his hands were so clumsy he knocked it onto the rug. He thought about bending down to pick it up, but another part of his brain wanted to stomp on it instead.

Neither Black nor Cullen moved, or stopped watching him. George felt detached from his body. Panic rose inside him. He was dimly aware he had no idea what the two men were actually capable of, or what they intended to do next. Nodding brusquely to them, he turned and rushed from the room, desperate for the protection of the anonymous darkness outside.

10

"That was my fault, William. I'm sorry," Black said.

Cullen placed the cup George had dropped back on the table, murmured a few remarks to Black's manservant as he pointed out the spilled tea, then returned to the sofa. Cullen could be magnanimous following a disagreement, though only when he was proven right.

"Don't worry, Joe. Just give the boy some time. He didn't sound particularly enamoured with our foe."

Black sighed. "That should put me at ease. But it's so long since I was his age, William. I don't know what a boy like George will decide to do next."

The two men sat in silence. Cullen finished his glass of wine.

"You said Lord Ross spoke with you? Any word on your chemical laboratory proposal from above?"

Black shook his head. "Nothing definite one way or another. Young agreed to raise the issue with his patron, and at the very least determine who is digging their heels in. It always takes a while to convince the Town Council to dispense with money for scientific pursuits: they think we seek little more

91

than to extract sunlight from cucumbers and cajole spiders into weaving silk cloth."

Cullen chortled. "They have no grounds to refuse you, Joe. No one disputes your stature."

* * *

Black's dark thoughts hadn't cleared by the next morning, so in the chilly pre-dawn light he made his way to the library cellar.

Black went straight to the shelves at the furthest end of his chemical storage space. On the bottom shelf was a small leather trunk, concealed behind a row of oversized emerald distillation glassware. Most of the glassware back here was too cracked or opaque for use in lectures, though Black hated to discard such valuable objects. Moving it aside, he eased the trunk out onto the floor.

He'd not touched this trunk in decades. It wasn't good to dwell on what he'd cast into history. Black was careful not to be too explicit in what he wrote down for posterity, knowing how dangerous his words could be if they fell into the wrong hands. The contents of the trunk were the briefest notes, existing only to stimulate his memory. He had wanted to do this yesterday, but the appearance of that student had changed his plans.

Black reached to unlock the trunk, but as he touched the lid it fell open. The precursor of sunlight was only just reaching the cellar. Black raised a now-alight hand.

Someone had forced the lock.

Instinctively Black looked around, but of course the cellar was deserted. It had been years since he'd come near the trunk, hadn't it? The glassware he'd just moved was all coated in an even layer of dust—no recent hand marks. Neither he nor the young man who helped him arrange his new Wedgewood jars had come this far into the cellar yesterday.

Black peered into the trunk, then pulled out the small folio of papers. Riffling through them, he couldn't say for certain any were missing, though if anybody came looking for incriminating evidence, they wouldn't find it here. Given that Black and his assistants only came into the cellar once or twice a day in the mornings, intruders who knew his schedule would have the leisure to copy anything they found.

After deliberating for a moment, Black removed all the papers and replaced the trunk on its shelf. He suspected Cullen would want to make use of his notes.

Black made a careful circuit of the cellar, but there were no other obvious signs of disturbance.

Any preoccupation with the boy George Stephens was cleanly removed from Black's mind, given the scope of the issue presenting itself to him.

Suspicious symbols carved onto Bennie, and when Black went to consult the decades-old notes he thought relevant to the situation, he found someone had got there before him. His and Cullen's problems went beyond Brown now.

The dark chymists were back.

* * *

In a small courtyard wedged between the Chapel of St John and the High Street, Black pushed the curve of his back into the wall and dared to look up at the window above him. A patina of green slime coated the wall a little to his left where runoff from the roof made its mark, and the courtyard smelled of damp stone. The air was crisp, winter settling into the ancient city.

Unlike Cullen, who flourished as the hours grew shorter, Black was a great believer in early nights and early mornings.

He was out and about later than he'd like, but he needed to be this late to avoid attention, and also because Brown would have finished his Masonry business by now and would be leading the conviviality in one of the Masonic lodge rooms.

Black pulled his felt cocked hat down past his eyebrows. With his sombre black attire, only a glint of his pale skin would alert the casual passerby that he was hiding in the shadows. Suitably positioned, Brown's voice carried easily through the open window.

So far, not even Cullen had considered following Brown and listening in to his conversations. Now that dark chymists were in the equation, the two had agreed such action was prudent. If Cullen hadn't a dinner engagement tonight he would be huddled against the wall with Black.

"Aye, they picked a champion alright. Boy nearly shat himself on two occasions."

"Three!"

"Aye, three it mighta been."

Black knew they were talking about George Stephens. Maybe Black was misinformed of the boy's military conduct: he had told the boy repeatedly that Brown wasn't going to retaliate in the middle of a crowded tavern; he shouldn't have been so fearful. Though it was a relief to know the boy was scared of the Brunonians: if Brown thought he'd join their ranks, he would surely be bragging about it.

"They've got no power," Brown was now telling his friends. It wasn't hard following along—most people in the room were listening, not speaking. "Old Spasm performs no more than tricks, and his—heh—*black lapdog* is too scared to do anything at all."

It was a shame he'd hidden the boy's proculopathic talents from him: if George hadn't stormed off, he could have been the one listening in on Brown this evening.

"Aye, aye," Brown said, shushing an interlocutor. "No one

at the college wants to admit it's all an illusion, that there's nothing there. I tell ye, if their doctrines were so much better than ours...why can they no' prove it?"

That's not true in the slightest, Black thought, tensing and releasing his fist in the hope his concentration wouldn't falter. If it came to a demonstration of phlogiston-wielding abilities, William and he would win.

"Right." Brown's voice rose, and Black forced himself back from his reverie. "The secret decider will make it so clear even the blind fools in the medical faculty willnae be able to miss it."

This snapped Black out of his indignation. He hadn't heard Brown boast of a secret "decider" before. Was this a person or an object?

"...soon, soon," was the last distinct remark he caught. Brown's voice faded into the general swell of noise; if they returned to the topic, Black was not able to hear.

Eventually, the scrape of chairs and general movement told Black the Masons were departing the lodge, likely in the direction of a tavern. He withdrew from the light of the window, readjusted the collar of his knee-length coat, shook his aching legs and tried to make himself fade into the shadows.

A thought came unbidden into Black's mind: if the Brunonians wanted a demonstration of strength, he could give them one this very evening, right here on St James Street.

And why not? He'd eaten well this evening, had managed several large glasses of milk throughout the day to settle his stomach. Despite the privacy of the close, he was steps away from the still-bustling High Street and the protection those crowds afforded him. If Cullen were here, the septuagenarian would have tried to leap through the window by now.

But even as Black calculated the risks, reason quelled his wild notions. His and Cullen's refusal to descend to spectacle was what proved them better than the Brunonians, who wielded phlogiston because they craved status. His inclination to humiliate them was base, nothing more than a knee-jerk response to their taunts. Black must rise above such egotism.

The Brunonians started to file past him through the close and into the High Street. They were all laughing amongst themselves, paying no attention to the shadows in corners. Black didn't want to stare too closely, but he could see the outsized figure of Brown moving resolutely at the middle of the horde.

As they passed, Black was overcome with a belated urge to pursue, to step out of hiding and proclaim his challenge. But like the Brunonians, that too faded into the brisk night air.

II

The Medical Society met only a short distance from his lodgings at the College of Surgeons, but George arrived as late as permissible in the hopes of avoiding undue attention. Brown's hearty laugh came from the front of the room, packed as before within a crowd of Brunonians.

The Society met in a hall of modest size, though its high vaulted ceiling made the space seem more impressive. The walls were painted in green marbled effect, and the floor occupied by rows of benches facing the main debating area.

As the week rolled past, George had done his best to focus on studying and forget the physicians' squabbles. The morning after he stormed out of Black's house, a note from Cullen arrived at his lodgings, which George immediately hurled into his fireplace. He regretted doing that almost as soon as the paper ignited, but reasoned he wasn't ready to deal with the professor's excuses or attempts to guilt him.

George remained angry at Cullen and Black for what they'd done to him, though his mind was woolly on what drove his rage. He didn't want to delve into his feelings, because parsing why he felt this way was the first step towards understanding why the professors acted in such a manner, and that was a step towards forgiving them for what they'd done. Which he wasn't ready to do.

He was then afraid the professors would show up at his lodgings or catch him about the college if he didn't respond to their message. After a few days when that didn't happen, he felt disappointed.

Entering the hall, he saw the unmistakable flash of James' pale straw hair in front of him, and as George took his seat, his fellow lodger motioned for him to come closer.

"What brings you here?" the boy asked. "I thought you preferred more...old-fashioned company of late." There wasn't outright rudeness in his voice, but he made no extra effort to be friendly.

"Dr Brown invited me," George replied. "I'm surprised word hasn't circulated."

James appraised him for a moment. "You agree on the scientific validity of our doctrine, then?"

George remembered being on parade outside Philadelphia several years ago, watching General Howe on horseback, his pale grey charger glowing in the early-morning light. George couldn't take his eyes off the horse, tossing its head as it trotted down the lines. His commander was entirely forgettable: George wished he possessed the haughty grace of that horse.

"Well, I'm prepared to be convinced on merit of the strongest evidence presented tonight," he replied with a lofty air that he hoped projected the same pride. "Not just by the most forceful rhetoric." How he wished he had Edward's confidence. If his friend saw him this evening, he imagined he'd be impressed with how assuredly he was conducting himself.

James turned up his nose. "Well, it's set to be a *proper* debate this evening. We're making sure of it."

George had first hoped divine intervention would get in

the way of tonight's debate, that he'd find a way to skirt Brown's invitation. Then it occurred to him he should be delighted at the opportunity to re-engage with the Brunonians.

"Say," George said lightly, "was Pierre a Brunonian comrade of yours?"

James frowned. While Pierre existed at the forefront of George's mind, his name required recall from everyone else.

"The student who died? He appeared at a couple of our gatherings earlier in the term. Tried too hard to impress us, didn't know what he didn't know. Was a shame he passed...but his attempts at intellectual discussion amused us."

George pretended James wasn't comparing him to Pierre with that assessment.

"Why did Bennie and Pierre both fall to fever?" Saying this, George didn't know Bennie was even alive, but no rumours circulated to the contrary.

"Maybe they caught it from each other," James retorted, eyeing George's stupidity with contempt. "Bennie wasn't much smarter. Can't believe Dr Brown gave either of them the time of day."

Hunger for approval made young men do foolish things, George realised with a shudder. He hated seeing himself in the Brunonian victims, but there he was. If Brown knew he was risking lives, why would he endanger his most valued supporters? Approach the orbiters, the objects of in-group derision. Imply respect could be earned, all Brown needed was a brave volunteer...

From the front of the room came a few thumps of Brown's stick. George slumped as low as he could.

"Esteemed gentle-fellows...lend me yer ears."

Not content to stay seated at the head of the debate, Brown paraded in front of the students as if he were delivering another lecture course.

"Are ye ready, Howell? As ye know, Mr Howell agreed to present his paper on the use of opium as a stimulant in treating pneumonia. Ye also know our *esteemed* professor friend says opium only acts as a sedative, so maybe Howell will explain how such an obviously wrong conclusion was made. Not that any of 'em would admit they were wrong, not even after seeing irrefutable evidence with their own eyes!

"Dr Cullen only cares about himself and his reputation: shame on me for not seeing the Old Spasm's duplicity sooner. Aye, but when I did, I set him a test to prove his loyalty beyond question. Of course, he failed it."

The others must have heard the story a hundred times, for they gave an appropriate outcry in support. George hoped no one was monitoring his reactions.

He had scant sympathy for Cullen. Maybe if those old professors actually told those around them what was going on, they wouldn't stumble into such conflicts. But several of Brown's students were dead, and Brown appeared culpable.

Brown spent a few minutes addressing the room in Latin. George didn't understand what he said, though the rest of the crowd made appreciative noises.

Finally, Brown made his way to the presiding chair and bade Howell—a reedy scholar with an escaping hairline and rat-tail queue—to rise.

The reading of Howell's paper proceeded smoothly. George tried to bite down his personal disdain for the Brunonians and concentrate on their theoretical arguments. Begrudgingly, he thought Howell presented a large amount of convincing evidence that opium acted as a stimulant when given to pneumonia patients, and he was confused as to why anyone would claim otherwise.

After the reading, audience members rose to ask questions. The room was filled with a steady murmur of approval with each query and response.

Then an older medical student rose to his feet, with the look of someone who'd waited to speak for quite some time.

"Sir, I'm curious as to why you didn't comment on the results from de Ferry's 1774 dissertation?"

At once the atmosphere changed. George had no idea what the dissertation in question was about, but jeers filtered through the air. Several students muttered "Cullenite" disapprovingly.

The medical student turned red, but didn't stumble. "I'm not a Cullenite in the slightest—but the only conclusion you could draw after reading de Ferry's dissertation was that opium sedated the nervous system."

Howell sneered. "I didn't waste my time with that: de Ferry's experiments were too flawed to bother rebutting."

The standing student—George believed his name was Cheltenham—now faced a rising onslaught of whispers.

Brown leant forward in his chair with an amused expression on his face. "Let the lad explain himself, Howell. Seems we have disagreement in the ranks."

"If you devoted the time to examining de Ferry's dissertation, you would find his results contradict the outcome of your experiments with dissected rats, and his explanations are a lot more compelling." Cheltenham looked uncomfortable, but some inner outrage urged him to remain standing.

Except enough time had passed for Howell to decide upon his clever comeback. "You don't need to couch your defence of de Ferry in such false objectivity, Cheltenham. Everyone knows your own medical dissertation is based off his hypotheses." The society hall now sounded a lot like The Mermaid.

"Delivered under the supervision of Dr Duncan, I might add, lest you make further slanders against my name." Cheltenham's voice rose as he strained to keep still. "And I'll have you know my findings support de Ferry's without question."

"What do you think, Stephens?" James smirked over his shoulder.

Startled, George tried to recompose his lofty attitude from a few hours prior. "Well, it's not a very compelling rebuttal, is it? Just measly quibbling over definitions."

"As if you know enough to understand what's going on," James scoffed. His brows knit together.

For the first time, George wished Edward was with them. He always had a quick retort, and knew how to put James in his place.

"I rather think it's you who is struggling," George managed, hoping the time he'd taken to think up his response wasn't significant. He was tired and disgusted with all parties, which helped the words rush out. "You're nothing but a jackal, James, who bares his teeth after his opponent expires. You tear others down because you wish to disguise the fact you're too useless to make a positive contribution to any debate. No one in this university will remember you after you've gone, except as an annoyance."

He thought he'd won that repartee, for James frowned and turned back to watch the unfolding argument.

Then James shot to his feet. "On my word, Cheltenham, you are a liar and a rascal."

At that, all semblance of decorum vanished.

George rushed forward, though the students sitting closer to the pair had already restrained them. James was thrashing to break loose, while Cheltenham cursed his opponent with vehemence.

"You dare call me a liar? You know what that means."

"Yes, I do," hissed James. "And unlike you, I won't need a pistol to prove my honour."

The room erupted. No one was keeping still anymore.

"James!" George yelled in his ear. "What madness is this?"

"Nothing of the sort," James screamed back. "This is the

ultimate evidence of Brunonian superiority—just you watch me. Unless Cheltenham is a coward as well as a liar?"

"Fuck your mother," Cheltenham spat. His voice lowered. "Somebody get me a pistol."

As James continued to thrash, George looked around for support. Surely someone would put a stop to this?

"Fine, James. Prove your stupid point. I wish you all the best."

Brown was nowhere to be seen.

12

As the medical students congregated in the street, George slunk away. James and Cheltenham were forcefully separated and disappeared with their seconds. It would take some time for pistols to be found and a field of honour agreed upon. Maybe cooler heads would prevail by then. But George didn't want to wait around to find out.

How many students heard his exchange with James? Why did he have to goad his unpleasant acquaintance? Edward could have put James in his place without provoking a duel.

For half a street length, George hated Edinburgh. He hated the overpriced, under-cleaned lodgings he had no choice but to inhabit; he hated the condescending professors who thought they were better than him; he hated the whiny, annoying students who thought the same. He hated medicine, its arcane theories and rules. He hated how stupid this city made him look. He hated how poor this city made him feel. He hated that when he tried to do the right thing and act like the right people, it all went wrong. The Brunonians were nothing but hot-headed fools who thought themselves better than everyone else.

George's chest hurt from the amount of unfocussed anger he held inside.

It was unfortunate that the only two men in this city who offered him acceptance and kindness were toying with him for their own amusement.

Yet even as that thought formed in George's head, it didn't stick with conviction. He didn't understand how Black's peculiar abilities served to mock him, only that they surely did. Black and Cullen may have used him, but that was the only time he'd had cause in this city to feel like an asset to anyone.

I don't need to play by this horrible city's rules, George decided. Edward is a natural: I don't have to sneer and act aloof because everyone around me acts in such a way. I shouldn't have burned Cullen's letter.

The hour was creeping towards midnight. George couldn't return to his lodgings yet—what if he ran into James? But Cullen kept late hours, and his house was only a few streets away, tucked in a close off the Cowgate.

Just go and talk to him, George urged himself. If he doesn't give a satisfactory explanation for Black's tricks then that settles the matter. But at least hear what he says.

George was let into Cullen's Mint Close apartment by Anna Cullen, a slight woman with dark curled hair and sharp eyes. She regarded George with a weary but friendly expression.

"Ye'll have had yer supper, Mr Stephens. My husband's in his study. I'll see if he wants to share a glass of wine with ye."

He wasn't sure how he would persuade the Cullen household to let him call upon its master, except that proved a non-issue.

Cullen's house was sprawling by Edinburgh standards, though the building showed its age. The ceilings were low, and wooden panels covered the walls. The floorboards wobbled under George's feet as Mrs Cullen led him through the house.

Like Black's study, Cullen's was a modest space, the occupants hemmed in by bookshelves. The carpet rugs were grey from wear.

George expected he'd find Cullen alone. Yet in the corner sat two young men with piles of books on their knees, scribbling notes on scraps of paper. George thought he'd seen them in the college in Cullen's orbit.

Cullen looked up from his letter-writing, surprised for only a moment.

"Why, it's Mr Stephens! The company tonight gets finer. You're acquainted with Misters Smith and Doyle? Fine gentlemen, the pair of them. They're preparing their doctoral dissertations." He spoke as if it'd been months since their last conversation. The men smiled, then dropped their heads back down to their reading. "I tell all students they have full use of my medical library. As Cicero says, 'A home without books is like a body without soul.'" Cullen had unbuttoned his waistcoat and swapped his physician's attire for a peach house-robe, but had not yet retired his leonine physic wig for the evening.

"Perhaps we could speak in private, Professor Cullen, if it's no trouble?"

"Yes! Yes!" exclaimed Cullen, rising to his feet. "Goodness, where is there an empty room? My sons are working on correspondence in the parlour, I have another student using the writing desk in my bedroom..."

This was probably why Mrs Cullen hadn't offered him much hospitality, George realised. She already had her hands full.

Eventually Cullen led George down the stairs and back out into the courtyard. Some residents of the close were milling about, but they had the space to converse without being overhead.

"Sir..." George thought he knew what he wanted to say, up until the point he tried to say it.

Cullen put a hand on George's shoulder and regarded him carefully.

"How are you feeling, George? I know we upset you the other night. I'm so glad you called. I know Dr Black was anxious about you."

"I don't...I'm fine, thank you, Professor Cullen." He wished he was better at articulating his thoughts, but he had precious little experience of doing so.

"The thing about phlogiston, one of the things at least, is it holds a kind of attraction to itself. It's like the phlogiston in one man senses what the other's is doing. Dr Black is very good at proculopathy."

That was what it was called. After Brown first mentioned the word in the tavern, George had had reason to wonder if that was what he was referring to.

"Can he read my thoughts?" George didn't like voicing such an insecurity, but he'd promised himself he would speak plainly.

Cullen looked amused. He patted George's shoulder.

"Dr Black can read most people's minds just by looking at them—he doesn't need phlogiston connectivity to do that. Wish I was as good at understanding people as he is."

George turned and looked up at the grand building Cullen lived in. It had once housed the Master of the Royal Mint. The courtyard was dark, but there was no sense of danger here.

"He communicated with me that way the first time we met. At my lodgings." It was the only way George could explain the odd moments and echoes in their conversation.

"Yes, some people are natural wielders of phlogiston. We don't know why that is—something about how they're built, perhaps—but I wager only one in a hundred can hear Dr Black's proculopathic messages without any training."

A series of thoughts snapped together in George's head.

"Oh, you were screening students? To see who could hear you?"

"Exactly," said Cullen.

"I thought it was my military experience you were interested in."

"That too," Cullen admitted. "I've taught some very focussed and self-disciplined soldiers over the years. It's a rare pleasure finding a student who listens with such control."

George wasn't sure what else to say, so he looked up at the constellations. It was a clear, still night.

"Dr Black and I were going to talk to you about your proculopathic abilities once we knew you wished to keep helping us," Cullen continued. "We should have told you at once...but lesson learned, as they say."

"You can do what Professor Black does?" George asked.

Cullen laughed. "What a question! Can the man who taught Dr Black everything he knows do what Dr Black does? *Why yes he can.*"

George jumped as Cullen's voice leapt into his ear, but the emotional recoil he had felt with Black didn't return.

Cullen winked at him.

"You're welcome to join me upstairs, drinking to the health of my students, though if you have engagements elsewhere, I'm sure Dr Black would appreciate a note or a visit when you have the chance."

"Actually, sir, the reason I stopped by tonight was because...well, I was at the Medical Society and I...um, the debate turned violent. James Campbell called out Silas Cheltenham."

"Good Lord!" Cullen looked shocked. "How disgraceful. Vile, in fact."

"I know I shouldn't have been there," George continued, determined to press out his confession. "Sir, I told James I wanted proof Brunonianism was the superior doctrine, and he said he intended to use phlogiston as his weapon of choice to prove the point."

"Merciful heavens!"

"And Cheltenham agreed to those terms, and it's all my fault."

"It's not your fault, lad," Cullen insisted. "Bruno has filled those students' heads with all sorts of nonsense, made them think they're invincible. Your acquaintance was looking for trouble long before you spoke, of that much I'm certain." He took a step back and looked around the close. "There's not much I can do. I have no connection with the gentlemen in question, but I can see if any of my friends amongst the student body can extend an influence."

"Yes, sir." George paused. "I'm sorry I lost my temper. I hope Professor Black doesn't think ill of me."

Cullen started to move towards the entrance stairway. George found himself following.

"Course not, lad! Dr Black thinks highly of you. As do I."

* * *

Sunday passed in a deep unease. James didn't return to his lodgings.

As the afternoon shadows luxuriated into evening, a cautious tap at George's door disturbed his poor attempts at studying.

Thomas' dark mop of hair poked into his room.

"Ah, George, I was just lending Edward my chemistry lecture notes." He nodded in a vague manner towards the hall. "Say, I heard yer friend James is holed up with a classmate on Bristo Street, intending to duel at dawn tomorrow. Ye two spoken?"

"What?" At first George was confused how Thomas held such information. Then he remembered Thomas lodged with

Brunonians: Bennie fell ill there. "No, I've not heard from James."

"It might be worth going to see him," Thomas said, his eyes wandering the room. "He's in need of sound counsel, I imagine. He can be found in the tenth building past the Kirk." His voice was unexpectedly gentle.

The silence deepened and itched.

"Well, I'll see. Busy with, y'know..." George flailed his arms in the direction of his untouched study materials.

Thomas appeared to wrestle with his tongue, but nodded and retreated. "Oh, and"—he rebounded back into the room —"I'll probably head across the street to the tavern with Edward shortly...if...?"

"Very busy, I'm afraid," George insisted, now desperate for Thomas to leave. "But, um, thanks."

He couldn't face anyone. How dare Thomas presume he could reason with James? After everything he'd said? What gave the Irishman the right to tell him where James hid?

George slammed his books shut, loud enough he hoped Thomas and Edward would hear him upstairs. But, of course, no one came back to his door.

* * *

As George left his lodgings the next morning, he spied a gathering of students a few doors down. There was something unsettled about them, so George edged closer. One of the students looked up.

"Hey, did you hear about the duel this morning?" George asked. He'd been awake before dawn, listening for sounds of disturbance that of course never came. The noise of a waking city—carts groaning through the street, messenger boys and water carriers hailing each other—consumed everything. Several hours slid past before George gathered the courage to rise from his bed. The absence of James in the lodgings told him his fatalism was deserved.

"I heard the Brunonian got shot," a student replied.

"Killed? Today?"

"No one knows." The student looked vexed at having to explain again what he knew, without prospect of having his own questions answered. "But several different people told me that, and no one is claiming the Cullenite fell."

The others in the knot weren't in a friendly mood, so George took his leave. He needed to find Cullen or Black. He had no idea what else he could do.

It was later in the morning than his usual departure time for lecture, and the streets around the college were quiet. George cut through College Wynd, the quickest route to the yards.

"Hope yer no' in too much of a hurry, young George," came a voice behind him.

George slowly turned around.

Of course it was Brown. He was leaning against the wall of the wynd, his cane drawing leisurely patterns in the dirt.

"Sir, I didn't expect to see you," George said. Which was a stupid remark.

"Ye know me, son: man of the people," Brown cheerfully replied. "No' like those college professors who must be carried everywhere, never touching the earth like common folk. Myself, I prefer to walk the fair streets of this city. Good exercise too, mind."

George tried to look around without making it obvious he was doing so. He couldn't see any of Brown's followers lurking in the wynd, but that didn't mean they weren't there. Brown's relaxed, smiling pose made it clear he knew what George was doing. His cane preoccupied itself with unearthing an oblong stone from the ground.

"What happened to James?" George asked. He knew he

should avoid provoking Brown, but he couldn't keep silent.

"Well, last thing I heard was a fellow man of letters pushed him into a duel against an uncivilised opponent at the Medical Society." Brown made a show of extracting a snuffbox from his pocket, turning it in his hands. "And once the damage was done, the instigator fled back to the professor pulling his strings."

George felt unmoored from his body, the exchange becoming distant and unreal.

Brown opened his snuffbox. A small blush of brown powder floated into the air. His oversized fingers took a pinch, spilling more in the process. "Now, unlike Professor Cullen, I try to be understanding. Perhaps the scholar in question didnae ken what his actions would lead to. Perhaps he didnae ken how fully he was being manipulated." Brown paused to rub the powder over his gums. "By God, Old Spasm is a crafty one: gives Satan a run for his money.

"When I was yer age, an unlicked cub about town, I was the same as ye. Guileless. Ye ken I used to translate medical dissertations into Latin for students? Once dear Dr Cullen saw how skilled I was...well, he took me in and I fell for his entreaties completely. His Latin was never great, ye see; he needed me to translate and draft all his letters. Wanted a Greek tutor for his young children. Couldnae get enough of me. Seems hard tae believe, eh?

"Before long I was repeating his lectures in the evenings to students I was tutoring. Old Spasm had the highest praise for what I was doing. Told me any faculty appointment was mine, I just had to say. Ha! See how that turned out..." Brown gave a rueful shake of his head, slipping the snuffbox back into his coat.

"What I'm saying to ye, son, is no one was there to warn me about Cullen like I'm standing here doing for ye. Ye dinnae have to repeat my mistakes."

"Where is James?" George shakily asked. His real question —*Is James still alive*—remained unasked.

"On whose behalf are ye concerned?" laughed Brown. "His, or yerself?"

"I didn't know James would challenge that other student to a duel." As soon as the words were out of his mouth, George knew he shouldn't have said them, for it was an admittance of involvement.

Brown gave an amiable shrug. "Let Pater Bruno give ye some friendly advice. Stay away from William Cullen. Ye may lack the social nuances to be around my Medical Society 'til ye've learned how to conduct yerself, but nothing good will come of yer association with Old Spasm. I ken ye've got enough smarts to see what I'm talking about."

George forced himself to nod.

Brown made an exaggerated tilt of his ear in George's direction.

"Yes, sir," George managed.

Brown bared his snuff-encrusted teeth in what passed for a grin.

"Well, then we have no further business." Brown started to move along the lane but paused. "Oh, and the honourable Dr Joe Black has his head so far up his former teacher's arse they're the same person, tae all intents and purposes. Stay away from him too." He tipped his hat and sauntered towards the light at the end of the wynd.

It wasn't until Brown disappeared from view that George remembered he too could leave. Since Brown went in the direction of Argyll Square, George had no choice but to continue towards the college. His route appeared unimpeded, but he didn't want to inspect the shadows too closely.

He tried to make sense of all the unspoken threats laced under Brown's jovial demeanour. Was Brown threatening to implicate him in James' demise? Was he now an enemy of all

Brunonians? Or did Brown intend to forgive him at a future date if he kept his head down?

Once in the college yards, on ground he still considered safe, George backed up against the old library wing wall, out of most casual observers' line of sight, and tried to think.

Had he already erred by continuing on to the college? Was he under observation? Brown wasn't going to take kindly to him warning the professors what had just transpired.

Unbidden, George's thoughts turned as they often did when he was overcome by despair to his father. Or at least the shadowy memories that remained.

It was easy to idolise the man. He died when George was seven, the shine of George's boyhood admiration never tarnished or challenged. As he grew, he saw how little his mother seemed to miss him, but he'd never had the time (nor courage, if he was being truly honest) to ask her how she felt about him. George liked to imagine his father was strong-willed and confident, that despite his illiteracy the towns-people respected him. It was only after George returned from the army that he noticed the townspeople's recollections didn't match that image. They told George stories of a jovial man, whose main exploits were witticisms in the tavern or hare-brained schemes from his youth. George tried to recon-cile such recollections with his own memories, and was distressed at how little they matched. His father may have been popular, but he was a source of amusement, not respect.

George didn't even know if his father would approve of him now: either as a soldier or a physician. His mother had urged him in her quiet way to pursue studies in Edinburgh.

"Your schoolteachers have always told me of your talents," she would say, leaning into him for balance more than empha-sis. "You shouldn't waste them." By then, his older brothers were carrying the farm, and she could afford to say such things.

George had gone to Edinburgh because that was what everyone told him he should do. From the teacher at the town school to Dr Pearson in the military hospital. George supposed they were right, but he'd been struggling ever since he arrived.

He thought that if he could just figure out which was the safest side to pick, he would be alright. Now it seemed that neither side was safe.

How other students like Edward could assume a neutral stance on Brunonianism eluded George. It was obvious the leader cared nothing for his followers. To assume the disdainful air of rationality was either moral bankruptcy or fear—George didn't care which. Maybe the other students would label him a fool, but now he could see it was preferable to his alternative.

George took a deep breath, holding it in then exhaling so slowly his body shook. Partial association, or changes of heart, wouldn't save him. He'd have to forsake Edward's esteem. He was going to throw his lot in with one side, and wouldn't back out later.

George cut through the library, hoping to find Black, whose first class of the morning would be over now. The college quietened as students filled their lecture rooms; he was in danger of arriving late to anatomy. Where could Black be?

Suddenly, a wave of nausea stopped him in his tracks. There was a strange smell in the air. George's hand clutched his throat as he tried to eke out enough control of his senses to locate the source of this onslaught.

"George, I saw you looking for me, but Dr Gregory waylaid me with some trivial yet pressing business."

George rotated to observe his surroundings, which compounded the nausea and dizziness.

Black's voice continued unhurried. *"I'm not nearby, you might surmise, but please call on me after two o'clock."*

There was a finality to that sentence which implied the message was complete. George expected the feeling of strangeness and the nasty taste in his mouth to subside, but it persisted. His nostrils itched. This hadn't happened before, but then again, Black hadn't communicated with him over any great distance.

While grappling the debilitating nausea, George wondered if Black was holding the connection open to invite a response. With the pounding queasiness, he hadn't the spare intellect to second-guess himself, and in this state he was willing to try anything to banish this.

George dug his fingers into his temples and pressed his chin into his clavicle. It was like trying to pitch your humming to another person's. Inside his head he tried to recreate the sensation of Black's voice next to his ear. Then he began to gag.

"I sensed something there. Very good indeed, George. We'll talk later."

The urge to vomit subsided, and George found he was able to move his limbs without gagging. Breathing deeply a few times to make sure the vomit stayed down, George hurried back the way he'd come, down the narrow stairs towards anatomy.

Monro looked like he wanted to object when George stumbled into the crowded lecture theatre, but became confused about what to say so returned to his demonstration. George sank into the bench and pulled out his quill, finally able to address the itching in his nose.

Then he realised the strange looks weren't just because of his lateness.

His nose was bleeding.

13

As the lecture concluded, George dared believe he could extract himself from the building without making this tragic day worse. Monro's sharp voice cut through such innocence.

"Mr Stephens, stay behind. Anyone wanting to talk with me, please adjourn to the waiting room—I'll call you back in when I'm ready."

George's heart pounded. The anatomy professor busied himself shuffling his lecture notes until the door was dragged shut by the last of his students. When Monro looked at George, there was no geniality in his eyes.

"Can you hear me, Mr Stephens?"

George gasped. By his sides, Monro's fists were working.

"Mr Stephens, if you can hear me, I demand you affirm."

"Yes, sir." George managed. The voice in his head sounded distorted, like the two men weren't in the same room, but it was still recognisably Monro's.

"Well, your friends have made quite the spectacle, there's no doubt about that. A report of your little stunt at the Medical Society made it into the *Edinburgh Evening Post*, you know. Have you no idea how much damage you're doing to the reputation of this school?" Muscles twitched across Monro's face.

George tried to wipe the last traces of dried blood from his nose, as if erasing the incriminating proof would stop Monro's assault.

"Sir, I—"

"Learned gentlemen acting like common street brawlers! No pretence at rational discourse. Well, you can tell Mr Brown I've had it with his posturing, but honestly I expected better from the students."

George didn't know how to begin telling Monro he'd been warned to stay away from Brown barely an hour ago.

"Outrageous, Mr Stephens," Monro continued before George could marshal his thoughts. "My conscience is clear on this: I won't support the education of Brunonians a moment longer."

It took George a moment to understand what Monro was getting at, and then his blood chilled.

"Sir, you can't—"

"That is where you're wrong, Mr Stephens." Of course: Monro had agreed George could attend his lectures for free, which meant he had the power to revoke his decision.

"Please let me explain," George begged. Without this anatomy course, he couldn't complete his degree. Despite today's threats, his assumption he'd continue his education hadn't wavered.

"You should have been more mindful of my generosity when you fell in with the Brunonians."

"I'm no Brunonian!" George protested, desperation finally forcing the words out.

"Then who taught you proculopathy!"

"Professor Black did!"

George hoped that would mollify his professor, but as he

spoke he realised Monro had taken time to get this worked up, so would take more yet to calm down.

"They're all as bad as each other!" Monro exclaimed, but it sounded like he wasn't fully convinced.

George kept quiet, hoping to avoid driving him back into anger. Monro focussed on his agitated hands for a moment.

"Yet you consider James Campbell your friend?"

"I...don't know, sir. We share lodgings, that's all." This was the first time George had heard of the newspaper story, and he wondered how much Monro knew of the duel.

"Well, your friend turned up in my ward at the Infirmary a few hours ago. You can tell Dr Black—or Brown, I don't care —that I want no part of this." Monro tugged at the slips of parchment on his table. He stabbed a quill into the inkwell. "The boy will not be my responsibility."

"Sir?" George tried to digest what Monro had just said. "James is alive?"

Ignoring him, Monro began scratching a message.

"Sir, he survived the bullet wound?"

"He wasn't shot!" Monro bellowed. George had no time to make sense of this before Monro continued, "Quite frankly I don't know who to believe in this sorry mess, so I am going to conduct my own investigations into your association with the Brunonians. I intend to get to the bottom of this by the end of the week. Let's see if there is anyone in this university besides Doctors Black and Cullen who can vouch for you."

He could have felt relief; instead George sank into despair. No professor besides Black and Cullen knew he existed, or showed any care towards him. Misery was plastered all over his face.

Monro looked at him intently, jowls quivering. "Of course, the obvious way around the question of which students I support as charity is for the offending party to remove himself from my charity."

George didn't see three guineas materialising into his possession within the next week. He turned his face away. Monro gave a triumphant humph and returned to the letter. He scrawled his final signature so roughly George thought he'd tear the parchment.

Monro began folding the scrap. "Ha, Joseph owes me a favour after I let him use the new anatomy theatre. Tell him that if he dares object."

George rubbed the final flecks of blood from his knuckles. "Can't you tell him, sir? Over distance, I mean?"

It was grimly funny, he thought. Just a few days ago I was struggling with what felt like an unspeakable violation by Dr Black. Since then, half the medical faculty have been stomping around inside my head.

Monro fixed George with the dirtiest scowl imaginable. Without breaking eye contact, he tossed his quill aside and brandished the folded scrap in George's direction.

"Take it. Take. It."

Monro wasn't going to move an inch. George edged towards the table and plucked the parchment from his hand. "J. B." was the only notation on the front. Bowing once, George fled the room, though the door required a few tugs before it let him escape.

George worried it would be improper to call on Black before their agreed-upon hour, but the addition of Monro's note changed his calculations. In the worst-case scenario, he could deliver the note and return later.

Black's servant let him into the dining room, where he found Black and Cullen already in conference. Black rose and readied to speak, before spotting the note George now held at some distance from his body.

"Um, this was from Professor Monro, sir. He spoke to me after anatomy. He was furious…"

"Old Sandy Monro's not a bad sport," laughed Cullen. "He's a lot easier to deal with than his father, in fact."

"My nose was bleeding when I got to class. He thought I was involved with the Brunonians, knew I could understand proculopathy."

"Very well." Black picked the note from George's hand, his expression carefully neutral. "Thank you, George."

George had no idea what Black and Cullen already knew. He saw Black's expression flicker and darken.

"James Campbell?"

"The boy from the duel, sir."

Cullen grabbed the note from Black's hand. It wasn't a long message. He swore.

"We better get to the Infirmary, Joe."

"I can manage this," Black insisted. "You may as well prepare the guest bedchamber for when I return. Morris can show you where I keep my medical supplies."

"I fear I offended Professor Monro," George admitted to Cullen as the two of them cleared the upstairs bedroom. "I asked him why he couldn't use proculopathy to communicate with Professor Black instead of delivering a note, and he reacted badly."

"Few men have the power of phlogiston our Dr Black has," Cullen noted with a brief smile as he inspected the contents of Black's medical box. "He makes long-distance proculopathy seem easy. Sandy Monro knows he's even more of an anatomical genius than his late father, so I doubt your ill-judged remark will trouble him long."

"It gave me a nosebleed and I almost threw up," George said. He wanted to make an excuse so he wouldn't be home when Black returned with James, but was angry at himself for such cowardice.

"With practice your body will adjust," Cullen replied. "It is quite incredible that you were able to send any kind of message back to Joseph. He reckoned he was over twenty metres away. He knew you had talent, but you surprised us both."

Black's manservant quietly came in, laying down a pile of towels and bandages on the dresser.

"You don't think James will be safe at the Infirmary?"

"Maybe not. If it's bad enough for Monro Junior to immediately relinquish a patient, then we can assume Mr Campbell is in a sorry state."

"Professor Monro is scared of Brown?"

"A little bit. I mean, lad, it's devolved into lethal duelling between Brunonians and everyone else—don't you think that sounds scary?"

"Yes," George admitted.

"Dr Black hopes the Brunonians are shaken by the outcome and will re-evaluate their cause. I'm less optimistic; I can tell you this because I told Dr Black the same thing. If we save the boy, the Brunonians will be embarrassed; if he dies, we shoulder all their wrath."

After an intolerable wait, Black returned, his servants carrying James upstairs. George was terrified of this moment, for he had no idea what he should say to him. However, as soon as James was set on Black's bed, George knew his fear was misplaced. Despite a few moans and twitches, James remained unconscious. His skin looked cold and damp. Although Monro claimed he hadn't been shot, one of his arms was coated in blood.

The two physicians leant over the boy. It was clear from

his posture that Black deferred to Cullen's lead. Black began to slice through James' sleeves with scissors, looking for the source of the bleeding.

There was a long, fresh gash down James' upper arm. Black stepped back to let Cullen inspect it.

"They tried cupping the boy," Black said flatly. He turned to the bandages.

"The hypocrite," Cullen remarked, his tone neutral for the benefit of the patient, who may still be able to hear him. "The Brunonians berate us for our reliance on bloodletting, only to resort to it themselves. And they've let out far too much blood."

Having seen cupping scars in New York field hospitals, George agreed that whoever had operated on his acquaintance had cut too long and deep.

There was a grimness in Black's face as he felt for the boy's pulse.

"We can step outside for a minute, George," he said eventually. "Let Dr Cullen work without us in the way."

Unsure he wanted to be alone with Black but too afraid of distracting Cullen, George acquiesced. Black motioned for George to stop on the landing, where their voices were unlikely to carry back into James' room.

"It's a bad time, but I owe you a proper apology, George. When I was a student I found proculopathy terrifying, and I couldn't trust my own thoughts for a while. I should have been more considerate of how withholding knowledge of what I'd done would affect you. I don't have an excuse for my actions, and I'm sorry."

George sighed. He'd gone almost a week hoping Black wouldn't apologise, yet here it was.

"I'm sorry too, Professor. I allowed Brown's comments to get to me, and I should have given you a chance to explain."

Black gave a ghostly smile.

"It's not looking good for our patient, Mr Stephens," he said. "Though I think you know that already. While Bennie had a lot of phlogiston in his body, it built up slowly, which curtailed the amount of damage it caused and led to a degree of reversibility. I hypothesise Mr Campbell was struck by a large quantity, possibly by his own hand: a failed attempt to raise and discharge phlogiston as part of the duel. We're left with a lot of internal damage."

George let the words sink in.

"I thought leaving the army meant I wouldn't have to deal with this again." George meant the way you had to shift your mind when someone you were joking with in the morning was dying by evening of battlefield injuries.

Black nodded. "As a physician you never escape it. It happened with one of my closest friends—I'm sure you know of the philosopher David Hume. He was plagued with colic issues throughout his life; it ran in his family. Well, when he fell sick a few years ago, he called for me to treat him. I wish he'd chosen someone else. Hume couldn't keep food inside him—he was wracked by intense stomach pains and bile obstruction. I was the one who had to tell him he was dying, had to see the shadow of mortality looming in his eyes. 'Am I going to suffer long?' he asked. I couldn't lie to him; Hume became my friend when I was younger than you. 'No,' I said. 'Having observed your symptoms, they force me to conclude your end will come within days.' He thanked me for that small mercy. I was correct in my diagnosis." There was a deep silence. "The death of patients affects Dr Cullen too, of course, but he can compartmentalise it better than any other physician I know." Black sighed.

"Does James have days remaining?" George asked, bracing himself.

"William may have a better sense, but my suspicion is no. His time can be measured in hours." Black paused. "I'm sorry,

George. We'll give Mr Campbell sedatives to reduce his pain, and I'll be with him throughout the night."

"I can stay too," George said. He didn't know how long he'd been at Black's house this afternoon, but the street outside was bathed in shadows. "It was my fault this happened. I told James I wanted to see evidence of Brunonian superiority; he called Cheltenham out in a bid to prove his point."

Black shook his head. "The blame lies with Brown for propagating such dangerous practices and convincing his students there's no risk. But to your first point, yes, if you wish to stay, you can."

George was about to return to the bedchamber when Black raised a hand.

"Having gone through this more times than I wish upon anyone...you'll regret anything in the coming hours you wanted to say to James and didn't."

When they re-entered the room, Cullen had finished binding James' arm and was measuring out liquids from the small bottles that made up Black's medicinal cabinet. Black approached his colleague, inspecting the labels only briefly.

Both Black's and Cullen's movements stilled, and a strange silence filled the room. They must be talking via proculopathy, George realised. Their hands flickered in punctuation of a wordless dialogue.

Cullen murmured something, administered the tincture to James, then left the room. Black took a few steps away from the patient, giving George space to approach.

The sedatives were already working. James was no longer whimpering.

He isn't going to wake up, George thought.

He took James' hand between his own. It was as clammy as he imagined it would be.

"I failed you, James," George said softly. "You didn't deserve this."

Barely a month ago he'd sworn to avenge Pierre, who died an unnecessary death at the hands of Brown. Protecting other medical students from the same fate was a small motivating factor in addition to that. Yet here was another dying student. George's selfishness hadn't protected his fellow lodger, and may even have contributed to what was happening now.

How he wished Black had left him alone, but George recognised the deep emotion in Black's warning to him, understanding the professor wanted to protect George, to ensure he wouldn't live with words inside him destined for a dead man that went unheard.

George had to think beyond Pierre, to recognise that his association with Black and Cullen meant assuming a greater responsibility. "Brown isn't going to hurt any more students. I promise you."

* * *

George hadn't slept well the night before, and he found himself slipping in and out of wakefulness in front of the hearth. It was around four o'clock in the morning when he was jolted from half-sleep by Black, who rose from the other corner of the room and walked over to the bed where James lay motionless. Black touched James' wrist and neck. There was a barely perceptible slumping of his shoulders.

Knowing what was coming but wishing it wasn't, George waited for Black to meet his eye.

A single shake of the head.

14

That evening, Black received a note. He studied the handwriting before breaking the seal, which gave him a good idea what the message contained before he took in the words themselves.

> If it pleases Dr Black, his friend desires his company for a walk around the Meadows early tomorrow morning.
> E. Ross

The sun was barely risen when Black met Lord Ross at the corner of the meadows near Potter Row. Mist hung over the expanse of grassland, and Black's fingers stung from the cold. Ross did little more than raise the brim of his hat in acknowledgement, before setting off in the direction of Middle Meadow Walk. The first few minutes were strode in silence.

Finally, Ross spoke. "What on earth is this business with the Brunonians? One of the duellists ended up dying at your house?"

News circulates fast, thought Black sourly.

"I don't doubt your good intentions, Joseph, I really

don't, but you and William chose to entwine yourselves deeper in this mess by treating him." Ross kept his gaze on the path ahead.

"At least one of my colleagues, probably more, refused to touch the boy," Black replied. "As physicians we have duties that go beyond petty doctrinal squabbles."

Black understood on an intellectual level that he could have gone to the Infirmary with the intention of changing Monro's mind, or stayed home. But he hadn't.

"Students do stupid things." Ross modulated his tone towards conciliatory. "Duelling is barbarous, but a natural consequence of the foolishness of youth. Those of us who were once foolish youths ourselves can tolerate it. But for the august professors to get involved? That's harder for the political men of this city to overlook and excuse. They wonder what hand said professors played in inciting the duel." He glanced pointedly at his companion.

"No hand whatsoever, my lord," Black retorted. His conscience was clear on this. "I wagered Brown would slide back into provincial obscurity if the medical establishment just ignored him, but I won't ignore dying students."

The two men reached the halfway point of Middle Walk. To the east, a crescent of light bisected Arthur's Seat as the sun rose, though it would be a few hours before the shadows were chased away from the park.

"The newspapers relish these sensational affairs," Ross said. "Grub Street and their Edinburgh ilk love nothing more than taking aim at the intellectual sect, and they know the semi-literate coffeehouse class will take equal pleasure in reading about the purported downfall of their social betters."

Dead students were a problem, Black noted, but overshadowed by bad publicity in the national papers.

"*The Sentinel* and the *Evening Courant*'s attention will last as long as we indulge them with outrage." Black forced himself to walk slower and measure his paces. "Better to keep our reaction muted and wait for the next scandal to bloom." He had enough to worry about: corresponding with the deceased wretch's family, fielding questions from the faculty and Town Council about the cause of death. As long as no one demanded to inspect the body, he could conceal the fatal phlogiston misuse from the wider public.

Although not looking directly at his companion, he could hear Ross' breathing beside him. He must still be walking too fast.

"The way you talk, you seem wholly unconcerned with the army of Brunonians professing abilities in phlogiston-wielding who are running around this town." Lord Ross lowered his voice a fraction, even though they were the only men on the path. "It's only a matter of time before someone's lips loosen."

Knowledge of Cullen's phlogiston-wielding seeped through the upper classes, and there wasn't much Black could do about it. Rich men passed dangerous secrets around their dinner tables like candies. Ideas deemed too incendiary for the poor were entitlements to them. Black imagined that if these rich men thought they could benefit from phlogiston-wielding, they would be a lot more demanding on Cullen and himself.

"The Masons manage to keep their secrets, and there is not inconsequential overlap between Brunonians and lodge brethren," Black pointed out.

"Come on, Joseph. Those halfwits will send bragging letters to the press at the first opportunity, telling the world about the powers they harness. Or at least once they find a peer who knows which end of a quill you put the ink on. They thrive on attention, and the clamouring to prove their superiority over the medical establishment grows. Can you not see the danger?"

This wasn't the first time Ross had expressed such fears in Black's company. He'd once questioned Black for an uncomfortable hour on the process Cullen used to select phlogiston-wielding trainees among the student population.

"Yes, the thought of people injuring themselves experimenting with phlogiston concerns me greatly." Right now, Cullen and he could assess students' natural aptitude for phlogiston-wielding, then make the decision to train those with sensible temperament. George Stephens was the ideal trainee in both regards, but boys like that were rare.

If the art of phlogiston-wielding broke into public knowledge tomorrow, there wouldn't be enough phlogiston-trained physicians to handle the ensuing casualties, Black thought. It would be awful.

A faint noise came out of Ross' throat. It sounded like exasperation. Evidently, he'd not assuaged his patron's concerns properly, but Black didn't see the point in trying to ascertain how he should have replied. It would only make him look weak.

"I don't doubt your sincerity, Joseph." Ross exhaled. "But you're making the new chemistry classroom business harder for yourself."

Black knew Ross would say this. The only surprise was that he had waited until they were this far through their circuit to raise the issue.

"It isn't even my doctrine they're arguing over, your lordship." After no sleep the previous night, Black had recovered only a fraction of the rest he needed to get through today in a civil manner.

"But we both know you aren't going to disavow your former professor either, not even for the benefit of the Town Council," Ross pointed out.

It has been over thirty years since William taught me chemistry in Glasgow, thought Black. Everyone in Edinburgh still sees me as an extension of him. "I know how these games work, Ross. We don't have to dance around the issues. What is the Town Council wanting from me?"

Ross chuckled. "This is why I enjoy your company, Dr Black. Get Brown under control. They don't want any more student duels—that goes without saying—and they certainly don't want to see university professors in the fight. They find you a lot easier to reason with than William; they have ever since you arrived in Edinburgh."

Most of today's city leaders weren't the ones in power when Black came through from Glasgow to Edinburgh to complete his dissertation. When the Edinburgh chair of chemistry became vacant a few years later, many in this city favoured the freshly minted Dr Black for the position over the established Cullen, who made it clear he wished to be lured from his teaching position in Glasgow. Black wasn't so vain to overlook the fact they thought him more malleable. But in the end, most of the city's powerful calculated it was better to have Cullen close, where they could keep an eye on him.

Though his tact and diplomacy never wavered, the same men never made the mistake of considering Black malleable again.

Now the current Town Council either thought Brown was a faculty problem or they lacked the ability to influence his patrons, whoever they were.

Black nodded. Deal. Ross rubbed his hands together.

"It's colder than I expected this morning. Winter in Edinburgh sneaks up quickly, doesn't it?"

Black extended his hand, palm up. Faint crimson flames twirled several inches into the air. Ross stared.

"These aren't as hot as regular fire, but they're better than nothing at all."

Ross cautiously reached out towards Black's flames, sighing as their warmth engulfed his fingertips. Black could make them hotter, but there was nothing to be gained by scorching a patron.

* * *

The fractures in Cullen and Brown's relationship had become obvious to Black and everyone else in the medical community four years ago.

On the night that exposed the rift, Black eased into the Nicolson Tavern on West Bow, where he found Cullen surrounded by a mixture of current and former students. Cullen raised his glass in a salute as Black seated himself in the alcove, but remained deep in conversation.

"...and of course I was stuck because correspondence was piling up on my desk and I needed to deal with that as well..."

"Brown isn't pulling his weight?" laughed one of Cullen's former students from across the table.

Cullen gave a rueful head shake. "No, his gout is playing up again. Had another attack several weeks ago, and hasn't fully recovered. He swore to me he was following my advice to cut meat and alcohol from his diet, but I'd trust Bacchus himself to follow such a directive more than I'd trust John."

Everyone around the table broke out in laughter. Black permitted himself a smile.

"Pro-fess-or Cullen!" a guttural voice boomed over the tavern clamour.

Black looked over with a disinterested glance, then remembered that this was in fact an unexpected sight.

Leaning heavily on his cane and limping, Brown thumped towards Cullen's table. By the time he came into Cullen's sight, Black remembered Brown was supposed to be indisposed with gout. Indeed, pain drummed in his eyes with every step, but he retained a cheery expression.

"John?" Cullen waved, as if that would pull his former

student towards him faster. "I didn't expect you to join us tonight. Your attack finally cleared up?" Unlike Black, he'd not noticed the difficulty Brown walked with.

"No' in as many words," Brown grunted as he collapsed onto the bench, other medical students scattering to make room. He nodded greetings around the table—his eyes skimmed over Black, as they usually did—then cast around for the tavern keeper.

If Cullen heard what Brown had just said, the full meaning didn't sink in.

"Well, I'm relieved the dietary restrictions finally paid off for you, John. You really should refrain from drinking much tonight, until the symptoms clear. The gout was still troubling you on Saturday, wasn't it? Goodness, it can hardly have calmed down enough for you to safely consume alcohol."

Beer secured, Brown turned back to the table.

"Aye, got lonely. The lady of the house and her bastards are agreeable company until three weeks' confinement, then ye crave proper conversation." Brown toasted the entire room. Many of the Nicolson Tavern regulars toasted him back.

By now, Cullen was focussing properly on Brown, and Black could see disparate pieces of information fitting together.

"John, your gout *has* abated, hasn't it?"

Brown gave a cheery shrug and tried to entertain the fifth-year student next to him with a bawdy joke.

"John!" Cullen leant his elbows on the table. "Has your gout cleared up?"

Brown's conversation partner faltered and looked back towards the venerable professor. Brown gave a nonchalant hand wave.

"Ach, it's no' gonnae clear up fae *weeks*, dear Professor. Disnae matter what I do. Figured there's no point making masel' miserable with oat broth and water on top o' the gout."

Black recognised the signs of disagreement forming within his fellow professor. What was usually stretched taut in Cullen's countenance and mannerisms crinkled rapidly.

Cullen's fingers grazed the side of his neck. "Are you sure about this, John? I mean, I'm the first advocate of moderation —good health depends on that balance between indulgence and deprivation, yes—but we've seen alcohol consumption make your gout worse before—"

"Naw," Brown interrupted. "I remember that time. I dinnae think it was the wine after all."

"In general, physicians recognise that alcohol and rich foods have a deleterious effect on gout," another former student interjected, probably suspecting as Black did that an argument was about to disrupt everyone's merriment. "Dr Duncan was lecturing about one of his patients just this month—"

"No' in my case," Brown snapped. The interrupter sitting opposite Cullen winced. Brown turned his attention back to Cullen, a calmer expression returning. "And a cup or two of beer willnae make things worse. I drank some claret yesterday and nowt happened."

At this admittance, Cullen frowned. The conversations on either side of the pair trailed off. Black recognised Cullen was trying to wrestle his emotions under control. No one risked an attempt at lightening the mood or steering the conversation, for fear one or both men would snap at them.

After a couple of fraught seconds, Cullen shook his head and busied himself with his glass. "We'll talk about this later, John. Watch how much you drink, at least?"

Brown grunted, then launched into another bawdy joke. Someone next to Cullen leant in and asked him a question, to which he chuckled and started on a digression.

The night wore on. Despite Cullen's sideways glances of concern, morphing over the hours into tutting disapproval,

Brown kept drinking. Black spied him surreptitiously dripping the contents of a dark, palm-sized vial into his glass. By the time Brown retired for the evening, alcohol and laudanum seemed to have numbed his pain, and he strode out of the tavern faster than he had entered.

"Has Brown disregarded your medical advice prior to this?" Black asked Cullen when the table thinned out enough for them to shuffle closer and engage in a semi-private conversation.

Cullen shrugged. "He followed me to the letter during his previous flare-up of gout, but claimed his condition got worse. I think he blamed me for it. We were getting into a lot of arguments about treatments and causes."

"He still says he wants to be a medical chair?" Black asked, realising nothing he could say would soothe hurt sentiments on the subject of gout.

"Ha! Last month he was talking about moving to New York to join Samuel Bard's new college scheme; the month before that he wanted to study anatomy in Leyden. It's been a while since he told me he intended to take more botany classes, so I suppose we're due for that whim to resurface next. Brown doesn't know what he wants." Cullen took another drag of beer. "He was doing well with his tutoring and evening lecturing—I told him it was a shame to squander those opportunities by racing off to another city."

Cullen could get maudlin after three drinks. Black estimated he'd reached the end of his third glass.

"I think I'll summon a carriage now, William. I hope you'll excuse me."

No longer paying lip service to Cullen's recommendations, Brown threw himself back into heavy drinking and beef consumption. To everyone's astonishment, his gout attacks ceased. Up until that point, Brown had worshipped the ground Cullen walked on. Afterwards, he questioned everything his teacher taught, though in social affairs things continued on as normal.

The cracks and wrinkles in Cullen and Brown's relationship didn't shrink, but for a while it seemed they'd hold at the level of minor disagreements and divergence of personal philosophies without rancour setting in. Unfortunately, Brown wasn't able to keep his fermenting ideas to himself.

15

As agreed, George met Black and Cullen in the latter's lecture hall. James had expired in the early hours of yesterday, and already George was sick of hearing student gossip about him. Cheltenham was keeping a low profile, which seemed prudent. An uneasiness hung over the students observing Black and Cullen, who knew that the boy died at Black's house instead of in the Infirmary where he'd initially turned up.

The smallest comfort was that Black looked as exhausted as George felt.

George endured another round of questioning about his interactions with Brown, though this time he tried to be as cooperative and expansive as possible. He told the two professors the story Brown had shared with him in the tavern, since they wanted to collect every detail he recalled.

"...and he told me he could share many such stories about saving lives in such a manner." George wondered why, then, Brown was unable to save James. "But I imagine he is exaggerating such success."

Cullen set his quill down. "Well, I certainly hope Brown was exaggerating or lying about those patients he pulled back from the moment of death...because if not, it sounds an awful lot like dark chymistry."

George's skin felt tight and uncomfortable. Cullen's gaze remained on his inkwell, tracing its lip with his thumb.

"Someone searched my chemistry cellar," Black told George. "Looking for what notes I had about our previous dealings with that group. Brown would have no reason to know about the existence of those notes."

George recalled what Edward had told him atop Calton Hill about Cullen supplanting an older theoretical system when he first arrived in Edinburgh.

"Professor, who are these people?" George hoped the professors wouldn't deceive him again.

"How much do you know about dark chymistry?" Cullen asked.

"Nothing, I'm afraid," George admitted.

"Ha! Don't apologise. The less you know, the happier you will be." Seeing George's crestfallen expression, Cullen hastily explained. "What we call dark chymistry—not that its practitioners call it that—has its roots in the secretive work performed over a hundred years ago by illustrious visionaries like Hook, Newton and Boyle. At that time, they knew about elemental powers such as phlogiston and aether, but had no understanding of how they existed within the human body.

"Instead, these men developed sigils to draw elements such as phlogiston from the surroundings and manifest power. To burn a living or inanimate object you just had to draw a fire sign on it. Oh, but if only they stopped at fire! Draw two sigils, and a doorway between them opened. Draw another sigil to conceal an object—or a person, for that matter—from sight." Cullen was no longer speaking to George but delivering a lecture to the empty room.

"There were only a few men with such knowledge, and after enjoying the power it granted them...well, they didn't want to share. Despite the union of the crowns, and the bloody spasms of Jacobite rebellion, twenty years ago, political power in Scotland belonged to the men it always belonged to. Anyone who threatened their power knew vengeance could be wreaked upon them: an assassin enters a locked chamber, strikes a man dead then vanishes into thin air. The terrible power of their sigils was concealed in Latin and coded texts, limiting their use to a select few.

"Once inscribed, these sigils conferred immediate power. For that reason, they were only ever partially drawn out in the grimoires. The power of these dark chymists depended on their instructions remaining ambiguous to outsiders. Men had to translate them to understand how to draw the full sigils. 'Take the fire of Jupiter and bathe it under moonlight' could mean to add a straight line through the circle and place a concave line above that. Depending on the context of the remark, it wasn't always clear where the concave line should be positioned.

"This was how things stood as I began my academic career, as a young and oft-times headstrong man. I didn't set out to do such a thing, but during my investigations into the nervous system I developed a way of wielding the body's own phlogiston through physiological means." Here Cullen flicked his wrist. Crimson fire sprang from his palm for just a moment, before he clenched his fist shut.

"Everyone feared the dark chymists. Power was wielded by the elites, and intellectual curiosity was stifled among men of learning. Our education system had barely advanced since the Crusades. Everyone knew, only I was foolish enough to believe I could change the system." Cullen nodded over to Black. "Of course, I would have got nowhere without the abilities of Dr Black.

"First, we dismantled the dark chymists' monopoly on scientific knowledge. I never believed in concealing my discoveries behind Latin—I taught my students in English. Compared to the dark chymists, our phlogiston-wielding powers were limited, but even the sons of farmers could access them." George blushed.

"First the dark chymists ignored us. Thought we couldn't possibly unseat them. That bought us a few years. Then, when it became clear I intended to come to Edinburgh to challenge them, they tried to mock and discredit me. Once Dr Black and I reached the city, they tried to kill us. But they were so convinced of their own superiority, their own power, that their complacency was what allowed us to get the upper hand.

"Every single one of their grimoires, we burned. Those that tried to fight us regretted it."

For a moment Cullen seemed triumphant, revelling in the victory. Then he stepped away from his pedestal. "But now they're in resurgence. The marks on Bennie's body were a crude attempt at channelling dark power. You saw that, Joe?"

"Of course, William."

"He's working with the dark chymists—he has to be. If he lived a thousand years, Bruno could never display enough originality to come into such ideas alone." Cullen scratched his bottom lip absent-mindedly. "Whatever the surviving dark chymists are up to, they need willing bodies. And despite our best efforts, that's what Bruno has."

Black looked tense. "Twenty years ago I was in much better fighting shape than I am now. And like you said, it will be younger men at the helm now."

"They have us on the back foot, that much is clear." Cullen paced the room. "I think it's time we call in the princess."

Black's eyebrows rose.

"I didn't expect that suggestion to come from you before

it came from me, William. But yes, that's an excellent idea. I don't imagine she will be aware of what is happening."

Cullen snorted. "The fact that the princess hasn't beaten a path to our door tells me she remains ignorant. Do you want to do the honour of composing a note, Joe?"

George noticed Black had perked up at Cullen's suggestion, and already his mood was lightening.

Black looked at George. "Our friend in many ways exists against the laws of God and nature, but that is why she's so useful. She is a formidable character."

"Dr Black here is one of her favourites," added Cullen. "He can say things to her that would provoke the decapitation of lesser mortals."

George assumed Cullen meant this as a figure of speech, but he wasn't entirely sure.

"I'd better conjure up some errands to get Alice out of the house this afternoon." Cullen sighed. "The last thing we need is that distraction for the princess."

* * *

George had no experience with princesses of any nationality, let alone Russian ones, but Princess Dashkova matched none of his preconceived ideas. She was a nondescript woman in her late thirties, with dark eyebrows and a face that wouldn't be amiss among the Grassmarket fish sellers. Her lilac hair was piled on top of her head, held in place by a complex network of braids and ribbons. She wore a flowing sack-back gown with red and white stripes, and though he was sure the material was fine, neither the dress nor the fashionable hairstyle struck George as especially regal.

He also hadn't expected her to lapse into French more often than Russian, or to sound so permanently angry.

"...and you think I don't notice you send your housekeeper away when I call," Princess Ekaterina Dashkova continued. "I do notice, and it offends me greatly. You know me, Monsieur Cullen—it is the women with dark hair I care for. And that is only when I am under great stress or feeling very sad. For shame that you would think so little of me and my attentiveness!"

Cullen bit his lip and wisely said nothing. Having observed how reluctant Alice was to leave the house once she overheard discussions concerning Dashkova's impending arrival, George wondered if the distraction Cullen feared was not of the Russian princess towards his blonde and comely housekeeper, but rather the other way around.

"We apologise for not being clearer in our letter," Black began. "But we suspect enemies have their eyes and ears upon us, and thus we are acting with discretion."

Dashkova gave a noncommittal nod. In the Cullens' modest parlour, her dress seemed to consume the sofa, its bright hues standing in contrast to the dusty bookshelves and tired furnishings.

"The dark chymists are back," Cullen interrupted. "We think they're tied up with John Brown in some way."

Dashkova let out a Slavic-infused curse at low volume.

"The problem is, we don't know who is at the top of this," continued Cullen. "And their motives are opaque."

"They want to kill you," Dashkova said. George couldn't tell if she was asking a question or making a statement.

"Their power is much diminished," Cullen added, ignoring the interruption. "But several students from the college turned up with markings on them that reminded Joe of their sigils. They seem poorly done."

Dashkova nodded, assuming a thoughtful air. The room was narrow enough that George, seated opposite the princess, panicked at the thought of his knees bumping hers.

"We need to find out who is behind this, and stop them from carrying out more damage. A group of Brown's men attacked us in Adam Square last week, so we need to watch ourselves."

"Ahhh," exclaimed Dashkova, switching from restrained disinterest to excitement. "There *are* threats on your lives. Well, we have defences against that!"

Angling her body away from the men, Dashkova reached into her bosom and dragged out a large dagger from her stomacher. With a flourish, she pulled the blade from its scabbard.

"Look at this, gentlemen! What do you see?" She seemed excited.

The three men recoiled slightly, realising she intended them to take the proffered dagger. Cullen, evidently aware he was at her displeasure for dismissing his housekeeper, sighed and took it from her, only touching the object with his fingertips.

"I'm not sure what we're supposed to be looking at, madam," he admitted.

"Oh, but Joseph sent me such a thoughtful and lively letter describing the properties of phlogiston when I was in England. I did not say, some of those experiments with metal were ingenious."

At this hint Black was the origin of whatever insight Dashkova wished to share, Cullen handed him the dagger. Black let his fingers curl around the hilt and brought it closer to his face.

"Was that when you found that phlogiston could pass through some metals better than others, Joseph?" Cullen asked.

A light dawned in Black's eyes. He tapped and scratched at the blade, then ran his fingers along the fuller.

"Oui!" exclaimed Dashkova.

Black gave her a satisfied look. He passed the dagger to George, who took it reluctantly, trying to ignore how warm and damp its hilt felt. He repeated Black's examination. There was a ridge in the fuller, a wire embedded within the blade itself that ran from the quillon to the point.

"Was it a zinc or silver thread you added?" Black asked.

"Silver, my wonderful friend. It is not like the cost is such a concern for me."

George had to admit the dagger was of fine quality and balance. It was not the kind of ceremonial or ornate blade he would associate with Russian royalty: a lot of money and skill had gone into its craft.

"You've tried it out?" Cullen asked, withholding appraisement.

"But of course! Dr Cullen, it is a thing of beauty. I lack the head of Dr Black for such experimental matters"—the princess laughed in a way that dared the others to agree—"but with it I can ignite targets from several paces further than if I were to use my hand. I think the flame burns stronger, too."

"She wields phlogiston? But she's a woman!" George thought he had intended to say something else, or maybe he didn't and the words came out anyway.

There was an embarrassed silence.

"Indeed," Cullen remarked. "And Dr Black helpfully assisted her." It didn't sound like Cullen considered Black's intervention helpful.

Dashkova shrugged. For a moment, George assumed the princess would fly into a temper at his ill-judged remark. Instead, she was acting like this wasn't the first time such comments had been made in her presence.

"I approached my friend Dr Black having already gained some skill in the use of phlogiston. He provided further instruction."

So Princess Dashkova had, through some unholy means, taught *herself* the basics of phlogiston-wielding. Given the fear of injury when the inexperienced handled phlogiston, Black had probably felt he had to provide guidance. Under no circumstances would George open his mouth again to enquire, though.

This morning George's interest in learning to wield phlogiston had soured. Watching James' unpleasant death from its misuse counteracted the thrum of pride he had felt after Cullen and Black complimented his proculopathy—given George's incompetence mastering medical topics, was he not guaranteed the same incompetence with fire?

"You want to guess how far I can fire phlogiston?" Dashkova asked George. She spoke with a strong accent; he couldn't tell if her tone was sarcastic, belligerent or neutral.

Yet here was a woman—a princess!—playing around with phlogiston. Was this divine mockery? He would have to accept the professors' offer of learning their craft now. What kind of man would refuse?

"This is a clever conceit," Black interrupted. "But such expense for a knife seems frivolous. What prompted this?"

"I did not just create this dagger," Dashkova said. "I refashioned my sword in the identical manner. I repeat myself: the money does not concern me."

Black's hand was already squeezing George's elbow in warning.

"But know this," Dashkova added, waving a finger. "You men are so reckless and forceful with phlogiston. This silver gives you great power and focus, with only a little—a little!— exertion. Too much phlogiston at once will overheat the silver wire and rupture it." She looked amused. "Perhaps this pretty conceit is of little use to men after all."

"We need your help to figure out who is behind all this,

Your Highness," Black said, turning back to the matter in hand. "Brown is a useful figurehead, but the real power is operating at a higher level of politics and power than us physicians."

"My salon next week: the perfect time," Dashkova declared. "Several of the lordships promised to attend. You must come." She appraised George for a moment, then nodded to herself. "Yes, you too. You will provide company for my son."

George tried to work out if this was a reward or a punishment.

As far as Dashkova was concerned, the matter was settled. She clapped her hands to signify as much. "And Joseph, my dear, don't forget to bring your flute."

As Cullen led him to the door, George finally felt able to ask the questions nagging at him.

"Sir, what did Princess Dashkova mean when she told Dr Black to bring his flute to the salon?" Was it a coded call for weaponry? Or perhaps an allusion to mystical texts everyone else had read?

Cullen's face contorted through several expressions. Finally, he laughed.

"She means what she says, Mr Stephens. She wants Dr Black to bring his flute."

"Oh." George tried to brush off his embarrassment in a bid to get through his list of pressing questions. "Why is she in Edinburgh?"

"Tensions were rising in the Russian court," Cullen remarked with a shrug. "The Empress and her mutually agreed it was in the princess's best interest she take an extended trip around Europe. She decided to reside in Edinburgh while her son completed his medical studies. She says the Empress is almost back on speaking terms with her."

George thought of his mother, toiling away on the land hundreds of miles away. He couldn't imagine his family dropping their livelihoods to follow him as he pursued his education.

"And her husband doesn't mind?"

"No, Prince Dashkov died several years ago. Bit unfortunate, since he and the princess seemed to like each other, but she's managing fine without him." Cullen shook his head and laughed to himself. "The princess is one of a kind. I'm certain she's destined for Hell...were it not for the fact Satan himself would be too scared to deal with her."

* * *

George was glad to rush up the stairs of his lodgings. The rain began when he was halfway home, and it soaked him within minutes. He looked forward to peeling out of his wet clothes and retreating to the parlour fire.

He was, therefore, surprised to open his bedroom door and be greeted with a chill blast. Cursing, George saw he'd left his window open. He rushed over to pull the sash down, flecks of rain blowing onto his brow.

As George fought to close the window, he had enough time to interrogate his memories: he didn't recall leaving it open this morning. The old wooden frames were swollen and it took considerable exertion to budge the sash. Maybe his landlady had come in while he was out, opened the window and forgotten to close it as the clouds gathered. Where she'd find the strength to open the sash this high, God only knew...

Then George turned, his heart accelerating out of control. The books and letters on his desk were sodden, but seemed to be where he'd left them. In his first glances around the meagre space there was no sign of disturbance.

It took him a while to spot it. Right where he laid his head to sleep, a dagger was buried hilt deep into his mattress, slashing wide enough to bleed stuffing.

They knew.

16

Despite assurances from Cullen, George's terrors were multiplying. It had never occurred to him he could end up inside the Palace of Holyroodhouse attending royalty, especially not at such a young age.

"You don't have to worry, it's not just nobility who attend these events. There are plenty of learned men like Dr Black and myself as well."

George had no idea why Cullen thought that would reassure him. He'd borrowed an embroidered coat belonging to one of Cullen's sons, and could only hope this whole spectacle wasn't another cruel trick at his expense.

He hadn't told the professors his lodging room had been broken into, that the Brunonians had left a dagger buried in his bed as a warning. He knew it was information he should share, but Brown's taunts about him running to Cullen in fear stung. George wouldn't give the Brunonians the satisfaction of learning they'd terrified him a second time.

Besides, he was a soldier. He should be stronger than this.

The advantage of Dashkova's salon was obvious: it was

one of the few times Black and Cullen could intermingle with nobility above their station without any pretext. George thought the two physicians must have a suspicion about who was involved, though they didn't share such knowledge with him.

Dashkova resided in the oldest wing of the palace, in the chambers once occupied by Mary Stuart. George expected grand, sweeping corridors and lofty plaster ceilings. Instead, he found himself ushered through modest oak-panelled rooms with low ceilings. Thick woollen silk tapestries depicting over-populated classical hunting frescoes covered the walls.

About twenty men dined with Dashkova in an intimate third-floor chamber; the son promised to George had not materialised, and when the claret came out, the men started to circulate and exchange conversation. George joined Black and Cullen underneath a vast painting of a half-naked woman standing next to an angry horse, in what appeared to be windy conditions.

"Sir Grey needs to be felt out," Cullen was saying. "He's a keen collector. The man's library of rare books is well known."

"Availability of books is not the same as reading them," Black remarked drily. "Nor is reading books the same as understanding them."

Seeing George's blank expression, Black added, "Sterne."

"I agree he's not known for his intellect," Cullen said, "but I wouldn't put deception past him. He's cunning with what wits he has."

Cullen departed towards a cluster of well-dressed men, who parted with cheerfulness to let him into their conversation.

A few metres away, Dashkova coughed in Black's direction and made a couple of motions with her hands.

"Looks like I'm being called upon," he remarked. "I'll let

you make the acquaintance of some of these celebrated guests."

George blanched. Being left alone was the situation he wanted to avoid.

"Talking to these gentlemen philosophers is not too strenuous an activity. Show interest," Black explained, "but of the polite, restrained variety. Treat everything as if it's only the second or third most interesting thing you have heard that evening. If there's a question you don't understand, or someone asks you an opinion on a subject on which you are ill informed, either tell them you defer to their expertise on the matter or ask what they think."

With that he headed off in the direction of Dashkova. George took a deep gulp of claret and turned to the men nearest to him.

It turned out Black played the flute rather excellently.

After surviving a couple of minor conversations, George was broken from his reverie by a coquettish tap on the shoulder from Dashkova, who bade him over to a young man with dark eyes who had wandered through the door.

"Pavel, mon cher, where have you been?" Dashkova exclaimed. She kissed her son rather aggressively, George thought, on both cheeks.

"Out with friends, Maman," the youth carelessly replied.

"You haven't been gambling, have you?" Dashkova asked. "You know I don't approve."

"I know well enough, Maman."

Possibly pretending that her son had answered her question, Dashkova changed the subject. "Here is Mr George Stephens, who I was telling you about."

The two men bowed to each other. George recognised

Pavel from the college. They hadn't interacted, and George wouldn't have guessed the young man was the royalty other students gossiped about.

"You will excuse me, I must retire to my room and adjust my outfit," Pavel said. "I look forward to speaking with you shortly, Mr Stephens." With that he took off, bowing to Black, who was moving to rejoin Dashkova and George.

"He was such an easy child," Dashkova sighed. "As was my daughter. Now, I don't know them at all. Always arguing. Always running off."

"Pavel is a very bright man," Black said. "He's doing very well in his studies."

"Oh yes, I'm proud of him." Dashkova sounded impatient, as if the brilliance of her son remained beyond reproach. "But when I was his age I'd already borne three children. His life is so different from mine. Any luck with your inquiries?"

"Sir Grey seems to have taken time off from Town Council duties," Black said. "Hasn't shown much interest in university matters. It could be a ruse, but his family came to political prominence after the dark chymists were routed—he had no connection to them. I think Dr Cullen is speaking with Lord Ross for a change."

Dashkova took a step closer to the others. "Lord Ross and his friend Sir Henry only started attending my salons last year," she said, lowering her voice. "Before that they were rumoured to only be interested in hunting and expensive art."

Black's eyes swept the room before he spoke. "Lady Argyle's cousins were dark chymists. The family tends to keep to themselves. The Dundas family, on the other hand, they've never loosened their grip on political power in this city, not even for a moment."

George felt uneasy. Everyone he'd spoken with had treated him with civility, reasoning that his presence at Dashkova's salon indicated his social worth. But some of these men had reason to wish ill on Black, Cullen and, by extension, himself.

"Well, others wish to engage you, so we will reconvene later," Black said, giving Dashkova an elegant bow. To George's surprise, Dashkova let out a trilling laugh in response. That was the kind of laugh he'd expect from a princess.

"My mother hasn't performed any...eccentric displays in my absence, has she?" Pavel asked, reappearing at George's side. Dashkova was already engaged with another cluster of men.

"Not that I'm aware of," George replied carefully. It sounded like an allusion to phlogiston-wielding, the prince unsure if George knew such an art was possible.

"Good." Pavel cleared his throat. "Such mesmeric tricks are rather coarse, in my opinion. My mother sometimes thinks she's above the rules of polite society."

Pavel's manner of speaking and casual posture indicated he considered George something approaching an equal: perhaps assuming that anybody brought into his presence must be.

After engaging in pleasant chitchat with Pavel Dashkov about his studies, the young prince attempting to gauge his interest in horse racing, George took brief leave to refuel on claret and sate his dry throat.

He paused to let someone past, and found himself within earshot of Cullen.

"Come on, Charles, you know better than that!" Cullen cajoled.

"Ahaha, you've got me, my dear sir," laughed one of the conversationalists in good-natured response. "Still," he added, "her ladyship was quite adamant on the subject."

"It was not my intention to offend her," Cullen replied in an equally light-hearted tone. "She's always found my recommendations helpful, and her gout was notably improved last time I called upon her."

"Yes...she said she also consulted with him prior to that visit, and thought his advice led to those improvements. Of course, your prescriptions led to modest relief—she is grateful for that—but she wants to try these alternative regimens."

"But Charles, those regimens are in direct contradiction to everything a true physician recommends! Her ladyship is lucky to enjoy a temporary reprieve of her complaint, but this new approach will cause lasting harm."

"I have the greatest respect for you, William, I really do. But maybe established wisdom is wrong on this count? I apologise, I have to take my leave and speak with Philip."

Cullen bowed. Only once he'd taken a step back and caught sight of George did he let his cheerful countenance drop. His long face lengthened.

"Damn that man."

"What happened?" George asked.

"Bruno stole another one of my clients," Cullen groused, sipping his drink. "Over the treatment of gout, of all things."

"He managed to cure the lady?"

"Doubt it," Cullen said bitterly. "He tells patients what they want to hear. No meagre diets, drink as much alcohol as they want, use laudanum to treat inflammation instead of exercise. It doesn't do me any good to lose these patrons, but I can't promise to make them young again, or whatever Bruno is saying to them."

Cullen liked to complain about all the correspondence he received from patients around the country seeking his advice on their ailments, but George guessed he profited handsomely from such consultations, or else why would he continue indulging them? How many of Cullen's patients could Brown steal away before causing his former teacher lasting damage? George could see how these nobles gossiped amongst each other, how interconnected their dealings seemed to be. Perhaps it would only take one powerful patron enthusing about Dr Brown's treatment for them all to follow.

Cullen murmured something about needing to speak to someone else and set out back across the room. Several metres away, his voice sounded jubilant again.

Scanning the room, George noticed a tall, periwigged fellow stepping into his line of sight. Instead of looking away, the man raised a hand and moved towards him.

"You arrived in the company of Dr Black?" he asked cheerfully.

"Yes, my lord," George replied. "You're an acquaintance of his?" Although this man appeared to be one of the gentry, he seemed more informal in his bearing. There was a roughness about his scrubbed hands suggesting he engaged in practical amusements. The fact he sought out George with a pleasant manner also made him less daunting.

"A long-standing one at that," the man conceded. "He's helping me with ongoing soil analysis of my Hopetoun estate. Perhaps Dr Black has discussed the undertaking with you? No? Well, I discovered a fascinating seam of pyromorphite in the upper-northwest quadrant of my estate where we expected a galena deposit. Anyone acquainted with Romé de l'Isle's seminal texts would know how peculiar this was. Then Dr Black's chemical analysis revealed that what we thought was standard pyromorphite in fact contained a novel lead carbonate morphology, which bore closer physical resemblance to the vaterite interspersed with Ordovician greywacke we thought could only be found in south Devon. Naturally I wondered if that meant cerussite could be found at lower altitudes on my estate, since they are more traditionally expected to coexist with carbonate minerals."

The man beamed.

George wracked his brain for something to say in response that sounded like he'd understood a word of it.

"South Devon, you say? Interesting…"

It was as if someone had thrown open all the windows and cold night air rushed in. The man's jaw clenched. He took a step towards George, who instinctively cowered.

"Excuse me, sir? Pray, share with me your credentials. Astound me with your wealth of personal insight into the topic."

"I…Sir, I'm sorry…"

Despite George's protestations, the sarcastic onslaught continued.

"No, please, my good sir, expound upon your vaulted opinions. For I am most curious as to what I have overlooked." Other men were beginning to look up from their conversations and even turn to witness what was happening.

A gasp warned George he had almost bumped into someone behind him. His implacable foe continued to close the gap George was desperate to widen, mouth curled ever so slightly. George began to gauge paces between them, estimating who among the nearby bystanders would rush to the nobleman's defence…

"There you are, Mr Stephens." A hand was clamped firmly above George's elbow. "I need to introduce you to Sir Grey before he gets occupied again. Forgive the interruption, my lord." Black didn't need to apply further pressure, because George eagerly let himself be led to the other side of the room. The murmur of conversation bubbled back to normal levels.

Once they'd covered enough ground, Black manoeuvred George in a circle so his line of sight to the aggrieved party was blocked, then let go of his arm. "Mr Stephens, what on earth is going on? The Earl of Hopetoun is a valuable friend of mine."

"I don't know, sir," George said, panicking. "I was telling

him his soil-analysis plan was interesting and then suddenly he got angry."

"Hmm," replied Black. After a moment, he added, "When speaking with the Earl of Hopetoun, did you remark, 'Your soil-analysis plan sounds very interesting,' or did you just reply, 'Interesting'?"

"The latter, maybe, I'm not sure. Why?"

"Yes, I can see why he may have taken offence." The stern expression faded. Now Black looked entertained. "Depending on tone, the response 'interesting' can mean the observer finds what they've just heard to be the *opposite* of interesting, perhaps even foolish. Lucky for you, since the Earl of Hopetoun is a good friend, I will explain that you meant no malice by your remarks. He'll laugh once he realises the misunderstanding."

Which means he'll laugh at me, George thought, blushing. Though becoming an object of mockery was probably better than becoming one of hostility.

"If you ever wish to provoke a fight, the quickest way is to tell your opponent, 'I'm *surprised* to hear you say that.' The inflection matters, of course. Wait until you're alone to practise, mind."

"I don't think I have the intellect for this," George said quietly, watching the proceedings.

"It's not a question of intellect, Mr Stephens—"

"Or the social stature."

"It's not a question of social stature either. Although both of these things help. It's about acting as if you possess the worthiness to rise above these strictures." Black raised his cane in a sweep of the room. "And you're more worthy than many here."

"I'm not sure I can complete my medical studies," George admitted, lowering his voice. "I'm unsuited to these learned pursuits."

He hadn't told anyone about Monro's threat to remove him from anatomy class. The past few days he'd been wracked with gut pains, waiting for the inevitable dismissal. But aside from a few scowls, Monro hadn't said anything to George, shooing him away when he sidled up at the end of Friday's class.

The older professor sighed with amusement, unconvinced by George's protestations of inadequacy.

"You appear more suited to medicine than myself, Mr Stephens." George looked over at Black in surprise. "I was a terrible scholar of medicine. I hadn't the stomach for dissections—I still don't, if I'm candid. To avoid it, I declined to pursue advanced anatomical studies in London that would have done wonders for my clinical practice."

Was the calm, composed Dr Joseph Black really this hopeless a medical student? Anatomy dissections were one of the few aspects of his education where George thought he held tolerable skills: to learn that Black feared them was a revelation.

Black continued, taking no notice of George's expression. "In fact, as the time drew towards submitting my doctoral dissertation, I spent three weeks convinced I should quit medicine and become a painter."

"A painter?" George couldn't help himself. "Sir, I didn't know you could paint."

"But that's the funniest thing: I can't!" Both men laughed. "Anyway, once you know what doubts the greatest minds have struggled with, you'll find your own case in no way peculiar."

With that, Black slipped around George and disappeared into the crowd.

"Thank you, sir," George mumbled.

. . .

At long last the salon wound down, and men began to take their leave of Dashkova. George overheard many of them speak to her regarding scientific matters, but with a degree of gallant flirtatiousness suggesting they didn't care if she understood or not. In return Dashkova giggled, giving delighted exclamations or pretty little replies depending on how seriously the men sought to engage her.

A hearty pat on the back nearly caused George to spill his drink. Once he saw it was the Earl of Hopetoun, he flinched so wildly claret ended up on his borrowed coat.

Now the earl was shaking his head and smiling to himself.

"Ah, to be young."

It looked like Black had managed a successful intervention, but George was too spooked by their first encounter to venture any remark for fear it too would be misinterpreted. The earl thumped George on the back a few more times for good measure, then dropped a heavy object into his pocket.

"Something more for the benefit of our mutual friend, but you too may find it...*interesting*." He took off cackling, leaving George to his crimson shame.

Reaching into his pocket, George curled his hand around a lumpy piece of rock, with smooth bubbles mixed around hard edges.

Beside him, Dashkova and Cullen engaged in whispered conversation. Perhaps from a distance it looked like all her other conversations, but George could hear how sharply focussed Dashkova's replies were.

"No, Sir Henry expressed scepticism about your aether theory. He told me this himself."

"Yes, yes, but he complimented my treatise on nosology when it came out. Went out of his way to do so, in fact."

"That was four years ago; much has changed since then. Anyway, no one can find fault with your nosology treatise—he would be an idiot to criticise it. Quite a few people have found fault with your aether theory, however; Herning's rebuttal to it at the Royal Society contained many valid points, but no friend of yours would publicly repeat them."

"Ah, George, how are you feeling?" Cullen asked, beckoning him over instead of responding to Dashkova. "Made some new friends?"

"Well, the Earl of Hopetoun just gave me a piece of pyromorphite, so maybe."

17

An unfamiliar nurse led Black across the Dispensary ward to Bennie, who was sitting up and reading. A warm hue had returned to his skin.

Based upon Black, Cullen and Dashkova's probing at the salon, there were three or four members of the gentry whose recent behaviour and family history raised the spectre of dark chymistry dealings. Dashkova had offered to invite them to call upon her in the next week, giving her the opportunity to ask more questions.

Not long after, Black was hosting Cullen in his study, a space less suitable for entertaining guests than his parlour, but the fire was well stoked and the wind outside was unduly cold. He was thinking about their next steps when his servant knocked at the door and handed him a scrap of folded paper.

Black unfolded the note.

Dear Sir,

It gives me great relief to convey this message: Benjamin's fever broke last Friday and he is recovering well. I will be discharging him within days.

Your obd servant, etc,
A.D.

"Good news," was all he said, passing the note over.

"Good news indeed," breathed Cullen once he read Duncan's message.

Black was already at his desk, sharpening a fresh quill. "I'll send a reply to Dr Duncan requesting another chance to speak with his patient. I assume he'll agree."

"Sensible idea, Joe," said Cullen. "See what Bennie can tell us before Brown has a chance to pour poison in his ear again."

An hour after Duncan's assent reached his study, Black was in a carriage heading down Nicolson Street.

"Got the appetite for your studies back?" he asked Bennie with a smile, noting the book in front of him concerned medical theory. "I'm sure we could arrange to bring some textbooks if you're short on material."

"Well, my concentration isn't where it should be," Bennie admitted. He appeared bemused at the sight of a college professor in the dingy ward, but set the book down on his knee and tried to perch forward.

"I visited here last week, to consult with Dr Duncan over a patient," Black said, omitting that Bennie was the patient in question, "and learned of the grave state you were in. I'm glad to see you recovered."

"Thank you, Dr Black."

Black eased into the spindly chair beside Bennie's bed.

"I hope I'm not the only visitor to enliven your recuperation, though since you've taken to your books, I fear I might be."

Bennie smiled politely. "The fellow on my left is sleeping now, but we've managed a few card games."

This answer implied the Brunonians hadn't called on Bennie, through underhand means or otherwise. After overhearing the Brunonians in the college library, Black had taken his concerns to several faculty members who taught in the Royal Infirmary. Muted outrage spread fast. Within days, several nurses were dismissed from employment, and a few Town Guardsmen were roped into monitoring the grounds after sunset. Town Guards were considerably more expensive to bribe than nurses, so Black predicted the Brunonians wouldn't be causing mischief there any time soon.

Crucially, his name was kept out of the sordid business.

"Your cuts are healing well, I presume?" Black asked, keeping his tone light. "Some of those marks looked to be deliberate, and I wondered if they were in any way connected to your illness."

Bennie fidgeted.

"Why, those were silly little injuries, Dr Black." He began tugging his sleeves over his wrists.

"Did Dr Brown carve those marks on you?" Black asked suddenly.

Bennie's eyes darted frantically. The book slipped off his knee. He stared at Black, trying to assess if he was joking, but Black remained silent and still.

"Dr Black...I..."

"I'm not angry at you, Bennie, nor are you in trouble," Black said firmly, catching his book before it slipped onto the floor. "But I am concerned that Dr Brown or his students are endangering lives."

"It's not like that, it's..." Bennie continued to look around like a cornered animal. Finally he slumped back against the wall. "Sir, I volunteered for an experiment. I wanted to be helpful, and Dr Brown was looking for assistants. He asked me if I was sure, and I told him I was. But I really don't think the experiments are what made me ill."

"What experiment was this? Do you recall falling ill afterwards?" asked Black.

Bennie frowned. There was a long pause.

"I don't remember much," he admitted. "I told you before, Dr Black, I don't know if I have the head for philosophical inquiry. I didn't understand everything they told me about the experiment, but they showed me the knives were clean and I think they helped dress my wounds afterwards. So I doubt they got infected."

"No, they probably didn't," Black agreed. "Why did they carve symbols on you?"

There was another long pause. Bennie seemed agitated.

"I don't remember. I know they told me. I remember it hurt when he cut me."

"What else can you remember from the day of the experiment?" Black uncrossed and recrossed his legs.

"It was a normal Sunday. I met up with Dr Brown in the afternoon after church. We must have gone to the private clinic space, because I remember being there and getting ready for the experiment. But I'm not sure if I remember getting there..." He trailed off.

"It must be distressing to have gaps in your memory, but such losses are common after severe illness, as yours was. Often those memories return upon some distance from the fever." Black saw Bennie's eyes welling up. "Do you remember if the experiment just involved carving marks on you? Did Dr Brown do anything else or make any particular observations?"

"He did a lot of speaking." Bennie sniffed. "I don't think he used any apparatus."

"This being Dr Brown?"

"No, this was all Cornelius Pyke." Bennie seemed desperate not to dwell on his memory loss. "Dr Brown had to attend to Masonic lodge business that afternoon; I knew all about that ahead of time. Cornelius performed the experiment following Dr Brown's instructions."

The name was familiar, and Black was sure he'd pin it

down once he had time to focus on the matter. For the moment he kept asking questions. "Was it unusual for Cornelius to do this kind of experimentation on Dr Brown's behalf?"

"Yes and no, sir. He's been Dr Brown's assistant for a while, but they usually work together." Bennie stopped. "Cornelius wouldn't act maliciously, Dr Black. He takes Dr Brown's teachings very seriously, and I used to take tea at his lodgings. Of course, that was before he sought sanctuary at Holyrood for debts."

"I agree, that doesn't sound like Cornelius." He was a former medical student, Black now recalled. "I don't want to fatigue you, Bennie, so I'll take my leave. Please follow all Dr Duncan's recommendations to complete your recovery."

Bennie wiped his eyes. "I don't want Dr Brown or Cornelius to get in trouble, Dr Black. None of this was their fault. Dr Brown has always been kind and generous to me."

"Don't worry, Bennie, just get as much rest as you can."

Black didn't like doing this. Men often constructed these facades of memory to protect themselves, and it was distressing to see them realise the false stories they'd told themselves. Black knew he couldn't tell Bennie to stay away from a mentor he thought was protecting him—but he could perhaps coax him to the realisation that Dr Brown didn't have his best interests at heart.

* * *

An academic dispute over the treatment of gout shouldn't erupt into violence, but with hindsight, the warning signs were there.

From his vantage point at the back of the senate chambers, Black had watched Brown strut into the room alongside the other faculty members. His bellowing laugh drowned out everyone else's demure whispering. The chambers were of modest size but airy and well lit, with creamy green walls and sculpted plaster coves. While the musty smell in other college rooms gave the impression of neglect, in here the odour conferred refinement. This wasn't a room for uncouth merriment.

Brown held a stack of manuscripts in his hand. He set them on Cullen's table near the front of the room; Cullen barely glanced up from his conversation with the provost to acknowledge him, then paused.

Safely unobserved, Black raised his eyes skywards. Over the past week Brown's boasting about his suitability for the medical theory chair had grown from tavern bravado to something a lot like serious intent. The manuscripts he returned to Cullen were an excuse to get himself in front of the gathered medical faculty to canvas support. Anyone with half a wit could see this. But the way Brown paused and patted his waistcoat pocket—he'd not yet added that cinnamon monstrosity to his wardrobe— made Black wince. Brown thought he was being subtle.

"Dr Bruno, I see!" the chair of botany quipped. Brown beamed and made a jocular response. This would be the first time many of the faculty saw him since he obtained his doctorate from St Andrews.

Brown kept talking, acting as if he hadn't heard the mockery in the botany chair's tone. Around him, the other faculty smiled to themselves, their eyes twitching towards the intruder.

Looking down at his notebook, Black wondered if he should intervene. Warn Brown that his strategy was going to backfire and urge him to leave with his dignity intact. He hesitated. Such guidance was really Cullen's responsibility. But the man who employed Brown as his ad hoc secretary remained deep in conversation with the provost.

In the front row, Monro was watching Brown with the intensity of a cat edging closer to a pigeon. Black couldn't see the anatomy professor's face, but he knew enough of his body language to feel uneasy.

He'd have to act. Black pushed his chair back, trying not to make a noise. He hated situations like these where he was reacting to others, not in control of the unfolding events. He had less than ten paces to invent a lie that would distract Monro from his quarry.

His hesitation cost him.

"Much effort spent acquiring that lauded honour, Dr Brown?" Monro asked loudly. "I hear dinner for six university senators and a principal can strain a man's purse, even in the wilderness of Fife."

The smile on Brown's face ground to a halt. Half risen, Black sank down into his chair.

"They invited me tae St Andrews fae the same oral examinations they give their students after reviewing my letters of recommendation. I composed the required essays, in Latin I might add, over the course of an hour. They said my aphorism commentary was one of the finest they'd heard." Brown glared at Monro, challenging him to claim he too could produce such a fine Latin essay in under an hour.

Monro leant back in his chair, confident he held the attention of the majority of the room and feeling no need to let Brown distract him.

"And after an hour at the bottles, I too tend to declare everything I look upon to be the finest I've seen. Especially when I'm not the one paying for the bottles."

Brown's face darkened, his smile slipping into a grimace. The snickering of onlookers worked their way into Black's ears.

"Oh come on, Sandy," Cullen interrupted. "Dr Brown

here isn't the first gentleman to obtain his medical degree from St Andrews in such a manner."

It was a partial defence of his former student, but the way Brown's chest heaved suggested Cullen's interruption came too late. The whipcrack of Monro's tongue had been heard round the room.

Brown turned to Cullen, bowed stiffly as if the only reason he'd waited in the room was to receive his acknowledgement, then strode out the chamber.

At the front of the room, Cullen and Monro dissolved into bickering.

"...needlessly cruel, Sandy—"

"Well, how long as he been a student, William? Ten years?"

"Not consecutively, no—"

"And then you listen to his rambling medical theories and wonder if he absorbed a single thing we lectured on in all those years."

"All the same, *rudeness* isn't necessary..."

Most of the learned faculty in that chamber lacked experience with brawls or boxing matches. But the way Brown's eyes had slipped in and out of focus reminded Black of the nastier street fights he had witnessed. When a fighter's eyes blurred like that, they were usually seconds away from snapping, crushing their opponent into a bloody pulp.

At the time it seemed ludicrous that Brown could conflate the senate chamber with a boxing ring, humorous even.

A few months later, it wasn't funny at all.

18

It was nothing more than luck that George learned of tonight's plan ahead of time. A few days earlier he had watched Black stride across the yards in the direction of Cullen's lecture room. He could either follow him and risk intruding or go home and fail at studying. He was quick enough in his decision that by the time he found the two professors huddled in a corner of the yards, Black had barely begun speaking.

"Cornelius Pyke?" Cullen asked, motioning for George to come closer so he wouldn't have to raise his voice. "He's still in Edinburgh?"

"Just about," said Black. "According to Bennie, he recently sought sanctuary in Holyrood."

Cullen grimaced. "Bad business, Joe, I tell you."

"Cornelius studied medicine a few years ago," Black explained to George, after recounting what had transpired at the Dispensary. "Bright scholar, but preoccupied with the accumulation of, and pretensions towards, wealth. Unfortunately, the pretensions won over accumulation. He dropped out midway through his studies, and according to Bennie entered Brown's orbit soon after."

"Bennie's sure he's an Abbey laird?" Cullen began rubbing his hands together. Black nodded. "Well, it should be easy enough to wring the truth from him, we just have to contrive a setting where he's...strongly induced to cooperate."

George wasn't sure he'd heard correctly. Was Cullen plotting the torture of a former student?

Cullen didn't notice George's alarm, because he kept on talking.

"In the city of Pamplona in Spain, they have a hundred-year-old tradition they call the Running of the Bulls: every summer, scores of young men hoping to prove their virility are chased down ancient streets by a herd of bulls. In the fine city of Edinburgh, we have a similar feat of athleticism every Sunday at midnight that I call the Running of the Scoundrels."

George was vaguely familiar with this arrangement. Debtors granted sanctuary in Holyrood had amnesty on the Sabbath to go about business within the city, but on the stroke of twelve o'clock, any debtor not past the boundary at Girth Cross could be apprehended by creditors. The only chance some creditors had of regaining lost money was to catch the debtors on their flight to the Sanctuary.

Cullen was warming up to his thesis. "Given Cornelius' tendency to arrive late for my practice of physic lectures, I speculate a threat of delay at the foot of the Canongate on the cusp of midnight may be enough to loosen his lips."

This seemed a plan as wild as the aforementioned bulls, but Black gave a thoughtful hum. "Cornelius was often late for my chemistry class, too."

Therefore, tugging his coat sleeves down over his hands, George found Cullen at the junction of Horse Wynd and Abbey Strand. The professors had requested George meet them here an hour after nightfall on Sunday. Behind him, the crags of Holyrood Park loomed dark and motionless.

The Abbey Sanctuary buildings that housed the debtors were just paces away from where Cullen and George now stood, parallel to the Girth Cross.

Cullen continued to explain his plans as the two men waited. "Dr Black will be concealed several hundred metres up the Canongate, and will alert us by fire signal when he spies Cornelius. You will then attempt to waylay him, and I'll be behind you in case you require assistance, and to conduct the questioning."

George wished, and was surprised at himself for feeling that way, it was Black who would be backing him up. Cullen must have observed his doubtful expression, because he added, "Dr Black has better eyesight, and will recognise Cornelius quicker than me."

The use of a fire signal rather than the more discrete proculopathy was unexpected, but George supposed the professors hoped to avoid inflicting choking and nausea on him again. He wasn't going to question their strategy.

"And what of Princess Dashkova?" George asked instead.

"The princess will be up the street near Dr Black, distracting any debt collectors in pursuit of our target, giving us time to perform our interrogation."

"But this is the middle of the night in Edinburgh!" George cried. "Who knows who will be out? Imagine the horrors that will ensue when they encounter a solitary lady!"

Cullen gave a dispassionate shrug. "Way of the world, lad. Most of the debt collectors deserve what she'll do to them. Ho, that looks like our carriage."

Black descended and made his way to the corner of Horse Wynd, at about the same time as Dashkova emerged from the gates of Holyrood Palace on foot.

The princess wore a dark blue bodice that exposed a

precarious amount of cleavage, even by current fashion mores. George wasn't sure how she could retrieve a dagger from down there.

She caught him staring.

"…Won't you catch a chill, Your Highness?" George asked, once it was clear Dashkova wouldn't stop staring back until he said something.

Dashkova tossed her head. "You think I am ill prepared for dangerous affairs? Let me tell you, I dealt with men at the Russian court this way, and tonight will be good practice for when I return."

George looked away to conceal his reddening face. Dashkova wrapped a black woollen shawl around her shoulders. With her black cloth cap, she almost melted into the shadows.

After a brief conference between the physicians, Black and Dashkova departed up the street. Black disappeared into the mouth of a close and Dashkova kept walking until she crossed the road and vanished out of sight. George and Cullen were left in the middle of the square.

"Everything clear? Excellent. Stay on the lookout in White Horse Close and I'll be in that doorway." Cullen pointed to an alcove several houses down.

"Actually, sir, it might be better if you hid behind the Cross, or on the other side of the street," George said hastily. "Because if Cornelius sees me, he'll cut to the other side of the square away from you."

His heart pounded into the silence.

"Yes, actually, you're right, George," Cullen said. "I'll stay underneath the Cross. Forgive me, lad, it's been an aeon since I last read Tacticus."

. . .

It was a tedious wait. As their watch began, a few men made their way down the street, some accompanied by wives or friends, who parted with them outside the Sanctuary. With the hours wearing closer to midnight, men started to come in smaller groups. The pace at which they crossed the city boundary became brisk.

George didn't want to know what the time was. Every distant ring of St Giles told him it was earlier than he wished.

Eventually the rate of debtors slowed to nothing. George was sure they'd either missed Cornelius or he wouldn't leave the city at all.

Then, in the distance, he detected a person making their way down the Canongate. George looked past them to the close where Black was concealed. There was a burst of crimson light from the shadows. Blinking, George scrambled to his feet.

Maybe the man caught Black's signal, or perhaps he detected movement, but he broke into a jog. Cursing, George saw him drift to the further side of the square, away from the shadows of White Horse Close. George had lost all element of surprise.

He barrelled into the street, but Cornelius skipped to the side and kept running. George turned in time to avoid tripping, but now Cornelius was several metres ahead of him.

Just as he was about to lose his quarry Cullen emerged from behind Girth Cross, hands glowing. He lowered into a crouch and waved his hands through the air in the direction of Cornelius' legs. Cornelius twisted awkwardly to avoid what Cullen had fired at him, and as he stumbled, George grabbed on to him. The two men flew through the air. They were at the very bottom of the High Street, at the point where the city runoff pooled, so George felt cold mud and water splash onto his face and the wetness seep into his clothes.

The two men scrambled, but George was able to crawl on top of Cornelius, pinning him face down on the ground.

"What the devil?" cried Cornelius, kicking and writhing. Despite his shabby garments, he looked like the kind of man who had spent his childhood indoors. Having noticed his absence of a chin, George couldn't blame him.

George pressed his knee into Cornelius' back.

"Don't try anything too creative, young sir," Cullen warned, his outstretched hands still alight. "I doubt your phlogiston abilities are as swift as mine."

"Professor Cullen?" Cornelius asked in astonishment.

"The very same. Listen, Cornelius, we know you are conducting lethal business with John Brown, and we need some answers."

"We didn't mean to hurt the boy," Cornelius wailed, renewing his resistance. "That wasn't our intention at all!"

"Then what was your intention?" demanded Cullen, taking another step forward.

"Please! We were studying Bruno's texts—"

"What texts?"

"The ones on creating phlogiston vessels. I don't know where he got them, but they said the procedures were safe. I swear on the Bible we didn't mean to hurt Bennie—he volunteered to receive the markings. Please let me go, don't kill me."

The shock of his ambush had left Cornelius temporarily forgetting that he had the ability to strike back against his assailant with phlogiston, George realised. Fortunately, Cullen wasn't giving him enough time to remember.

"You didn't notice you brought the poor boy to death's door?" Cullen snorted.

"Bennie was fine when I left him." Cornelius' breath came in ragged spurts. "It was a simple procedure, one we'd successfully done several times before. I placed the markings on Bennie's torso where Dr Brown advised me to. They were trifling scratches that stopped bleeding before Bennie had the chance to get his shirt back on. We kept him in the clinic for a few hours for testing, but he seemed fine: no fever, nothing. Told him to come back tomorrow morning or call for Dr Brown if he fell ill that night. Next thing I heard he was rushed to the Dispensary before Dr Brown had a chance to treat him."

"Yet you know the procedure killed Pierre," George interrupted. Cornelius was no longer resisting the knee on his back. Instead he seemed to be cowering into the mud.

"No, Pierre survived the procedure several times before. Most of the Brunonians have." Cornelius' wet hair was sticking to his face, and he flicked his head, trying to remove it from his eye. "The previous times he had nothing worse than a headache the next morning. He wasn't supposed to go through it again; Pierre was looking for other recruits. But that night he came to Dr Brown saying the student in his anatomy class was a worthless lead after all, and offered to try the procedure again. I wasn't there that night."

George pressed his kneecap deeper between Cornelius' shoulder blades. He wanted to demand Cornelius tell him which anatomy student Pierre had considered and discarded, put the truth out in the open. Yet as Cornelius whimpered with renewed discomfort, George knew the truth wouldn't help him.

If Cullen sensed any change in George's demeanour, he didn't remark upon it.

"Why did you go along with this criminality, Cornelius? Don't insult me with false protestations that you didn't know how dangerous Dr Brown's procedures were."

"Everyone knew there was a risk!" Cornelius insisted. "But if the texts were right, they'd gain incredible power once Dr Brown fine-tuned the procedure."

"What texts are these?" Cullen pressed.

"I don't know!"

"Not a good enough answer, boy!"

"They're old, they're written in Latin codes that even Bruno struggles to decipher sometimes. I don't know where he got them. Please let me go. I can't be caught here after midnight."

A squelch to George's left told him Cullen was shifting on his feet. "Why try to dam the body's natural phlogiston?"

"Dr Brown wanted to move beyond the old phlogiston vessels." Cornelius spoke quickly, deciding cooperation would secure his release. "He said he would be to phlogiston what some journeyman in Birmingham—I forget the name—was to the Newcomb engine."

Cullen muttered several rude words. Recognising he wasn't in mortal danger, Cornelius renewed his attempts to break free. Still angry, George pressed his forearm into Cornelius' neck.

"And that's what they were all about?" Cullen demanded. "Creating phlogiston vessels?"

"What?"

"The texts, boy!"

"No, there's other procedures, but Bruno says they're too risky to try before he's fully cracked the code."

George had been keeping his eyes firmly on Cornelius, but he realised Cullen was standing over them both.

"Let the boy turn over," Cullen said softly. "He's going to drown in that puddle of horse piss."

George shifted some weight off his knee. Cornelius flopped onto his back and groaned.

Cullen crouched down beside him. "Listen, Cornelius, I know you. You have the potential to become a fine man if you apply yourself. We know you didn't intend to hurt Bennie, and praise Providence he seems to have made a full recovery. Resume your studies at the university: I'll put in a good word with the other faculty, and we'll see about waiving some of your course fees. Dr Brown is playing a dangerous game he does not fully understand, and cannot control the forces he's playing with. I would urge you to cease your involvement with him."

The sudden onslaught of compassion took the fight out of Cornelius, who rubbed his eyes.

"Think about it anyway, will you, lad? George, let him be on his way."

George rose, careful not to lose his balance. Cornelius lay in the mud for a minute like a dazed deer, before shakily standing. Cullen's hands still glowed, but his body language was less tense. The professor reached into his coat pocket and tossed something to Cornelius.

"That should be enough to keep you out of trouble for a bit, at least until you've had time to consider your options." Cornelius nodded, then began to edge away. He didn't fully turn his back on the two men until he reached Abbey Strand and finally succumbed to the shadows.

Cullen gestured for George to direct his attention back up the High Street.

"That was good work again, Mr Stephens. We'll regroup tomorrow."

George wanted to hurl something after Cornelius, a rock maybe. So much for avenging Pierre's death. The boy he'd considered a proto-friend was as contemptuous of him as everyone else—he'd simply died before he had the opportunity to insult George to his face.

"What did he mean by phlogiston vessels?" George asked. He wanted to take his mind off the exchange, seeking reassurance that Cullen didn't consider him a worthless scab.

"Like I said the other day, the dark chymists rely on sigils for their power; they can't manifest phlogiston at will. They used large earthenware pots, baked from a particular kind of clay, to draw and store phlogiston. Using a living animal as a vessel would be a step ahead of what the dark chymists mastered," Cullen noted.

"What difference does it make whether the vessel is human or inanimate?" George wondered.

"Well, lad, those old phlogiston vessels couldn't store their power indefinitely; they remained at maximum strength only a short while. There's not much you can do with a cumbersome pot: it stays in one place and any operator has scant control over its discharge. Theoretically, the animal nervous system could store phlogiston longer if there was a way to contain it without causing harm. That's an avenue of inquiry I've thought about and drawn many a blank on before I even started."

In the course of George's military service, steam-powered engines had gone from an academic curiosity to exciting commercial investment for Cornish mining companies, simply because someone found a way to keep the heat inside the contraption long enough for it to be useful. In Cornelius' awkward analogy, Brown was experimenting with ways to magnify the power of phlogiston, and in doing so, open up unknown avenues of application.

Just then, loud, incoherent swearing pierced the night. A man in shabby workman's clothes was pelting down the hill as fast as he could, clutching his hat. It was hard to tell in the dark, but there were signs of scratches on his face.

"Bricon! Fis à putain!" Rustling down the Canongate, Dashkova followed, struggling to hoist her skirts clear of her legs. Despite her moving remarkably quickly, in George's estimation, the man was accelerating towards Holyrood away from her.

Suddenly Dashkova dropped to one knee in the middle of the street.

"Ekaterina, no!" In the distance, Black sprinted towards her.

Ignoring him, Dashkova pulled a knife from her stockings, peering down its hilt like she was aiming a rifle. A silent, smokeless flash of light flew down the blade and out through the air.

Whipping his head around, George thought Dashkova had missed her shot, because the man kept running. Then a blaze of light broke upon his head. His screams reached the onlookers just as he knocked his burning hat and wig to the ground and stumbled around the corner out of their line of sight.

Black bent to a halt beside Dashkova, gasping for breath. He dropped a mud-caked purse into her spare hand. After appraising it and finding its weight satisfactory, Dashkova rose and fixed him with a cool expression.

"You see, I did not kill him, my dear Joseph. I try to learn patience from you."

19

If Cullen left the Canongate fuming after his interrogation of Cornelius, by the next morning he was erupting.

"A grimoire, Joe! Brown's been holding on to a grimoire this whole time. How could we have missed one?"

"Difficult to say at this point," Black demurred, breaking his ratafia cake from quarters into eighths.

When Anna Cullen had let George into the house this morning, her eyes and tight mouth flashed out a warning that the master of the house was in an ill humour. This wasn't a surprise. What caught George off guard was that he wasn't the first student welcomed into the Cullen household that day. A second-year fellow from Cornwall was holed up in Cullen's study, copying a medical treatise as fast as he could get ink onto paper.

Cullen brooded to himself until Black and Dashkova arrived.

"We thought it was just a question of experimentation subjects," Cullen continued. "No, it's Bruno's Latin fluency they're after. Damn his limited genius. He'll be right at home digging into those arcane texts. No allusion will be too obscure for him to miss."

Black nudged the food around his plate. There was a reddish tint to his eyes suggesting he'd suffered another night of poor sleep.

"Shame Cornelius couldn't identify which grimoire, or how it came into their possession," Cullen said with a sigh. The majority of his ire was expended. From what the two professors had said, it was unlikely Cornelius would resurface this week. While Cullen believed he wouldn't return to the Brunonians, Black didn't think Cornelius would cooperate unless the professors helped clear his debts.

Cullen's parlour was chilly—George felt a draught through the window on his neck. Cullen's blood ran so hot most of the time it was unlikely he noticed, though. Not for the first time, George wondered how he'd survive his full Edinburgh winter. He was used to the cold, and could survive the wet, but the unique melding of the two in Edinburgh was harder to endure.

"Where is the grimoire now?" Dashkova asked. She'd already demolished two ratafia cakes.

Cullen hadn't bothered to dismiss his housekeeper this time. But perhaps his initial concerns were misplaced. Princess Dashkova stared rudely at poor Alice whenever she entered the parlour, causing her no small degree of agitation.

"We're not sure," Cullen admitted. "The Brunonians don't have access to the city hospitals or teaching wards, but Cornelius implied they had a space for medical procedures. Should have asked him while we had the chance, though maybe he'd hesitate to reveal that information." The Brunonians appeared to have abandoned the College of Surgeons for good. Cornelius was certainly afraid the professors pursued retribution against Brown. With good reason, George noted.

"Are you still meeting Sir Grey and Lord and Lady Argyle this afternoon, Your Highness?" Cullen asked.

"Indeed," Dashkova said. She scowled at Alice when the housekeeper tried to offer her another plate of cakes.

"Maybe I can come too," George blurted out. Cullen raised his eyebrows. "I mean, I was talking with Prince Dashkov after anatomy class, and he invited me to call upon him. Perhaps I can be present at the meeting." He wanted desperately to be useful to the professors, and thought that his restraint when handling Cornelius had won him more respect.

"Hmm," Cullen said after a pause. "They might already be aware of your involvement in this affair—it is a little too risky. But a good idea, lad." It appeared his restraint counted for less than he'd hoped. Black gave him a sympathetic look.

"We'll keep you informed, George. You should prioritise Dr Monro's class this week."

George caught a glimpse of Alice in the kitchen after Dashkova left, on the verge of tears.

George couldn't deny the professors' reasoning in keeping him away from Dashkova's salon, but it was still a disappointment. Especially since they'd given him no other tasks to occupy himself with until their next meeting.

But as he returned towards his lodgings, George was struck by an idea. Instead of heading indoors, he continued on towards Candlemaker's Row and Livingston's Coffeehouse.

James had mentioned he met with several Brunonians at the coffeehouse, and they were often there on Monday morning. George wondered if that meant the Brunonians' clinic was located nearby.

By the time he was descending into the West Bow, he was almost convinced he should turn around and return home: he was no friend of the Brunonians, and they knew he was still involved with the professors. Eventually he convinced himself that the seedier elements of Brown's entourage—the boxers and armed thugs—were less likely to be here. James had made it sound as if it was only the medical brethren who frequented this coffeehouse.

There was also a smaller part of him that *wanted* the brutes to be there, because it would allow him a chance to redo his humiliating encounter at The Mermaid and challenge them for breaking into his lodgings.

George made his way into the coffeehouse, trying not to look like he was searching for anyone in particular. He settled on a table near the back with a discarded newspaper and set to reading.

He had almost finished his disgusting coffee, which he'd no desire to savour, when a handful of half-familiar voices rose.

The Brunonians had been sitting on the opposite side of the room the whole time behind a pillar, so George hadn't noticed them. Now they were leaving.

Checking all of them had vacated the table, George crept after them. He rushed to the opposite side of West Bow and cast around. The Brunonians were heading down the hill towards the Grassmarket. The street was busy enough that George could follow them from a distance and know he wasn't attracting attention.

With juddering heart, George saw the three Brunonians turn into a close. From his vantage point across the street, at the foot of Greyfriars Kirkyard, George watched them enter one of the buildings. There was someone standing by the door who nodded as the men passed, and George thought it was one of the men who had attacked him in Adam Square. He didn't want to loiter in view, so skipped to the side. It didn't look like the men were going to come out, and now he worried that other Brunonians would spot him. It seemed like he had the location.

George didn't have time to congratulate himself on a job well done, because as he turned to walk away, he was rudely grabbed on the shoulder.

"Doing more of Dr Cullen's dirty work?" Edward taunted.

"No. What is the meaning of this?" snapped George. He had been within seconds of striking whoever had assailed him from behind, and only the realisation that Edward was unaccompanied stayed his hand. "Why are you following me?"

"As if!" snorted Edward. "It's just my luck to encounter you when I was going about my business."

George swiped Edward's hand off his shoulder and took a step back. Edward usually carried himself with ease, a knowing smile fluttering at all times. While his clothes and periwig were neat as ever, there was something dishevelled in his manner today.

"Have you been drinking?" If Edward's breath smelled of anything, it was cloves—but George couldn't understand what else would cause such belligerence.

Edward's eyes narrowed.

"Don't try and deny this, Stephens. I know you ratted the Brunonians out of the Infirmary."

"I...what?" George was too confused to act the part of a wronged individual.

"Oh, they were furious alright," Edward continued. "The Town Guard patrolling the Infirmary, the nurses who supported them dismissed from service? Damn it, Stephens, that's impressive vindictiveness."

"Edward." George gritted his teeth to slow the words and impress upon Edward his sincerity. "I have exactly zero idea what you are accusing me of."

He was thinking desperately, trying to conceive a thought

or memory that would link "Brunonians" with "The Infirmary" in his mind. All his thoughts swirled back to the Public Dispensary, because that was where Bennie was treated: the subject of numerous conversations between the professors.

George could almost see the steam rising off Edward. Of course, implying an angry man was an idiot didn't usually do much to dispel their anger, but at this point George felt more enraged than fearful by Edward's nonsensical allegations.

"Well who else could it be?" Edward swung his arms. "After the Brunonians accosted me, it all made sense. You asking all those asinine questions about them, then spending an afternoon with them in The Mermaid and getting yourself invited to their debate. All before you recommence crawling around Dr Cullen's place. Oh, and just this minute I interrupt you spying on the Brunonians from afar."

On the one hand, this whole exchange with a hopping-mad Edward felt ludicrous: Edward had managed to stitch together a string of truths into a whole-cloth falsehood that still didn't make any sense. But George's heart was pounding, because he didn't understand what was actually going on, or how much danger he was in.

Then George's brain caught up with his ears.

"Wait, Edward...the Brunonians accosted you?"

Edward laughed bitterly. "They thought I was responsible for ratting them out to the Infirmary physicians, didn't they? I shared lodgings with James—caught him in Mrs Collins' kitchen one day smuggling pies out, which is how I learned they were sneaking into the Infirmary to treat patients using Brunonian principles. Not that the subterfuge bothered me: not my patients, not my problem."

There was a redness partly concealed by Edward's neck scarf, George noticed. The kind of mark you'd acquire after being grabbed by the throat.

"What did they do to you, Edward?" he asked, his outrage channelled in a new direction.

"And my friendship with Dr Cullen attracted their suspicion," Edward continued as if he'd not heard George. "No thanks to you, Stephens." He almost spat the last sentence out.

George cursed himself for his blindness. With that outburst, Edward's oscillating treatment of him finally made sense.

"What gives you the right to undermine my friendship with Professor Cullen?" Edward demanded. "You know how important he was to me, and you flaunted your usurpation."

I shouldn't have drawn attention to the fact the Brunonians threatened him, George thought. He's ashamed of that and is going to refocus his shame onto me.

"My time with Dr Cullen had no consequence on your friendship with the man," George retorted. "How could it?"

"Oh, you insouciant puppy! You took pleasure in asking me all those questions about the Brunonian and Cullenite doctrines, knowing how little I knew of the whole affair."

Two heartbeats ago I was a spy exploiting him for information about the Brunonians, George thought. Now I'm a snake who took pleasure in exposing his ignorance about them through my questioning. This argument bore an unwelcome resemblance to the ones he had with his mother: changing her points of contention whenever a new idea came into her head, more concerned with defeating her opponent than being right.

Edward's handsome face was an unflattering, puffy scarlet.

It was incredulous to think that all this time George was envying Edward's standing with the medical faculty, the green-eyed monster's eyes pointed back at him too.

George took a deep breath, letting each mouthful of air settle in his lungs. He wanted to punch Edward across the jaw, and he suspected Edward was equally keen for him to lash out in anger.

If Edward resented his semi-legitimate parentage, he'd never exposed it for George to see. There was one night Edward loitered in Mrs Collins' parlour after one too many hours in the tavern. The other lodgers were eager to ingratiate themselves with the social ringleader while he was in a voluble mood, and crowded into the room to engage him in their smartest repartee. At some point Edward let it slip he had an older sister still in Jamaica. The revelation stunned George, who couldn't ask more because Edward was bellowing with laughter and had already changed the subject. How many female siblings did Edward have? Did they share a mother? How did he navigate relations with his father's relatives and in-laws now he was back in Scotland?

For the first time, George saw some of Edward's insecurities laid out on the street. How fragile his confidence was, and how easily it could be threatened. Given what he knew of him, the truth shouldn't have been as astounding as it was.

A few weeks ago, George would probably have settled this argument with his fists, delighted to take a pompous youth down a peg or two, like he did to everyone else. But there were other ways to take the fight out of a rival, and George knew he didn't have to play by the rules Edward and his ilk set.

"You're my friend. Listen, Edward! I was envious of your friendship with Dr Cullen and the other professors. I still envy it, as a matter of fact, because I know how highly Dr Cullen thinks of you. He still does. Not once has he disparaged your poor knowledge of Brunonian or Cullenite medical theory."

Edward opened his mouth, but once George had caught his breath, he decided to keep talking instead of listening to his fellow lodger rant.

"I don't know who ratted the Brunonians out to Dr Cullen or the other faculty members. Frankly, I don't rate

Brunonian discretion to begin with." A tiny smile appeared on Edward's face at that, before he remembered he was supposed to be angry.

That could have been enough for one outburst, but George decided to keep talking while he still burned with courage. "Not everyone is out to mock you, Edward, and you shouldn't be out to mock and denigrate everyone either. It's neither becoming nor necessary of you."

Edward was silent. He rocked on the balls of his feet and looked everywhere but at George.

The argument was almost extinguished; George thought for a moment about how to stop it rekindling. "Professor Cullen will be at home tonight. I was going to call on him, but I have no urgent business that requires his attention, and I'm sure he'd be delighted to see you." That wasn't strictly speaking true, but his information could wait.

Edward's fidgeting motions were subsiding. He settled on looking several feet to the left of George's head. "You don't have to disinvite yourself from Cullen's home for my sake, George. Maybe we can make our way over there together later?"

This was probably the closest to an apology Edward would give right now. George found himself smiling. "That would double the agreeableness of the evening's company."

Allowing himself to be buoyed by his success, George permitted himself a small act of defiance. He made his way down the High Street and presented his card at Holyrood Palace.

It wasn't as if the professor had forbidden him from calling upon Prince Dashkov today, and he was confident Dashkova's guests would have long departed by now. Not that he didn't fantasise about creeping into the palace and eavesdropping on Dashkova's conversation with the men, but that sounded even less like something the others would entertain, and George knew he lacked the courage to attempt it.

This was around the time the prince had suggested as suitable for George to call, so no one could criticise him for it. But it still felt like a defiant act.

When he was led into her apartment, Dashkova didn't look surprised to see him. She shepherded him to a tiny room off her bedchamber, which she'd outfitted as a study.

"Ah, George, you must not leave with my son until I have offered you tea. There are honeycakes too. Please sit down." She flapped her arms until George sank into one of the gold-embroidered chairs, located underneath a portrait of King George the Second. Less than a minute later, Prince Dashkov threw himself into a nearby chair.

"Pah, why can you not be my son, George? Pasha, you see how well-mannered our guest is—are you not ashamed of yourself?" Dashkova nudged the plate of honeycakes on the table in front of her until George leant forward to take one.

"Evidently not," replied Dashkov, winking at George.

Dashkova let out a brief admonishment in a mixture of Russian and French, which Pavel tried to laugh off.

"You must forgive my mother, she is very demanding."

"I think," George said delicately, "your mother, erm, Her Highness, is deserving of great respect, and her concern is wanting the best for you."

Dashkov laughed with the same good-natured looseness, but to George's surprise he wriggled upright in his chair to match George's posture.

"Do you hope to return to Saint Petersburg next year?" George asked, hoping to avoid getting drawn deeper into a family squabble. His own mother would never let him dismiss her in such a way.

"It is too early to say," Dashkova said, stirring her tea. "After Pasha graduates this summer, well, I wish to travel to Ireland first to visit my friends. The Empress is still claiming I played no part in the coup that brought her to power. She knows the truth as well as I do, but refuses to say it." She took a small sip of her tea. "Pasha wants me to make nice because he desires a military position, but I'm not convinced that is a good idea. You don't really have the self-discipline for such responsibility."

"Not true in the slightest, Maman." Pavel laughed again, as if there was no offence to be taken from his mother's harsh assessment. "My friends tell me the European service is a lot of fun. And have I not come home early every evening this week, as requested?"

"Because there is no horse racing in Leith this week," Dashkova muttered. "George would never cause his mother this much heartbreak, I am sure of it."

George had never been simultaneously so flattered to be compared favourably to a prince and so glad he was not part of this royal family.

"These honeycakes are excellent, Your Highness," was what he said in response. "This green tea reminds me of the Hyson blend I drank at Dr Black's house last week."

"Ah, you noticed!" Dashkova exclaimed. "I told Joseph to order that tea. It's very good, is it not?"

* * *

George had traversed most of Edinburgh today, and it proved a long drag up the Canongate back towards his lodgings. A light shower was dampening his face, with the promise of heavier rain to come if he dawdled.

The most convenient route home had him turn down the wynd nearest to Cullen's house to cross the Cowgate.

Everyone else kept their heads down and pushed on through their business before they were soaked.

All except for one man, sheltered in Chalmer's Close, on the opposite side of the street from South Gray's Close. His dark green coat caught George's eye, and one glance at his dark hair under the low-brimmed bicorne was enough for him to recognise the man. He stood with his arms folded; George couldn't tell if his wrist was still bound under his long coat sleeves.

George forced himself to keep moving, but he knew he'd been recognised. The Brunonian gave him a deep, ironic bow; rivulets of rainwater spilled onto the cobblestones at his feet.

George sped up his pace as the man returned to watching Cullen's close.

20

Black respected the swiftness with which faculty gossip spread, but the business with Brown and the medical theory chair served as a painful reminder that students, with the vigour of youth, were capable of spreading it just as fast.

It was over a year since the death of Dr John Gregory vacated the chair of medical theory, and like many learned men in the city, Black assumed Brown never put his name forward, despite bragging that the appointment was his for the taking. Perhaps his humiliation at the hands of the medical faculty had cooled his ardour. Dr Gregory's son James assumed the chair after the usual burst of behind-the-scenes manoeuvring: conversations in hallways, bargains struck over lavish Old Town dinners where the scent of claret hung over the table.

Until one night one of Black's students stopped by to greet him at the Theatre Royal. Louis Grey was the son of chief justice Sir Grey, and sauntered through his medical studies with the relaxed air of one who didn't need any kind of distinction to do well in life. This gave Louis a genial, easy nature that made his conversations very pleasant. He was capable enough that Black forgave his indifferent attitude towards studying.

"Well, Dr Black, you wouldn't even be the last esteemed professor I see tonight, because I promised to call on Dr Cullen once the performance ended." Louis raised his voice to be heard over the orchestral interlude.

"You should find him in good humour," Black said. "As you are no doubt aware, he's entertaining John Brown this evening." This was one of the days Brown tutored Cullen's children, and afterwards he hung around well into the night.

"No doubt!" agreed Louis. "It's wonderful to hear they're still on good terms, what with the faculty chair dealings and all."

Black frowned. "I don't understand you, Louis, I'm afraid." The hiring of Gregory Junior was business he'd not had cause to dwell upon in months.

"What Dr Cullen said regarding Brown's candidacy?" Louis' tone indicated he was belatedly realising he'd made a passing remark on something that was not common knowledge. "You know, Dr Black, I shouldn't have mentioned it. Pray forgive me. *Illiterate* it from your memory," he added, quoting a line delivered from the stage earlier that evening. "This was something my father told me, and I didn't appreciate it was in confidence."

"Oh no, several faculty members alluded to the incident," Black lied, "but I confess at the time I didn't enquire as to the...*perpendiculars*"—another rejoinder from the play—"and so remain ignorant." If some sort of incident with Cullen was being spoken of by men at the top, Black needed to know what it was.

Louis looked relieved. "Oh good, I was worried I'd betrayed my father's confidence again. He gets rather vexed when that happens. It was just that the Town Council asked Dr Cullen what he thought of John Brown when he put his name forward for the medical theory chair. According to my father, Dr Cullen first"—Louis affected an impersonation of Cullen in a pose of exaggerated contemplation—"then laughed and said, 'Why sure, this can never be our Jock!' When my father heard about it, he thought it hilarious."

"I see," said Black. The Town Council had little sense of academic affairs: they wanted to know what standing Brown enjoyed among the physicians of the city. Cullen, unofficial chieftain of the physician cabal, had made it clear he didn't consider Brown one of them.

"Well, I should leave you to enjoy the performance," Louis concluded, glancing around. "I'm delighted I ran into you. I'm relieved to learn that the business between Brown and Cullen isn't a secret—I feel a bit silly now for keeping it hidden. Good evening to you, sir."

Oh dear, Black thought, massaging his temples. Off Louis heads, straight for Cullen's.

21

"There was a man in Chalmer's Close as I returned home yesterday. He was one of Brown's ruffians and I know he spied me." George paused to wet his lips. "They were surely on the lookout for you, Dr Cullen."

"Most likely indeed," agreed Cullen with a cheerfulness George was dismayed to hear. "Keen eye you've got, lad."

"Did you see anyone as you came today?" Black asked.

The professors weren't reacting the way George wanted them to. "No, sir, but..." He trailed off, not sure how far he wanted to belabour the point.

"Don't worry on our behalf, Mr Stephens," Cullen said. "They won't learn much from our movements."

George wanted to protest that these were the same men who'd confronted them with knives and fists, but the professors were sweeping the conversation along past him.

"Tell us, Your Highness, anything useful from your afternoon with the Argyles and Sir Grey?"

Dashkova dispelled a long shrug.

"I'm less sure of their involvement with dark chymists. It

was clear from their conversation they knew little of natural philosophy."

"Sir Grey could certainly feign ignorance," Black noted, his brows creasing.

"Yes, but had you heard the lengths he expounded on personal ignorance he mistook for genius, you would not believe that," Dashkova replied after a sip of her tea.

Black gave Cullen a sharp look as if to say, We have to trust her on this.

After a moment, Cullen broke eye contact. "Well, you intended to ask them of Brown, so anything illuminated?"

"We spoke a little," said Dashkova. "Under the pretext of perhaps consulting Dr Brown for a health complaint. They both know of him through the Masonic brotherhood. If anything, Brown is annoying Sir Grey with his proposal for a new chapter that conducts its business entirely in Latin. Brown thinks a new chapter will help preserve the classical tongue; Sir Grey thinks it's little more than a vanity project."

Cullen scoffed. "The only use for gossip that flimsy is occupying old wives, Your Highness. It tells us the lords have little fellowship with Brown and his patrons, that is about all."

Dashkova released another shrug and resumed sipping her tea.

George looked at Black to see his opinion. Black was already rising from his repose by the fire.

"Thank you, Your Highness, for your delicate work." He picked up his cane and hat. "I should have done this sooner, though I understand he was occupied yesterday, and call upon Dr Duncan to explain what I deduced about Bennie's injuries. Andrew was more generous than he needed to be in all this."

"Yes, to his credit he was," Cullen agreed. Then he stopped. "Today's Tuesday, is it not?"

George imagined he could hear Cullen's heart sink through his pelvis all the way down to the floor. Although the sun was shining outside, a coolness and lengthening of shadows warned that afternoon was merging into early evening.

"I won't be doing this, Joe. I'm not dealing with more of that Beggar's Benison nonsense. He will be preparing for the evening's meeting and be in one of his *humorous* moods. In heaven's name, Joe, why couldn't you have called upon him yesterday?"

"He's with the Horticultural Society on Monday nights," Black said.

"Well, Joe, you're welcome to call upon Andy now. In fact, knowing what time the Beggar's starts, I won't detain you a minute longer." Cullen made a show of sitting down and scrutinising a piece of correspondence.

"My friend is venerable in years," Black sighed, "and my great affection for him precludes me from forcing the issue." George couldn't help noticing Dashkova appeared lost in her cup of tea, like she couldn't hear what Black was saying. "Unfortunately for you, Mr Stephens, you will not be let off so lightly. You're coming with me. It pains me to say it, but I think there may be a thing or two you can learn from Dr Duncan."

* * *

There was no guard outside Duncan's house when they arrived, and a servant ushered them through a grand entrance hall to the dining room. Duncan had decorated the place in the Oriental style, with delicate porcelain on the mantelpiece and folding screens concealing cupboard doors. In the middle of the room was a large table, piled with silverware and small stacks of paper. Black went to inspect a painting of a hummingbird on the far wall, leaving George stranded amidst preparations for the evening's Beggar's Benison.

George leant over the silver platter, doing his best to ensure no part of his clothing touched the plate or table. He was right: the silverware engraving *was* that of a jocular penis.

"Initiates place their members in the 'Test Platter' for public inspection during the initiation rites," Black remarked from the other end of the room. "On other occasions they gather round and masturbate into the platter, with emphasis on who can ejaculate first, or produce the largest quantities of semen."

George shrank back, then looked over in alarm.

"Professor Black? Sir, how do you know of these secret Beggar's rituals?"

Black frowned.

"Secret rituals? No, these take place at the ordinary Wednesday evening meetings: they record it in the society minutes. I don't know how they occupy themselves at the secret meetings." He chuckled. "But if you are curious, it won't be shame preventing Dr Duncan from divulging the information."

George shook his head.

A small book, pages greasy from use, was propped open on the lectern at the head of the table. George wondered if Duncan had forgotten it was there. He peered at the open page.

> He thrust the table imperceptibly from between us, and
> bringing his chair to face me, he soon began, after preparing
> me by all the endearments of assurances and protestations,
> to lay hold of my hands, to kiss me, and once more make
> free with my bosom...

Oh, George realised. Oh. He tried to ease away from the lectern so as not to draw attention to the fact he'd been reading it at all.

"Ah, I see you've found the sacred word of Our Lady *Fanny Hill*." Duncan chortled behind him. George felt the familiar blaze of embarrassment seep in, but without Cullen's mortification it was easier for him to focus on Black's unblemished expression and try to replicate his calm. "The Beggars receive a portion of her holy wisdom every meeting. I tried to get Dr Black here to come and provide musical accompaniment to the readings on his flute, but he demurred."

Their host was dressed in another silk banyan and turban, though this time he appeared clothed underneath.

Duncan opened a lacquered cabinet to his right and pulled out a letter.

"While you're here, Joseph, I wanted you to take a look at the message I received from the Town Council last week and the response I drafted. They had questions about my city asylum plans. I think I know what they're getting at and responded accordingly, but, well, you always have a better sense of these matters than me."

Black nodded and slipped the papers into his pocket.

"Thank you, Andrew. I'll review this and send you a note."

Black paused.

"Forgive me, Andrew. I never explained our business with you last Tuesday night, nor properly in our subsequent exchange of notes. Bennie was involved with John Brown, and there were some signs on his body of improper phlogiston-wielding."

Duncan gave Black a sharp look.

"That was *Bruno's* doing? You are sure about that, Joseph?"

"...It fits a pattern," Black replied with care.

"What do you mean?"

"Several students of Brown's have fallen ill this year. All of them with symptoms that could be mistaken for seasonal fever. I suspect Bennie was not the only one with unusual markings on his torso."

Duncan furrowed his brow. He didn't challenge Black's accusation.

"It seems the number of Brunonians arguing with me in lectures or examinations has only increased this year," Black continued.

"Oh, Joseph, you aren't exposed to the half of it! Try lecturing on medical principles, then you'll hear all their wild opinions. They want to argue every point I make; I'm like a whore continually stopping to readjust her merkin. It's maddening."

Black made sympathetic noises. As with the last time, George was paralysed in front of Duncan, but now it was with fascination. Every word of Black's was like the silent footfall of a hunter, tracking its prey into a clearing.

"You must have thought about what to do about the Brunonians, Andrew. After I realised how many students of his were getting injured, and worse, I wondered if the school should take some kind of action to stem the promulgation of Brown's teachings. The Medical Society business convinces me something should be done."

Duncan shrugged. "Aside from failing students who resort to Brunonian doctrine in their medical examinations, I'm not sure what the school can do. He's at liberty to teach privately, as are the students to debate theories."

"You think a ban on Brunonian doctrine in medical examinations would work?" Black asked, leaning forward and frowning slightly. "Up until now, examiners have at least tolerated Brunonian arguments if they're well thought out. I wasn't sure the medical faculty would unite behind such a ban."

Heavens, he's good, George thought.

Duncan laughed. "You'd know better than I on matters

of the medical faculty, Joseph"—George had almost forgotten Duncan was a private lecturer like Brown—"but if they agreed Brown was a big enough threat, I think they'd act."

"It certainly took me a long time to realise how many students were falling victim to him," Black admitted. "He hides his sick and dying flock well. I'm not sure what Monro Junior, Gregory, Young and the others know about the extent of Brown's influence."

"Sandy hates the man, though he hopes he'll go away of his own accord. You're saying there's several students ill thanks to Bruno—"

"More than one died, Andrew."

"By Jove's cock, Sandy would raise a fit if he knew about all of that! As would the others, I wager."

"It would be interesting to determine what Monro Junior and the others already know about Brown's students, if anything. If they've pieced together the illnesses and deaths. Then we might have a better sense of how well supported a ban would be." Black continued to affect a nonchalant tone, tinged with concern.

"Well, tomorrow I'm on the register at the Infirmary. I usually see Sandy then, so if he's there, I'll ask. See if he thinks the ban would be a good idea."

Black smiled. "That sounds like an excellent idea, Andrew. I can confer with Gregory." He looked around, as if startled from a reverie. "Gosh, I've taken up far more of your time than I planned, please excuse me. You'll have preparations to attend to."

"Don't apologise!" Duncan protested. "I'll manage in time. Oh, talking about Sandy Monro reminds me—he was asking after you, Mr Stephens."

"Really?" George asked, his voice faltering.

"Indeed! Was asking just the other week. Told him not to

worry, that he was a young man who knew his pintle from his baubles." Duncan winked at George.

Well, George thought, that might—just might—explain why Monro hadn't banned him from his anatomy class, or demanded he pay course fees.

"I'm grateful you vouched for me, Professor Duncan," he replied, with total sincerity.

"Think nothing of it, young sir." Duncan ushered his visitors towards the door. "You know you're always welcome as an honoured Beggar, Joseph. The stories I hear about your wrist action in chemistry lectures is astounding: you shouldn't be so modest about your talents."

Black let out a laugh of what seemed to be genuine amusement. "You don't need to flatter me like that, Andrew! You know I'll get that letter of yours back to you as my first order of business." He patted his coat pocket.

"What is the business with the letter?" George asked once they were back in the street.

"One of Duncan's close friends, Robert Fergusson, suffered from lunacy and died in the workhouse because there was nowhere else he could go. This was almost ten years ago, but Duncan still feels a lot of guilt over it. He wanted to create a public asylum in Edinburgh so other unfortunates would avoid the same lonely fate. He's been trying to generate support among the political class of the city for quite some time now. Progress in these sorts of things is always slow."

The two reached the end of the square. George found himself looking into the closes and shadows, even though it was a bright afternoon. Of course, no one was lurking.

"Sir?" George didn't know what he was even asking. "They're going to ban Brown's theories?"

"Well, it doesn't even matter at this stage what the medical faculty does or does not decide," Black remarked. "There won't be any immediate decision. The important thing is that word reaches Brown that the faculty are considering such a step. Which could happen within days. Duncan may even start talking to the Beggars tonight."

"Brown will be furious," George sighed. Brown already thought the medical establishment was out to crush him; the news would play right into his fear.

"Undoubtably, but it'll be the warning he needs to temper his doctrine. He'll argue and object, then we can negotiate."

"You're sure all this will work, sir?" George didn't know how Black could be so confident of Brown's reaction.

"How else can he react?" Black patted his shoulder.

22

Black's memory of the day Cullen and Brown's friendship ruptured for good was a vivid one.

It was an early spring morning, the kind that lifted Black's spirits as soon as he left the house. The sky was already a cheerful blue, and the steady rumble of pedestrians, carts and carriages outside the college seemed charming as opposed to cacophonous. It was the type of spring morning that lent itself to thoughts of a pleasant summer.

Black sought out Cullen at the conclusion of his practice of physic class. It was a trivial matter: faculty members horse-trading time slots for oral examinations.

As he entered Cullen's classroom, Black was surprised to see his colleague shoo away the pack of medical students crowding around him.

"Not right now, my dear fellows," Cullen was telling them. "Pressing matters to attend to."

Black caught his eye. Cullen was affecting cheerfulness, remembering to laugh when the students made witty remarks, but the way his eyes were downcast and slipped out of focus suggested much on his mind.

Once the last student was coaxed through the door, Black shut it and stepped towards the podium.

"Is everything alright, William? Doctors Gregory and Young gave me their availabilities for the Saturday, and I reckoned you'd like to get your preferences in now. Both wanted done by two o'clock. Dr Hamilton wanted to come after four, but I think he could be persuaded otherwise if it meant avoiding Monro."

Cullen regarded the list in Black's hand. "Thanks, Joe. I have to deal with Brown this afternoon, so I hope my answer isn't urgent."

"Monro Junior said he needed to consult with his secretary anyway, so I imagine it can wait." Black studied Cullen's face. "But what is the business with Brown?"

Cullen did his best to downplay the situation. "Nothing. Just a misunderstanding that needs to be smoothed out."

"Something happened between the two of you? He was at your house earlier this week; I thought relations were improving." Reports of Cullen's comments to the Town Council had now hit Black's ears from several approaches, though he hadn't dared repeat the allegations to the man himself. Brown's feelings on the matter weren't known. All Black knew was it'd been months since Brown joined Cullen's table in the Nicolson Tavern.

"Was it this week? I thought it was the week prior." For a moment Cullen hesitated, bent over his lectern, and Black was struck by how old he looked.

"No, I remember stopping by on Monday or Wednesday night when you were sharing a drink. You said it was fortunate it was me who called, because any other guest would have expected some of the brandy and would be offended to learn you'd just finished the bottle."

"Must have been this week then. But regardless, I need to call on Brown."

Black hadn't wished to intrude further on Cullen's time, and Cullen wasn't in the mood to talk, so he bade leave of his colleague.

* * *

Black was preparing for dinner when he heard a knock at the door. He wasn't expecting callers, and the particulars of his conversation with Cullen from the morning had faded from his mind, so he was surprised when his servant's voice rose and footsteps drew towards his study.

Anna Cullen was shown into the room. Startled, Black scrambled out of his chair and bowed.

"Mrs Cullen, what a pleasure. Forgive me, I was not expecting guests. Can I offer you some tea?"

She shook her head and remained standing in the doorway. "Don't trouble yerself, Joseph. I stopped by because I thought William might be with ye."

Black paused as he rubbed his neck. "Not today, Mrs Cullen. He said he had business with John Brown; I imagine that's where he is."

"Aye, but it's been several hours now," she told Black with a note of impatience. "I would have assumed no matter could consume that much time."

Anna Cullen and Black remained locked in eye contact for a moment. Black took in her stamping feet, crossed arms and a roughness to her lips that looked like excessive biting.

"It might be a good idea for me to check up on him then," Black said gently. "You don't need to trouble yourself." Brown's house was closer to the Cullens' than Black's—in fact, they were only a street away—but he recognised the same tension in Anna Cullen as he'd seen on her husband that morning.

"Right," agreed Anna, trying not to tremble. "You're very kind, Joseph."

* * *

Brown's wife, Euphemia, ran a boarding-house for students just off the High Street. She was in the kitchen when Black arrived. Black gave her a brief nod. He didn't know the Browns well—they were Cullen's friends, not his.

Euphemia balanced her youngest, Will, on her hip. Was she with child again? It had been a while since Black last saw her, and he couldn't remember if Cullen had mentioned it or not.

He assumed a diffident pose. "I was searching for Dr Cullen. I fear I forgot the correct time we agreed to meet. Is he still consulting with your husband?"

Euphemia stirred the contents of the pot a little too vigorously. Mushroom ragout spilled onto the floor. She didn't look at Black.

"Would imagine so. They've no' left his study since Dr Cullen arrived."

Black waited to see if she'd pause her cooking. It didn't seem likely. Euphemia was one of the typical Scotch wives who would turn their sharp tongues as readily on King George himself as on a maid, if the monarch came into their house without due courtesy. She was a lot like Anna Cullen, Black thought. Most men were whittled down to nothing by strong-willed wives like these: Cullen and Brown were honed by theirs.

"If it's alright with you, Euphemia, I'll head upstairs and present myself to the gentlemen."

Euphemia shrugged and jerked the ladle around her pot. The baby on her hip whimpered.

"Hush yerself, Willie. Where's yer sister? Lizzy!"

Reaching the foot of the stairs, Black understood why Euphemia Brown had retreated to the kitchen. He could hear raised voices several floors up. Brown's guttural shouts, Cullen's agitated entreaties.

At the top of the stairs, Black considered knocking, but settled on quietly easing the door open.

Brown's study was extravagantly furnished with green velvet upholstery, gilded lamps and Chippendale mahogany. From his estimates of Brown's lecture earnings, Black knew most of this was acquired on credit. The other two ignored him as he stood in the doorway: Cullen pacing like a tiger, Brown standing and pounding his cane into the Persian rug. A glass tumbler lay shattered near Black's feet; he couldn't tell if it had been knocked accidentally or thrown.

Rage, opium and alcohol had rendered Brown almost incomprehensible.

"Who else could it ha' been? Yer in the Phila-sophical Society—e'rrybody kens the eminent Doctor Cullen has the final say in aw Phila-sophical Society membership petitions, his word is God. Ye say 'the Society' would reject ma petition —ye *are* th' Society!"

"I told you, John, they would have made a mockery of you. The committee has rejected membership applications before; I don't know why you think your acceptance was ever guaranteed—"

"'Cause ye told me tae apply tae aw they things, ye two-faced cur! Ye told me the medical chair wis mine, smilin' as ye did."

"No, I never—"

"Aye, an' ye thought auld Brown wuid never hear wha' ye said behind ma back. I'm here in front of ye now, why don't ye stab me in the front this time forra change?"

"John, be reasonable—"

"Instead of honest dealings, ye and yer cronies at the

medical school launch against me this dark Catiline conspiracy—"

"It can't be that," Cullen snapped. "Because Senator Catiline's conspiracy to ouster Cicero failed."

The metallic scent flooded Black's senses so fast he thought his eardrums would rupture. Diving forward, he collided with Cullen, and the two men slammed into the bookcase just as Brown's blast of energy smashed the window. Black felt it tug his queue.

"William, we're done here," Black yelled in his friend's ear. Cullen pushed him off and stumbled away. Black saw his hands were balls of scarlet flames. "William!"

"Nice ye've got someone guarding yer back," snarled Brown, sparks rotating around his forearms. "Wonder how tha' feels."

A faint crackle in Black's ear caught his attention. Flames were licking the books next to him, where Cullen's hand had been seconds before. Black reached out and hastily tried to pull the flames up into his body. He was almost sure he'd succeeded when noise in his other ear caused him to look back at the other two men.

"Lizzy!" Euphemia's footsteps reached the top of the stairs. "John, have you seen our daughter? I—"

Already halfway across the room, Black managed to get in between Cullen and Brown before the next projectile was launched and before Euphemia's scream reached his ears. Seeing Black in the way of his target caused Brown to jerk his hand and send smouldering books flying off the shelves. Crouched only a few metres away, where she'd dropped into a terrified ball, was Brown's five-year-old daughter.

Black scooped up the child and turned so he was between her and the men. She smelled of starch and violets in the way that only small children can. Almost immediately, Lizzy was yanked from his arms by Euphemia, who stormed out of the room without Black getting a chance to read her expression.

On Brown's face, however, there was nothing but fury. Black hadn't had time to decide if he expected gratitude from the man for shielding his daughter from a blast that could have knocked her out the window, but in those few seconds he'd only served to throw Brown's inadequacies back in his face.

"William!" His colleague's arm was hot to touch, but Black gritted his teeth and steered Cullen onto the landing. The further they got from Brown's study, the less resistance Cullen offered.

As soon as they were out of Niddry Wynd, Black dragged Cullen into the nearest empty doorway.

"What in damnation was that all about?" Black demanded. "You didn't even notice his infant daughter was in the room with you."

"Since when did you ever care for children, Joe?"

"That is entirely irrelevant to the point I'm making, William, and you know it."

"S'blood, that man is a wrong-headed lunatic."

"And you're no better than a right-headed lunatic, if such a thing exists. Why did you let him petition the Philosophical Society for membership in the first place? Such a venture was destined to end badly." Black glanced around, but no one was observing them.

"I'm not his father, Joe. I warned him several times the Society wouldn't look kindly on his petition; he chose to ignore my hints."

Black gritted his teeth. The fact Cullen delivered nothing more than hints was half the problem. Right now he was exhausted, jittering with adrenaline from the confrontation. Black didn't have the strength to press the issue.

"I've wasted hours on this pointless argument with Bruno, Joe—I'm not going to repeat the exercise with you."

Black let out an exasperated sigh. "I don't know what you were thinking, provoking that fight, William."

"Well, that phlogiston blast came from Brown's hands, not mine." Cullen finally shook Black's grip. "Goodnight, Joe."

* * *

In the months that followed, Cullen never once made mention of Brown. Never in the lecture halls, but neither did Brown's name cross his lips late at night in the tavern, or in the privacy of his study at one o'clock in the morning, as far as Black could tell. For Cullen, his former student and Latin assistant ceased to exist.

That was until one lazy July afternoon when the college was sleepy in the heat but a kind of sadness hung in the air: because days this perfect reminded everyone summer couldn't last forever and winter would be here soon. Black was sheltering in the cool dampness of his chemistry cellar when soft footsteps approached. It was only then Cullen broke his silence about Brown, after shutting the cellar door with a careful backward glance and leaning so close to Black that not even their shared thoughts could be overheard:

"He killed one of his students, Joe. I'm sure of it…"

23

George rose the next morning with no greater sense of approaching calamity than what he experienced most mornings.

He'd persuaded Mrs Collins to let him have James' old room, which was on the floor above his, up a particularly creaky flight of stairs. There was no difference in size or appearance between them, but his landlady, deciding it was no more than a strange fancy, agreed.

Following the warning left in his old room, George moved the dresser every night to block the door, but despite these precautions his sleep was still troubled, and he entered his room with trepidation every time, checking the corners for intruders.

Today he needed to purchase another roll of parchment, which was why George headed down the street in the opposite direction from the college, at an earlier time than he usually left. And why he spotted the gaggle of Brunonians rounding the corner into his street a few seconds before they saw him.

George nearly froze mid-step. The Brunonians moved swiftly, a tight pack focussed on their destination. George didn't need to regard them long to know a plan was afoot. Yet despite his paranoia, for a moment he wasn't sure if these grim men were coming for him.

Fortunately, George had his answer as soon as the first man in the pack spotted him and paused. They immediately broke into a jog. It was about the same number of men—attackers—George had faced on that night in Adam Square, but this time there was an alacrity to their approach that warned him they weren't going to flee so readily. Besides, now George was alone. He turned and sprinted down the nearest wynd.

The men didn't bother to shout at George to slow down. There was no pretence as to their intentions towards him.

The wynd was barely wide enough for a man to squeeze down, and George's feet skidded over the clumps of refuse and human waste. Night temperatures hadn't yet dropped low enough to promote ice formation, he assured himself. The clamour of his pursuers echoed behind him.

George thought the easiest route of escape would be to turn left towards the Grassmarket, cut up West Bow and run onto the High Street, where he could count upon crowds to submerge himself in, but he realised that route would take him dangerously close to the Brunonian headquarters, so instead, once his feet squelched into the mud of the Cowgate, he turned right towards the Pleasance.

The Cowgate occupied the lowest cleft in Edinburgh, ramshackle tenements rising up on either side. Daylight was hours away from reaching these cold depths. The air smelled rotten.

The tendons of his left knee twitched alarmingly. Looking behind him would slow George down, so he dared not.

Aware of the long shadows concealing closes and wynds, George tried to keep away from the walls. Given the Cowgate was the main thoroughfare into Edinburgh, this proved tricky.

Despite the reek of the open drains, George thought he could smell the pursuers a few steps behind.

Thinking swiftly, he swerved into the middle of the street in front of a horse-drawn cart. The driver hurled curses as he jerked on the horse's reins.

The cart immediately behind it, piled high with garnet-coloured cow carcasses, was also forced to slow. George recognised the mule pulling this one was young and flighty, so he veered as close to the animal as he could, smacking its rump as he passed. George almost slipped, but got past the cart before the yelling mule started to spin it.

An onslaught of thuds and vile language from behind told George some of the Brunonians were tripping over the carcasses or colliding with the carts. He couldn't assume he'd delayed them all, though.

Now George couldn't hear much above his own ragged breathing, and he could no longer tell whether the Brunonians were gaining or losing ground. George had slipped out of military condition as soon as he slipped out of the military: he could feel the strain running was putting on his body, and soon he'd have no energy left to fight. Any cramps in his sides would paralyse him.

A warming of the air told George he was approaching the High School Yards and the city walls. Maybe the men would abandon pursuit, but beyond the Flodden Wall the slimy Cowgate turned into arable meadows, where he would be entirely exposed. If any of the Brunonians carried pistols, that would be when they paused to take aim and fire.

As his legs stumbled forward, George fumbled in his coat pocket. His hand closed around the dagger he'd taken to carrying wherever he went. If he was lucky, he'd manage to escape this encounter alive, with only a serious injury—which was only to be expected when an exhausted man faced five or more armed opponents. George started assessing the closes ahead. He had only seconds to decide whether they could offer the momentary concealment necessary to await his pursuers, granting him the thinnest margin of surprise required for survival.

His absorption in this exercise meant he didn't realise the street was blocked by someone until he was almost upon them.

"Oh, good morning to ye, George," Thomas remarked in mild surprise. He was walking idly, perhaps in no deeper reverie than wondering what he might enjoy for dinner. Then Thomas noticed what must have been a wild expression on George's face as he was forced to slow to avoid tripping over the Irishman's feet. A few frantic twitches of his head were enough hint for Thomas to look over George's shoulder and take in the men sprinting towards them.

"Ah!" Seeming to grasp the situation, Thomas bundled George back into the close he'd just emerged from, and through a door only a few steps beyond that.

The noise of footfalls rose in the street as Thomas carefully slid the lock into place behind him and braced his palms against the door. This must be the Irishman's lodgings, George realised. It had the musty odour he'd come to expect from Edinburgh lodging-houses, at least.

After a few minutes frozen in place in the entranceway, Thomas appeared satisfied the receding noises outside meant danger had passed. He crossed his arms and leant his forehead against the door.

"Ye got gambling debts, George?" Thomas asked with a bemused tone that wasn't entirely condemnation.

"What? Heavens no!" protested George. He couldn't decide why that was the first conclusion Thomas jumped to. He took a breath, aware he was shaking. "Those were Brunonians after me."

He wasn't sure what reaction that would provoke in his

fellow student. He knew Thomas engaged with the handful of Brunonians in forced proximity to him, but it wasn't clear how deep his sympathies towards their doctrines ran.

Thomas shook his head and laughed to himself. "That seems even less probable, young Stephens. But who am I to judge?"

It finally came to George's mind that he should thank Thomas for extracting him from that dangerous situation.

"Not a bother," Thomas said with a wave of his hand. "But I'm about to be late for chemistry." Alarm rose in George again at the thought of venturing back into the street, but Thomas settled him with another wave. "If you don't wish to accompany me to the college, my wife might be persuaded to serve you tea while you wait for the coast to clear."

George's main preoccupation was not fear for his life— since at this instant his security felt assured—so much as the sense he must warn Cullen and Black. He wasn't far from Cullen's house, but the old professor's classes began soon. Would it be more prudent to go to the college or call on Mrs Cullen and arrange to send a message?

As George's fighting instincts abated, he took in how calm Thomas seemed, lounging against his door in a state of what appeared to be relaxation.

"The Brunonians might have seen enough of you back there in the street to recognise you," he warned. "I don't know what their intentions were towards me, but they are in the habit of carrying weapons."

Thomas looked amused, and gave his head a little shake. "I'm sure there won't be an issue. I hope your day improves, George. Send word when you can." With that, his fingers found the key and guided him out into the close.

24

Black used the deep silence between his morning classes to prepare solutions for the next round of demonstrations. While he thrived on his students' awe and excitement as he taught, this precious stillness allowed his nerves time to spike and abate, as they did in the minutes leading up to every class.

Unlike the old anatomy theatre, the new classroom was above ground: a spacious octagonal room built into the yards only a few years ago. Polished wooden seating rose towards the ceiling around his table in the centre, looking like an onion from above. Light from the broad windows gave the theatre a warm golden glow. Even though this was one of the most spacious new rooms at the college, if his class sizes continued to expand at their current rate, in a few years students would be forced to sit on the floor again.

On the table next to his bottles and flasks were several modest lumps of raw metals: silver, zinc, lead. Today, Black would explain the differing properties of these metals. Some were for display, others would be dissolved in beakers of acid and precipitated back out. Black found the lawyers in particular were captivated by shiny metals laid on the table, especially gold.

Black could understand Monro's wariness in loaning him the use of this space, given how hard the anatomy professor fought the Town Council to gain building permission. That said, Monro would struggle to find any trace of Black's morning chemistry lectures by the afternoon: it was a point of pride that he rarely spilled a drop of liquid or left behind a mote of powder on the table.

Then he felt it. A build-up of phlogiston left an unnatural lingering aftertaste in the air, like sugar mixed with blood, and pricked the skin on his arms and chest. In what he knew would be the last moment of stillness, Black grabbed two larger chunks of metal and stuffed them into his sleeves.

"I would have presumed today's chemical lecture too facile for you, Dr Brown." Black pushed a knowing chuckle out of his throat, despite the noise of blood pounding in the back of his head. He forced himself to not immediately look up, acting as though the intrusion was no cause for alarm. The taste of phlogiston had appeared out of nowhere, as if he'd discharged it himself. Even the pressure of it surrounding him felt aggressive.

"Aye, we warned the gathering students today's lecture was unlikely to take place." Black could hear the thud of Brown's cane making its way through the ground-floor door towards his table.

There was a second door into the anatomy theatre behind Black, leading students into the top row of tiered seating. He could hear light footfalls spilling into the rows behind him, crossing the space faster than his students would.

Keeping his eye partially downcast, Black tried to pinpoint how many Brunonians—who else could they be?—were now in the theatre. He heard a few thuds as men leapt down the tiered seating towards him, before all the footfalls blurred together. Now he could see the Brunonians prowling around the lowest row of benches. At least ten of them, maybe more, were spread out around the theatre, only a few metres from Black. He couldn't tell how many were behind him, but the skin on his back burned with anxiety.

Throughout this, Brown stood in front of him, leaning on his cane and watching the chemistry professor without blinking. When he raised his face properly, Black thought Brown would be smirking at him. Instead, the interlocutor's face was dark crimson.

Black tried to mirror Brown's stillness, but he knew his nerves were showing. His was the superior phlogistonic talent —Brown knew that as well as him—but he was outnumbered. Brown's followers were rudimentary and crude in their skill, but he couldn't keep his eye on all of them.

Somewhere behind him on the left, Black heard a soft click.

And at least one of them had a pistol. This wasn't good at all.

Black kept his voice low, as if it was only Brown in the room with him. "Tell me the meaning of this, John."

"Ye got my attention alright." Brown leant heavily on his cane, twisting it into the floor. "Taking medical degrees away from my hard-working students? Must have made ye aw laugh when ye came up with that."

"Well, that's easy enough to rectify if you only—"

"I'm no' rectifying shit, Joe! I know I'm right. Why should my students pay lip service to the outdated theories taught here?"

After meeting with Andrew Duncan the other day, Black had played several scenarios in his mind concerning how Brown would react and what he'd do next. Some of those scenarios were imagined for his own petty gratification: Brown bellowing with impotent rage in his study; slinking to the professors in a sulk. It was only as he adjusted to the room filled with Brunonians and took in their founder's words that he realised this wasn't an eventuality he'd prepared for at all.

Brown had come for a show of strength. "Why are all your students dying, John?" Black asked, raising his voice. "Why are Pierre and James dead? It was only thanks to my intervention that Bennie didn't share their fate." He hoped this was news to the other men.

"I warn my students this is dangerous business." Brown shrugged. Black tried to keep an eye on the Brunonians within his line of vision, but they didn't appear to react. "Ye dinnae hear about the hundreds who follow my advice, do ye? I'm not responsible for what Pierre and James did in their own time." He paused, his tone less defensive than Black had hoped. "Bennie wis never gonnae die, and yer meddling slowed his recovery."

There was no way to force realisation onto this man, Black realised. Even if all his students dropped dead in front of him, he'd blame them for failing to follow his instructions. The men in this room must know about the deaths of their comrades, and not care.

He tried to get the confrontation back onto the course he'd envisioned. "So you want your students to receive medical degrees? That's why you're here?"

"This whole university is corrupt, Joe!" Black tried not to flinch when Brown called him that. "I wis stupid to think I could sit on ma arse from the outside peering in and hope to prove Cullen wrong." Now the true extent of Brown's rage bled into his voice. "Not only do you have to stop this absurd talk of censoring my students, ye need to give me back the chair ye stole from me."

This was new information.

"Dr Gregory's chair?" Black thought most of Brown's gripes had made it back to his ears. While he knew Brown considered his failed bid for the medical theory chair to be a bitter blow and proof of his discriminatory treatment, he'd never expressed the public sentiment that he still wanted it. "Be reasonable, John, you know he's not going to resign his father's chair for your benefit."

"He isnae, ye say?" Brown took a half-step towards Black. "Well, perhaps I'll have to create a vacancy. Unless ye want to do some of yer famous diplomatic work."

This must be what this act of intimidation intended to achieve. The threat of withheld medical degrees was enough to wound Brown's pride and spur him into action, but Black guessed he wasn't so blinded by rage he would threaten a faculty member over just that.

"Those threats are ridiculous. And I'm not your stooge." Black smoothed his academic gown, wincing as the uneven lump of silver dug into the soft tissue of his wrist. He wondered if he shouldn't have admitted Brown was threatening him, if acknowledging the danger weakened his ability to diffuse the situation.

A minute smirk appeared on Brown's face. "Aye? Yer Cullen's stooge, so I know ye cannae pretend it's no' in yer nature."

Every one of Black's anticipated negotiations with the Brunonians started with him being the one in the position of power. Being mocked by Brown to an audience of his thugs was not part of it.

"Who's lending you the money for this, John?" Black asked calmly.

A gunshot rang out.

Black tried to duck and run at the same time, but the loose circle of men surrounding him reared forward and he froze. There was no sensation of a flying bullet or impact, so it dawned on Black the pistol was only discharged in warning. Could they see him shaking?

"Well, that's an impudent question, Joe!" Brown laughed. He heard the clunk of the pistol being reloaded, and knew the next shot wouldn't be wasted so. "But let's just say the name will be a familiar one."

Of course it will, Black thought. Dr Young had come back from a call with his patron bearing the name of the sole individual urging the other Town Council members to hold back on approving his chemical laboratory proposal.

Black hadn't wanted to believe Dr Young's information—hoping there was another reason his laboratory proposal was being blocked. This no longer appeared to be the case.

He wondered if Cullen or anybody else had noticed the disturbance in the anatomy theatre. Would one of the chemistry students think to summon help? How many more men did Brown have waiting outside? He could try calling for help via proculopathy, but without a direction to target Cullen, it was unlikely he'd reach him. Brown would also notice what he was doing.

"I won't have you threaten me, or the other faculty," Black said. "Please leave. We can discuss this like civil men later." He knew he couldn't capitulate in front of Brown and his men. Not when Brown was so keen to point out how weak he perceived him to be.

"Ye won't weasel out from under me without making a few promises first, Joe." Taking his eyes off Black for a minute, Brown looked around the room at his supporters. A few of them shuffled in their stances. "I fear ye dinnae understand how serious I am, and I may need to demonstrate. I know yer a professor who loves big, clever demonstrations. No' me, mind: I prefer discreet yet compelling ones."

Brown was not a patient man. In sidestepping his first demands, Black was minutes away from witnessing the escalation of his threats.

"This business is foolish, John, especially since your grief lies with Dr Cullen. Can we not resolve the dispute like gentle-men?" Black wished his brain was working faster, that an obvious solution was available. He could just storm out, but Brown was partially blocking his way.

"Old Spasm himself!" The contempt in Brown's voice told Black bringing Cullen into this was a mistake. "It disnae matter how much ye love him, how many times ye stop over for a wee drink of brandy late at night like ye were his kin. It disnae matter how many of yer children ye name in his honour. Disagree with Cullen and he...will...discard ye." Brown stamped his cane as his voice rose. The Brunonians scowled. "It'll happen to ye just as sure as it happened to me. Oppose the infallible Cullenite doctrine and he will destroy ye."

"In most instances I don't disagree with Cullen," Black replied quietly. His mouth was dry, but he couldn't wet his lips in front of them.

"Ha! Dr Black disnae have the guts or head to think for himself in matters of science and physic—everyone knows he hasn't had an original idea in decades."

"We don't have to do this, John!" Something in Black's composure slipped, and for a moment anger overtook him.

Then that flash of anger blossomed until it connected with another angry thought inside his head: how dare they.

Brown had marched his cronies into the college knowing no one would stop him. Disrupted Black's chemistry lecture without fear of consequence. They knew Black would put up minimal resistance and do everything to maintain the peace. Because that's what he always did. He was the diplo-mat, the one who talked others down and strove for common ground.

The young men surrounding him weren't medical students. Maybe a Latin or Greek scholar in the mix, but these foot soldiers were culled from Brown's Masonic lodge or his boxing circles. Black thought he recognised several from the ambush in Adam Square.

Even the most ardent Brunonian heretics among the medical students would have baulked at attacking one of their most respected professors.

This time.

Brown made it look easy to force capitulation. He insulted Black in front of everyone. If Brown walked away from this with a ringing victory, next time he asked, no medical student would hesitate to join a similar mission.

The anger rose, submerging all fear.

There could be more than fifteen men spread around the lecture theatre, some at the back, others within arm's grasp. Black looked past Brown to the men either side. Some stood with folded arms—two heavyset men near Brown were surely boxers—and the wiry ones were touching the insides of their coats. He couldn't see any swords, but in close quarters these street thugs would prefer daggers and flintlocks.

If Black thought he had a chance of overpowering Brown's associates, he would have done so the minute they'd entered his classroom. The odds were terrible.

The biggest brute, his nose and brows crooked from countless bouts of fighting, uncrossed his arms.

Black took a steadying breath and let his fingertips trail along the edge of the table. He focussed on the sensation of the whorls and knots against his skin.

He hadn't meant for his body language to change, but Brown must have sensed a shift. Maybe that Black was too angry to continue begging, that his current level of menace had stopped working.

Black's fingers finally brushed against his physician's cane, which he'd propped against the table leg a lifetime ago.

His eyes were burning and he couldn't hide them. Refocussing on Brown, Black saw his opponent nod imperceptibly to someone behind him, just once.

That would be a signal to the Brunonian with the pistol. Black couldn't see him, but Brown had looked about forty-five degrees to his left, raising his head only slightly. The pistol-waver was in the second row of seating, two metres away.

Arm by his side, Black shook his right wrist as discreetly as he could. He felt the lump of silver slip under the cuff and into his wet palm.

They wouldn't put a bullet in his head. Not initially. The pistol would be trained on his arm or shoulder.

The only way he could break out of the anatomy theatre against all these thugs was by doing several things at once.

Black threw the lump of metal into the air. The first blast of phlogiston shot through his outstretched hand as he wheeled around, simultaneously dropping to the ground and sending a second blast behind him with his left hand.

That second blast deflected a shot of phlogiston which would have struck his back. Brown's men were closer behind him than he'd realised. Before anyone else had a chance to respond, Black's first fireball made contact with the silver. The narrow strip of it in Dashkova's sword magnified and focussed the phlogiston she fired. A round lump of metal provided no such directionality.

Black was able to duck under his table as the silver exploded.

His hand closed around his physician's cane before the blast shook him. Liquid dripped over the table edge, but he didn't have time to recall what chemicals he'd left out. As soon as the shockwaves abated and before the others had time to recover, Black swung himself out into the auditorium.

The one nearest to him got a cane strike to the groin. Black wasn't in the mood for fighting fair. He spun the cane in his hands and got in a follow-up hit to the man's *splenius capitis* muscle.

Now there was a rush of noise as the others jumped down from the tiered seating. He jabbed another in the liver, then twisted over his shoulder and grabbed the barrel of the pistol, yanking it aside. He yelped as the gun discharged in a blur of hot metal, pain and smoke.

Amid the flurry, one man remained motionless, with a wide-eyed stare locked on Black. Black clapped his hand on the man's outstretched arm, ignoring the raw pain of his burned palm, just as the pressure of phlogiston rose around him. As the pressure crescendoed, Black pulled the accumulated phlogiston from the man's body, a half-second before he discharged. In the second it took him to anticipate the blast, someone else punched him in the ribs. For a moment Black felt his body leave the floor, but when he was jolted against the table he directed the built-up phlogiston back into the man trying to fire it at him. A partially blocked blow to the face jolted his target in and out of focus, though Black watched him fall, blood seeping from his mouth.

I have to get out of here, Black remembered.

Someone swung in with a punch. Black dodged and struck the attacker's knee with his cane. He rammed it into the man's solar plexus, forcing him into two men behind him.

Either I try to leave by the side entrance up there at the back, which is an impossible ascent, or out the main entrance where Brown was a moment ago, Black thought. He couldn't tell if Brown was still there.

In the brief space around him, Black sent two phlogiston blasts to push the standing men against the seating. Someone tried to grab him from behind, but Black latched on to the hand and slammed it onto the table, which was still covered in broken glass and corrosive chemicals. Momentarily unaccosted, Black focussed on the open space ahead of him. He ran towards it.

He almost ignored another sharp rise in phlogiston in a bid to reach the half-open doorway, but realised anyone had clear aim at him. Black spun around and swept a trail of phlogiston across his body, diffusing the impact of the blast hurtling towards him. He tripped, scrambled to his feet, collided with the seating, kept running.

25

George stared.

Black hunched beside the fire. His lower lip was cut and swollen, and his delicate skin yielded a fearsome red bruise in his right eye socket that would be dreadful to look upon tomorrow.

"Professor," George whispered. "What happened?"

Black acted like he hadn't heard. "I believe ribs number eight and nine are broken on my left side. Torn right medial ligament, and my trapezius is sprained without a doubt." He grimaced into the fireplace. "Other than that, no lasting damage."

"Brown's men got him," Cullen said, bustling past George to hand Black a teacup filled with what George suspected wasn't entirely tea. "A gang of them showed up as Joe was preparing his lecture, looking to inflict misery and suffering. Fortunately, he had the wits to throw up a distraction. Edward suspected something was amiss in there and fetched me. We found him in the yards and brought him here."

After Thomas had left his apartment for the second time that morning, George turned around to see his wife watching him from the top of the stairs. She'd offered him tea and made surprisingly relaxed conversation with him—never once asking him to elucidate on the circumstances that brought him cowering behind their front door. After sufficient time passed, with Thomas' wife checking surreptitiously out the window and shrugging, George decided he should go directly to Cullen's and see what direction Anna could give. Instead, he arrived and found Cullen home, his eyes flashing as he crashed between rooms.

Cullen barely noticed his visitor, and it was up to George to make his way into the parlour, now dreading what he would find. Seeing Black in this condition was not outside the boundaries of his imagination by this point, but it proved no less distressing.

Black slurped the tea without his usual refinement. Finally, he looked up at George.

"Brown's men had me surrounded in my own lecture hall —one of them even brought a pistol to make a point. I distracted them with a small explosion, was able to grab my cane and fight my way to the door." He adjusted himself in the chair and hissed in pain. George started to move forward—not even sure what he could do—but Black held up his hand.

"When I was your age I could run home bearing injuries like this, drink a dram of whisky before bed and awake good as new the next morning. How I envy your youth right now." George didn't know how to respond.

"I'll tell Alice to bring another blanket, shall I?" Cullen said. "More to drink?"

Black nodded.

Cullen headed back out into the hallway. As soon as he'd left, Black sighed.

"Brown did this to me because he knew it would hurt William, causing him more pain than a physical attack against his person ever could. I know John feels the loss of William's friendship, sees it as a wounding betrayal. I became the object of his hatred."

"He intended to kill you?" George asked quietly. Black was silent. He wondered if he'd spoken too softly, but eventually Black replied.

"What Brown wants more than anything is a chair of medicine. He may not have intended to create a vacancy today"—Black grinned bitterly—"but he wanted to undermine his opponents and put Dr Cullen in a position where he couldn't block the appointment. Brown intended his coercion to be discrete, perhaps faking an accident. In that regard, he failed."

"Several Brunonians chased me down the Cowgate just a few hours ago on my way to class, sir. Thomas and his wife helped me get away. I thought the Brunonians ran in the direction of the High Street." George was starting to connect the scary events of his morning with what had happened to Black, and his heart rate was beginning to accelerate out of control. "Sir, I should have gone straight to the college, I'm so sorry, I didn't know...I mean, I didn't think—"

"Stop apologising," Black interrupted, with more sharpness than George thought him capable of. "What happened to me was going to happen, regardless of you."

They fell into silence. George wanted to apologise with all his might, but he feared Black turning more anger on him. Trying to distract himself, he cast his eyes around the room. Then he spotted Black's blood-slicked cane propped against the side of his chair.

"The men who attacked you, sir?" George whispered. "What did you do to them?"

"I did my best," Black said. It took a few seconds' silence before George realised he had delivered a complete sentence.

When George continued to stare at Black, the professor sighed and let his gaze drift back to the fire. "Twenty years ago this city was a dark place, George. Many dangerous men fought against the light Cullen brought. I've done worse than what I've done today in the name of survival."

"Joseph?" Princess Dashkova swept into the room. "*Sacré Dieu*, I came as soon as Dr Cullen sent word." She fumbled with a folded cloth in her hands as she approached the fire. "I know you told me it was oranges or lemons that got rid of the taste of phlogiston in your mouth, but I couldn't remember which. I'm afraid I only had an orange." She thrust the bundle, which George now saw was half a sliced orange wrapped in a napkin, into Black's hand before he could protest.

"That is very kind of you, Ekaterina," Black said softly. "And I did say oranges." George noticed that Black's and Dashkova's fingers seemed to linger against each other, before Dashkova grunted and pulled back. She set herself down in the chair opposite him, and did not make any further indication of concern. Likewise, Black said nothing more, nibbling at the orange.

Turning away from the two by the fire, George rose to stretch his legs. The door to the living room was ajar, and he noticed Cullen in the hallway, finishing a conversation with his servant. The servant nodded and disappeared into another room.

Cullen turned towards the living room holding a cup of tea, temporarily lost in thought. In the seconds before he realised he wasn't invisible, George saw the expression on Cullen's face.

This was Cullen's true emotion right now: what he hid from Black and the rest of them behind his physician's attentiveness and calm.

There was rage in Cullen's eyes. A ferocious, consuming rage.

"It's alright, Joe," Cullen said a few moments later,

tapping the sofa near where Black's arm lay. He set the tea on the table. "When the faculty senate meet tomorrow morning, we can organise a proper response to the Brunonian threat."

For a moment that placated Black, but then he gasped. The force of whatever had entered his mind was enough to propel him to his feet, but he cried in pain and collapsed back.

"The senate, William!" Black said as Cullen tried to comfort him. "That's what he's intending to do."

Cullen continued to ease him back into the sofa, but once Black's agitated words sank in, he froze. George felt scared, because he didn't understand what message was being conveyed between the physicians, but it was sending them both into panic.

"He really would, Joe..." Cullen was muttering to himself.

"He told me as much," Black replied, clutching his side.

Dashkova rose and put her hand over Black's.

"Joseph," she said with surprising softness. "What is Brown intending to do?"

Black gestured for Dashkova and Cullen to stop crowding him. Once Cullen had stalked over to his table and Dashkova reluctantly settled into her chair, he took a few breaths, probably to quell the pain in his ribs.

"We knew Brown wanted a faculty chair—he's never stopped wanting that, I don't think. Coercing me into supporting his bid for the theory of medicine chair was only half his goal this morning: if I didn't acquiesce, he'd settle for incapacitating me in time for the faculty senate meeting. We forced his hand with the medical degree business: he hasn't the time to perfect his human phlogiston vessel, but I imagine the inanimate vessel would serve his purpose, albeit with less poetic symbolism."

"You mean the weapon he bragged about?" Dashkova swayed her head. "But Joseph, no one has seen this weapon."

"It's not designed to be seen," Black groaned. "We're all

thinking about the vessels the dark chymists used, those unwieldy urns. Brown hinted to me that his vessel was smaller. I wager its purpose is to go undetected."

"He could have already concealed the vessel," Cullen said, unstopping a decanter on the table. "When he was in the college this morning." Amber liquid sloshed into his glass.

"What is he intending to do to the faculty?" George asked, unsure if he wanted it spelled out.

"Coerce them into giving him a medical chair," Black replied. "Except half his fighting men are out of action, so I imagine his revised strategy for tomorrow will involve less talking and more pistols."

"If he has a vessel in the senate, he doesn't need to waft the aroma of grapeshot around." Cullen gulped down the contents of his glass with a grimace. "A weaponised phlogiston vessel, even if it's just to intimidate, could cause serious injury to anyone in the room if used recklessly...which is the standard course of action for Bruno."

"But couldn't the faculty band together and stop him?" George knew it was foolish to seek reassurance when the professors had spelled out how deadly the situation could get, but he couldn't help himself.

"You've seen Monro Junior at his full power," scoffed Cullen. "None of the rest are any better. Certainly not when they don't know an attack is upon them."

George also wondered how strongly the rest of the faculty would want to oppose Brown, despite their disdain for his teachings. Why risk their lives if they could give him a faculty position and that would be the end of it?

"Besides," said Black, "under no circumstances are we letting Brown commence this plan. We have to destroy the phlogiston vessel and bring an end to all his schemes before he gets too bold."

"Curse Brown," Cullen exclaimed. "We need to regroup

after Joe has had time to recover. We'll keep in contact and try to figure out what should be done."

"That's a bad idea," Black said.

"Joe?"

Black swivelled slowly until his back was against the fire.

"Brown knows that he has tonight. By the time we're ready, so is he. That's why we need to act now, before he can prepare. Before his injured men can recover."

"Well yes, on a logical level that is the correct reasoning," Cullen fumbled, "but you're barely able to walk, Joe, and I don't see how I can face all the Brunonians by myself."

"We have Her Highness and George, do we not? And I can be of some assistance from a distance, I just can't move very fast." Crouched there next to the fire, Black was the frailest George had seen him, but there was a light in his eyes he hadn't seen before either. "I was stupid to think Brown could be reasoned with or skilfully guided like a fellow academic, and I paid the price for my mistake. We have no choice but to go on the offensive, and if we want that to work, we have to act now. Not just the phlogiston vessel: we need to destroy his grimoire."

"Tomorrow. We'll talk at first light tomorrow morning, once you've had at least some rest, Joe." Cullen went to lay a hand on Black's shoulder, but Black swiped it away.

"We're talking now. I guarantee Brown will be conferring with the Brunonians tonight. He knows where we all live. I wouldn't sleep a minute."

"I'm with you, Joseph," Dashkova said. "Those whoresons must be stopped, and I am ready."

Cullen threw up his hands. Then he paused and look carefully at George.

"There's four of us here, so that means four votes. Tell us what you want to do, Mr Stephens. Then it's either a majority decision or remains unresolved."

George looked around the figures in the room. The bruises on Black's face had already darkened since he first saw them. Making eye contact with Black, the professor's expression was blank, but not in the usual way that concealed emotion. For the first time Black wasn't trying to hide what he felt from George. Dashkova kept her eye on Black. She looked distressed, but there was no apprehension. Cullen was deeply worried, but George sensed it was more out of concern for his friend than because of what Brown could do to him.

"Sir, I agree with Dr Black. Several times in New York and Pennsylvania we drove the Americans back in full retreat, and then squandered our advantage by calling off the pursuit and giving them time to regroup."

Cullen nodded. He moved to squeeze Black's shoulder, and this time Black didn't swipe him away.

"Well, at the very least we give Joe here a few hours to rest. We then have the cover of darkness to our advantage."

26

George departed Cullen's place once to patrol the nearby closes in the intervening hours. No sign of anybody watching them, confirming Black's suspicion that the Brunonians were gathered elsewhere.

Returning to the parlour, George stumbled upon Dashkova talking quietly to Alice in the corridor. Unusually, Dashkova's voice did not carry. Alice was nodding along in agreement; her head couldn't stop bobbing.

"The mango ice proved especially popular last summer," Dashkova was saying. "I will send you a jar of the pickle so you understand."

"Yes, that would be…Yes, yes, thank you," Alice blustered.

Dashkova also left the house while Black recuperated, except she returned dressed in men's clothing. Her pea-green coat, vest and breeches were surprisingly well-fitting, which raised the alarming possibility the clothing was tailored to her. Floral embroidery spilled down her sleeves. As George approached, she was adjusting a scabbard at her waist.

Black stayed on the sofa next to the fire, though he took the opportunity to lie down and close his eyes. George wanted to ask him questions—so many questions—but he forced himself to leave Black alone until the agreed-upon hour.

Cullen entered the room. His eyebrows popped, but there was no further register of shock at Dashkova's dress.

"That coat is very much in the French style, Your Highness," was all he said, and it didn't strike George as a compliment.

"We are going to the senate room first, yes?" Dashkova asked, folding her arms. "To destroy the vessel?"

"Yes." Cullen waved his hand, as if it was foolish for Dashkova to question his strategy. "Even if we fail at everything else tonight, we have to foil the trap."

"You think the vessel will already be charged?" Dashkova asked.

"We have to assume so." Cullen began to pace as his brain sped up. "I was making some calculations and consulting a few books while Joe rested. I think Brown could have packed his vessel with gunpowder. Perhaps it contains the mineral-rich soil traditionally used in phlogiston vessels, but the object's purpose may not be to store large quantities of phlogiston so much as detonate the gunpowder."

Dashkova grunted.

Cullen had hauled George into his study as he came up with this, seemingly as an object for him to voice his ideas at. In doing so George had learned that Black or Cullen could sense a charged vessel: raising the general level of phlogiston in the room would lead to a spike in the trapped phlogiston. Cullen hoped this would help them find a hidden vessel more easily. However, if Brown's new design was more sensitive to phlogiston build-up, they risked igniting the gunpowder.

"We must be careful about wielding phlogiston in there," Cullen repeated to Dashkova, who grunted again at his lecturing tone.

While in the office, George stammered out his desire to

learn the basics of phlogiston-wielding before their mission, but Cullen rebuffed him.

"You've got your sword and proculopathic sensitivity, Mr Stephens," Cullen said, patting his hand. "That's what we need from you most tonight."

George clung to the shadows as he looped around the deserted college yards. It was unlikely the Brunonians had left anyone watching the senate room—they wanted to avoid detection, after all—but he knew if they were alerted now to their presence in the college, they would either launch an attack or change their plan to something less predictable and more lethal.

Apparently, the college was swarmed with Town Guards for several hours after the attack, more out of boredom among the personnel than civic protectiveness towards the esteemed faculty. However, no one could prove Black was in the anatomy theatre during the Brunonian invasion, and since Cullen had attested he was with him in another wing at the time, the Town Guard drifted off long before George and the others crept back. As far as the guards were concerned, Brunonians had assembled in the theatre and accidentally run afoul of the experiment Black left.

This innocent explanation would stand until someone important paid Black a visit tomorrow to enquire as to the nature of his unattended experiments and observed the state of his face. By then, however, that might be the least of their problems.

Another consultation between the three phlogiston-wielders had solidified Cullen's concern about the dangers of even a minor phlogiston build-up within the vessels. That's why only George and Cullen entered the senate room. Black and Dashkova kept watch nearby, forbidden from even communicating via proculopathy.

"Better to be too cautious than to become a martyr, lad," was how Cullen put it to George.

"And we really have no idea what the vessel might look like?" George asked. Again.

Cullen gave a sigh indicating he wished he could gift George that knowledge.

"No, lad. It may look like a dark earthenware jar, or they may have disguised it to look like something else."

George had never seen inside the room where the faculty senate met. His heart sank as he picked the lock and realised it was about the size of the Medical Society meeting place—filled with chairs, cabinets and tables. Everything was bathed in deep shadows; the windows let in what moonlight they could, but it was an overcast night.

If Cullen was daunted, he didn't show it. Instead, he clapped his hands together.

"Right, we'll start at one end and work our way along. Excuse the lack of candles, George—the last thing I want is for someone to spy us in here."

At first George was tense, afraid of hair-trigger explosions from everything his fingers brushed. After pushing aside every chair, turning cabinets inside out and tapping wooden boards with his feet, the tension faded. Then it was replaced with greater unease as he realised they'd both combed the room and found nothing suspicious. Not that George had any better idea of what he was looking for, only that the vessel couldn't be too small or the phlogiston stored wouldn't last overnight. Which made its lack of visibility all the more baffling.

Cullen gave only shrugs and grunts before moving to recheck the next item.

George didn't want to ask Cullen how long they had and add any more stress to the situation, but he knew they didn't have all night. If Brown was convening his men, they would disperse after a few hours.

Eventually, he saw Cullen stop searching and stand still for a moment, hand on his chin, breathing deeply.

Cullen spoke gruffly. "I think you best go join Joe and Her Highness in the yards, lad."

George started to ask why, but then he understood.

"Raising phlogiston is incredibly dangerous, sir..." As if Cullen hadn't been the one repeating that point to him over the course of several hours. "You told Dr Black and Princess Dashkova it was too dangerous to attempt."

Cullen gave a weary chuckle. "I said it was too dangerous for *them* to risk doing. I'm willing to shoulder the risk myself."

George wanted to protest that they had more time and should look again, but they'd fumbled around this room twice over and his hands were coated in dust. Brown and his men would have concealed the vessels for daylight conditions—here they were in the middle of the night without any good source of illumination.

"Of course, you don't have to go all the way over to Joe and Her Highness; just clearing the building will keep you out of harm's way. Heh, Joe will be furious if you tell him I'm doing this."

"If you're sure, sir, I'll wait just outside the building door." That way Black and Dashkova wouldn't realise what Cullen was doing. It was impossible to see Cullen's lined face in the meagre moonglow, but he nodded and tapped George on the elbow.

George's hand was on the senate room door when he paused.

Of course Cullen wanted to protect him and the others while attempting a risky procedure to uncover the location of the vessels. He was the teacher, the expert, while George was very much the student. He didn't for one minute doubt Cullen's assessment of the danger.

"Actually, sir..." George faltered, hand still on the door handle. "I think I should stay. I *can* sense a build-up of phlogiston, even if I'm not as skilled as you or Dr Black." He hadn't fully turned around. Cullen didn't respond so he plunged on, pulling the idea out of his head and finding to his surprise it was fully formed. "This way we can stand at opposite ends of the room, and maybe the one of us closest to the vessel will detect something first."

"You know you don't have to do anything you don't want to do," Cullen said, taking a step towards George. "It's not something you're trained in. The most important thing is keeping you safe, George."

George realised there was an unspoken question. He took a deep breath.

"I am able to detect the build-up of phlogiston," George repeated, with more forcefulness. "I've experienced it several times."

"If you're sure." Cullen pointed to a corner of the room. It was the less crowded end, away from where it looked like the bulk of the faculty would congregate. George nodded and moved.

"I'll start at levels too low for you to detect," Cullen said, sounding calm. "It might be better you close your eyes or look away, so you don't get distracted."

George nodded. He calmed his breathing and tried to dispel his fear. He wanted to believe Cullen would go carefully.

After what seemed like an eternity suspended in darkness —he was too far away to hear Cullen's breathing or other noises—George yelped and fluttered his hand.

"You felt something, George?" Cullen asked quickly.

"I—I thought I did." George ran his tongue across both

cheeks. Cullen must've immediately dropped the level of phlogiston, because the sensation faded back to nothing. "The start of something."

"Well, we'll repeat the exercise," Cullen said.

This time George let the metallic taste bubble on his tongue for all of a second before jerking his hand. There was no mistaking the build-up.

"You're sure, George?"

"Yes, sir."

"Right, I didn't feel anything. We should swap positions." Cullen began to move, and pointed to a spot in the middle of the room that brought the two men closer together.

"The vessel is sensitive," Cullen remarked, confirming the question on George's mind. "That was not much phlogiston at all."

George took in Cullen's firm stance, with palms splayed in front of his body, before closing his eyes again.

"Oh, I felt that," Cullen said quickly.

"I didn't feel anything," George replied.

The two of them stared into the gloomy shadows of their corner. There was a cabinet they'd looked through three times each. None of the floorboards or skirting felt loose. George went over to the nearby tables and ran his hands underneath them again, worried he'd confused one table for another.

This time George moved without Cullen pointing, taking up a place almost abreast of the older professor but several steps to the left.

When Cullen raised the phlogiston a third time, both men twitched simultaneously. There was a new tension in Cullen's posture. The metallic taste in George's mouth had appeared as soon as he'd closed his eyes, hanging in the air as he tried to lick his teeth clean. If they both felt the spike from the phlogiston vessel, it meant they were standing in front of it.

George looked around the corner of the room again, willing himself to see what he'd missed a dozen times.

"Sir..." The faint glow of moonlight on marble had caught his attention.

Cullen stood beside George and squinted up. "That's Monro Senior by the door, is it not? Should be Lord Drummond."

Well, that explained it. A bust of Alexander Monro the elder would have come from the Medical Society hall. George dragged over a chair.

"Careful, careful..." Cullen whispered.

The bust didn't feel unusual, but George wasn't sure how he expected it to feel. It was very heavy.

Cullen rubbed his hands.

"Right, let's move this and then check again..."

The search didn't take much longer, because as soon as the first marble bust was removed, Cullen noticed a second in the other corner of the room that he thought should be a former provost but wasn't. Cullen swept the room a final time, but neither he nor George could detect a third vessel. At last, with limited assistance from the seventy-year-old professor, George deposited the phlogiston vessels in the middle of the yards.

Black and Dashkova had crept over by the time the second vessel was set down. There was a tightness around Black's mouth. He was leaning heavily on his cane and touching his ribcage.

Cullen regarded the three of them.

"I say we retreat"—he pointed to the Jossie Steps linking the two courtyards—"and I'll discharge the vessels." Black nodded and limped away. He didn't offer to detonate them.

After the initial tension of searching for the vessels broke, George almost forgot the danger they posed. His arms ached from carrying two marble busts outside, and he tried to rub away the fatigue as he followed Black and Dashkova into the darkest recess of the college grounds.

Cullen didn't follow them all the way to the edge of the yards; once he got a good distance from the vessels, he stopped. When the others had retreated to safety, he turned to the busts, now barely visible in the shadows. George watched the professor raise a single hand, glowing crimson, and point.

A small ball of fire shot into the centre of the yards. For a moment the busts glowed red. George was sure that wouldn't be enough to ignite anything, so he was shocked by an explosion that sent Cullen toppling to the dirt and pushed him into the wall. Debris shot out in all directions. George, Black and Dashkova all ducked, Black hissing in pain.

George sprinted to Cullen, who was struggling back to his feet. Having cast up a wall of phlogiston to shield himself from the explosion, the old professor was shaken but unhurt.

"In God's name..." Cullen breathed, staring at the dark, smouldering remnants. "I didn't think Brown capable of producing an artefact that deadly."

The four of them didn't wait to see if anyone had heard the explosion. Instead, they cut through College Wynd and up the Cowgate to the Brunonian headquarters, stopping to shelter in a close off the Grassmarket. An initial inspection by George told them there were a couple of Brunonians standing guard in their courtyard outside their building.

"They almost certainly outnumber us, and there are several large rooms on the first floor," Cullen mused.

George knew the element of surprise was crucial to defeating a larger force. This was a military concept even these learned philosophers would be familiar with.

Dashkova turned towards the others. "Cover of darkness. We take out their lights."

Cullen grimaced. "That's beyond my power. While theoretically I could pull all the phlogistonic energy from the area, to do so from a distance where we remained concealed, it would require a lot of concentration, and the amount of phlogiston that entered my body would be dangerous."

"I wasn't saying you would do it," Dashkova scoffed.

"Well, Joe is too weak to do that and still be any use to us once we get inside."

George felt the rare flush of pleasure that came from knowing that despite his greenness, he was one step ahead of Cullen on this one.

"No, William. I will do it," said Dashkova.

Cullen spun to face Black.

"She can't do it, Joe."

Pain was clearly eroding Black's usual composure.

"Well, she says she can do it, William," he snapped.

There was an extended silence in which Black and Cullen launched into an argument via proculopathy. Cullen gesticulated; Black stamped his cane.

"I will do it," Dashkova repeated. Cullen made a distracted shushing gesture and refocussed on Black.

George wondered if Cullen would change his mind about his ability to perform the task in response to Dashkova's challenge, but eventually he let out a sigh and waved his hands through the air.

"Fine, Joe. Have it your way. Let her do it."

"I wasn't the one who suggested it to Her Highness," Black retorted, hobbling forward.

The quartet gathered in the shadows at the mouth of the close. Several shadows were patrolling outside the Brunonians' doorway. None of them looked their way.

"We need to act fast." Cullen was now communicating as if

this plan had belonged to him all along. *"Take out the lights and get past the guards into the building before the Brunonians upstairs have time to react. And it goes without saying, before the guards outside realise they're under attack."*

"If Her Highness aims true, the courtyard lights shouldn't be disturbed," Black added. *"Are we ready?"*

George nodded. Dashkova grunted and rolled her neck.

To George's surprise, Black stepped behind Dashkova and took hold of her shoulder.

"It's risky to Her Highness, but the phlogiston can discharge through me."

George took a step back and fingered his sword pommel. Cullen remained wordless. In the faintest illumination of the street light, George could make out some vigorous eye-rolling from the venerable professor. But then he too reached out and clapped Dashkova on the other shoulder.

"We've got you, Your Highness. When you're ready." Cullen sounded begrudging, but he set his cane against the wall and pointed his free hand into the darkest recess of the street. George took a second step back.

Dashkova raised her arms.

27

There was no time to determine Dashkova's success. The princess staggered, Black yelped, and the close was filled with flames and metallic bitterness. George didn't wait. As soon as the phlogiston discharged behind him he was running, skimming the walls and hoping he wasn't on fire. His sword already drawn, he dived towards the clump of Brunonian guards, who were still fumbling for weapons in reaction to the flames and noise.

Of course, George thought as the last sentry detached from the shadows. The meagre light from the lamps and phlogiston flares around him was enough to illuminate his still-bandaged hand.

But his assailant's other hand was rising, and the pistol was locking on his chest.

George swung his leg up in a crescent. The kick was unexpected enough that the pistol fired into the dark crevice of the close. Before the man had time to regain his balance and bring the weapon back to bear, George lunged forward so the tip of his sword came into contact with the man's neck.

"Drop the pistol, sir," George said calmly. He could run

his blade through the man's throat and be done with him forever, but that didn't seem right. Even if Black wasn't whispering instructions in his ear, he had to believe he was better than a hired brute.

His eyes didn't leave the man's face, but he heard the clatter of the pistol landing on the stones. A few tense steps and George angled the man so his back was to the close entrance. Then he stepped back a single pace, so his sword was now a hand's length from his opponent's throat.

The attacker eyed George for a moment, calculating whether he should retreat, or if there was a way he could get round George's sword and regain his fading honour.

"Leave," was all George commanded. His poise and the steadiness of his blade must have convinced the assailant it wasn't worth a second attack. He stepped backwards, keeping eye contact until his good hand touched the wall. Then he bled into the shadows and vanished.

There was a risk the man might return, perhaps amidst a larger armed gang. Though as George surveyed the fight, there was a cast of paleness over the Brunonian guards forced to reckon with the phlogiston-wielders striking from the darkness. There was a gap in their skills compared to the professors', and they were confronting it for the first time.

"No injuries, George?" Cullen appeared just as George noticed the courtyard was emptied. Two Brunonians lay on the ground; from his companions' attitude, George guessed they were unconscious, not dying.

Dashkova was opening the door, Black limping after her.

"If these rogues are still here when we're done, I suppose we can give them medical attention," Cullen said as he hurried through the closing door. "Rather hope they're not, though."

· · ·

Once inside, Dashkova froze, giving George time to take in the narrow stone staircase, a ground-floor door to a separate residence and the discordant noises from upstairs.

Panting, Cullen tried to get in front of her.

"There will likely be a second set of stairs on the other side of the building. Joe and Her Highness should find and block it." He pointed back to the courtyard.

Black grimaced. "No, we mustn't split up." There were new tracts of blood around his mouth, but he didn't seem weaker than he had been in the close.

"But we need to stop them escaping somehow," protested Cullen.

"No," Black repeated. "Let any medical students escape. They pose no danger." He adjusted his cane under him.

Cullen spluttered the beginning of an objection.

"We don't have time to argue!" Dashkova told them, plunging into the stairwell.

George ran after her, knowing a second's hesitation would drag him into an argument. He hoped Black could ascend the stairs without assistance. He didn't dare to look at Cullen's face as he left.

Back on the farm, the most dangerous animals he'd known weren't the bulls or stallions. It was the cows, sheep and goats who were cornered and injured. Nothing good came of cornering animals, not even the meek ones, when you had a choice.

Climbing the endless, lightless staircase, George thought he should be the one leading the charge, not the princess. It didn't feel right, exposing a woman to men who wouldn't hesitate to kill her. He heard Dashkova shriek—in rage, not fear—which told him she had found another opponent. His breath was hot and ragged in his mouth, but he could still taste the spike in phlogiston. Seconds later, a man tumbled down the stairs towards him. George hadn't the space to step aside or jump; he simply threw himself forward and over. The man slid to a halt, unconscious at best, and George clawed himself to his feet and kept moving.

On the second floor the stairwell led out into a corridor with a single door at the end, where Dashkova was already engaged with two men. Her sword moved through the air with little finesse but a lot of speed. The men struggled to land a strike, though with such artless swordsmanship, so would she.

Noticing George, one of the Brunonians, too haggard to be a medical student, stepped away from the combatants and raised a hand.

There wasn't room to dodge. George threw himself to the ground, the air scorching above him. He was an easy target on the floor, so plunged to his feet. There was a warmth against his back, and the smell of burning cloth.

George was mostly upright when the sword swung towards him. He buckled under the impact of the parry—why did his leg muscles feel so empty?—but he didn't fall.

His attacker would use phlogiston again if he could. George had to keep the man's focus on his sword. He lacked space for a diagonal blow, so George swept his blade at waist height, aiming for the attacker's legs. The man parried and drove forward. George twisted, but felt the sting of the blade against his ribs.

Not giving the pain enough time to register, George stepped left. The wall crashed into him—maybe it was just as well; the impact would extinguish his smouldering coat. The man was still falling forward, but in the process of recovering and pulling his sword in to protect his body. In the second before he refocussed, George saw his opening and stabbed into the man's shoulder socket.

"Step right, lad."

George obeyed, and a flash of white light shot through the air. George wasn't sure how Cullen managed it, but this was the second time he'd seen him use the white light to render an assailant unconscious. His wounded opponent fell.

Dashkova headbutted the other man, then stepped aside. Cullen took another few paces forward and a second white flash struck its target.

No other men came into the corridor, and as the pounding of blood in his ears abated, George felt silence washing out from the rooms ahead. His side stung, and his undershirt was already damp with blood, but the injury was no more than an inconvenience. Dashkova stood panting like a dog, the rage that had got her this far still burning. She sported no obvious injuries.

George looked at Cullen and Black behind him, aware more than ever of the sound of their breathing. The doors in front of them were barred. Finding his heart rate under control, George began his approach. Cullen and Black edged along the opposite wall.

George was about to kick open the doors when the other three flinched. Pain crossed Black's face.

"That can't be right," Cullen muttered.

There was a distinct, bitter taste in the air. A single drop of blood was trailing out the corner of Black's mouth.

"What's happening?" George asked, unsure how uneasy he should feel right now.

Cullen's eyes remained fixed on the door. "He's just charged up a phlogiston vessel."

"Get down!" Dashkova yelled.

George dropped to the floor as a blast of energy sent the door off its hinges. He just managed to cover his head. The ringing aftershock consumed his ears.

"We can't stay here," Dashkova hissed. "That door was our shield."

Glancing back, he saw the others were also prone on the floor. Black's dark eyes caught George's.

"Brown's somewhere behind that vessel," Cullen continued, ignoring Dashkova's attempts to shoo him backwards. "It'll take him a few minutes to repower it."

Cullen crawled forward to peer through the door. Dashkova grabbed his arm and tried to stop him. Black watched them without moving. In the scuffle, George managed to slide forward on his belly and glance through the doorway.

He saw a large room, full of beds, tables and chairs in the style of the Infirmary. A few relit oil lamps gave texture to the shadows. The makeshift ward looked abandoned in a hurry, but that could also have been the force of the explosion. At the end of the room stood a dark clay jar the size of a man. The air around it appeared fuzzy, like summer heatwaves.

"There's a large jar at the back of the room," George said. "It's giving off heat."

"Brown's in there?"

"I didn't see him," George admitted. He peered back inside. "There's a room behind this one." The door was little more than a black hole behind the vessel.

"If Brown can see us, he can time the vessel's build-up and discharge," Cullen said, wiping sweat off his face. "The infernal device feeds off phlogiston—our only hope is to destroy it by emptying its contents. Damn it. What do you think, Joe?"

Black was slumped against the wall, either because he was unwilling to lie all the way down again or because he didn't trust himself to be able to get back up from the ground.

"I can't shield myself against that device, let alone anyone else," he sighed.

"Your Highness..." Cullen adjusted himself on his elbows so he was facing Dashkova. "Can you get to the vessel? One of us must stay here with Joe. And young George has the advantage over all of us when it comes to speed and strength."

George wasn't surprised he'd been volunteered. Phlogiston vessels were too complicated to understand, but dodging surprise explosions as he ran was reassuringly straightforward.

The smell of phlogiston still hung in the air. Dashkova pulled herself into a crouch.

"You go behind me," she told him. George was taken aback to hear her communicate via proculopathy, though he knew he shouldn't be. Hopefully his legs had a few more minutes' use in them. He pulled himself to his feet.

George edged up to the damaged doorway and squinted inside. The vessel, the colour of raw umber, stood a metre from the furthest wall. There were in fact two doors at the far end, one to the second stairwell and the other to a side room. The stairwell door hung open uselessly, but the other door was ajar in a way that felt deliberate.

Nothing for it. George took a deep breath and ran inside. The hall was at least thirty metres long and Brown would be recharging the vessel; he'd have to hope he was fast enough.

He was only a few paces inside before several things happened simultaneously. The first was someone wrenching on his coat sleeve, enough to throw him backwards. The second was a pressure snapping in his ear and a flash of blue-white light leaping across the hall towards him. As George struggled to right his balance, the figure grabbing him stepped into his peripheral vision with hand outstretched. A ball of crimson light shot from their palm and collided with the blue-white light. The force of the collision sent George onto his backside, but since the first blast had taken off the hall door, he knew he'd been spared its worse.

"You idiot boy," Dashkova exclaimed in his ear and head. *"I said stay behind me."* She dropped into a crouch, her fist still full of his coat sleeve.

George wanted to protest, assure her it was his duty to protect a lady. The first thought that stayed his mouth was that Brown could overhear him, or strike again as they argued —for Dashkova would surely argue. The second thought was his fair companion was better able to protect him than he her.

Dashkova finally let go of his sleeve, and he indignantly thought she wouldn't be happy if he handled her delicate embroidered coat sleeves in such a rough manner.

The door at the far end remained ajar.

"We have to move," he hissed as quietly as he could. "Else Brown will—"

"*Shhh!*" Dashkova took off, vaulting to her feet and sprinting across the hall. It took George a second to get to his feet, by which point he thought Dashkova had almost reached the vessel—

As fast as she was accelerating away from him, Dashkova came flying back, a bolt of blue light almost touching her outstretched fingers. She smacked into George, sending them both back almost to the entrance.

"Argh!" Dashkova exhaled.

"*A third time I cannot do this—the force is too strong...*" She added something in Italian then trailed off.

Hearing her English deteriorating under stress was the most alarming part. While Brown may not be able to charge and discharge the vessel indefinitely, it appeared he could endure longer than his targets.

They had only a few seconds to catch their breath before the next discharge.

"We split," George panted. "He can't hit us both."

"*But you—Oh, pizdets!*" George was already on his feet and running, this time swerving to the left behind a table, jumping over a row of chairs. He could only hope Dashkova wasn't following.

He hated being exposed and leaving her vulnerable, but he had to trust she could protect herself.

"*Yaaaargh!*" That was all the warning he received. George dived headfirst to the ground, falling into a row of upturned chairs. Heat and force pressed him into the floor, but the noise and sensation of impact came from above and behind him.

The sounds of hangings crashing to the floor and distant cries from residents of the close were interrupted by the more proximal sound of ceramics shattering. Looking up at the same time the pain of his fall began to register in his limbs, George saw Dashkova standing over the upturned vessel. Its black contents were spilled across the floor, flickers of blue flame hovering above them.

Dashkova looked at him for a second to check he was moving, then turned towards the open door. She pressed herself against the far wall and brandished her sword.

"*No time. Joseph and William will deal with vessel.*" She focused on the doorway.

His forearms stung, but George was able to flex his fingers. Same with his knees. He jogged across the room to join Dashkova.

"*We go in now.*"

Not for the first time, George reflected that proculopathy gave Dashkova the advantage, because he wasn't skilled enough to object to her ideas using the same medium. Instead, he eased along the wall in her shadow, until the doorknob was within touching distance.

He wondered if Black and Cullen were even aware they had destroyed the vessel. Could they see into the chamber, or were they sheltering where they'd left them? He didn't have time to voice concern, because Dashkova was already tensing her body.

28

George pushed the door open with one hand, readying his sword with the other. Empty room. A breeze caught his face, and he saw the open window overlooking the rear close.

"He's escaped," George cursed, stepping into what looked like a medium-sized study. Brown wouldn't be far; he could chase him on foot.

"What?" Dashkova pushed past George towards the window.

Behind them the door slammed. George heard the click of a lock.

"Your Highness—"

An invisible force knocked him against the wall. His hand smacked against shelving, causing him to let go of his sword. Dashkova steadied herself faster than he did, glaring at where Brown stood, half submerged in the deep shadows behind a cabinet. The only light in the room came from the streetlamps outside, but George could see Brown's triumphant smirk all the same.

Dashkova took the final paces towards Brown at a run,

raising her sword. For a moment it looked like Brown was frozen in place, but then...

CRACK. The noise of Brown's fist colliding with the side of Dashkova's face reached George almost at the same time the princess' unconscious body hit the floor. George could only stand there blinking. Brown had moved far faster than he'd given him credit for; the punch was timed to perfection.

Dashkova lay motionless. George had seen a number of fighters felled with blows to the jaw or side of the head like this. Not all of them woke up, and some were never the same afterwards.

He didn't have a choice about what happened next. Neither Black nor Cullen was in any position to go up against their rival and could be minutes away from reaching him anyway. Taking a single deep breath, George began his approach, more cautious than Dashkova's.

Brown watched him with an intense expression, a dog primed to erupt into aggression once the intruder crossed its threshold.

"I'm no' one for hitting lassies...usually," Brown commented without apology. "But if they want tae play a man's game, I'm gonnae treat them like a man."

George wasn't sure what would come next. Would Black want him to offer his opponent a way out? He couldn't see where his sword had fallen, and there was no way to retrieve it without taking his eyes off Brown.

"We want your grimoire, that's all," he said, still out of striking range. "We don't wish violence against you."

"Aww, how kind of ye." Brown gave a mocking bow. "As if what yer doing isnae violence against me already." Brown must know he didn't have much time before Cullen and Black broke into the room.

The two started to circle. Brown kept a hunched position with low fists. His breathing sounded heavy, but that could also be anger. The amount of phlogiston he'd discharged within a few minutes would be considerable; he might not have the reserves for more. But as soon as he did recover, George had no doubt he'd blast him.

George swung. Brown pulled his head back. The counter-punch came in so fast George couldn't do more than raise his hand and drop his chin. Then Brown's second punch followed on the other side. The third smacked into George's ribs with enough force to lift him off the ground. Reeling, he almost tripped over Dashkova.

Brown didn't immediately strike again. He watched George with the same raging-dog intensity, huffing as he moved. George suspected he was waiting to see if his opponent broke and fled. His breathing was ragged, every deep inhalation painful.

Without breaking stride, Brown threw another punch on George's right side. Raising his arm drew a paralysing stab of pain, so George was only just able to roll the punch across his jaw. He let the impact send his body flying. His hip collided with the edge of a table. On the ground, George instinctively curled up, because Brown's foot was coming in for a kick. George rolled awkwardly under the table and out the other side.

He was losing this fight. His right side was out of action thanks to those broken ribs. There was a clinical ferocity to Brown: he'd use George's injury to press his advantage.

George edged around the table, trying to mask how weak he felt.

Brown said nothing. His eyes flickered, calculating. George hugged his right arm to his ribs.

The next blow Brown landed would finish him.

Why was George fighting him? Was it for Pierre, who didn't care all that much about George in the first place? James no doubt died believing the Brunonian doctrine the superior one, perhaps not aware it had killed him. Were any of the dead medical students worth fighting to avenge?

He took in a couple of weak breaths, gasping as the pain in his chest bit into his lungs.

It didn't matter, George decided. Even if the dead Brunonians collectively despised him. Even if Cullen and Black's approval was removed from consideration. Even if he died and no one knew what transpired tonight in this locked room. Brown was in the wrong, and George's principles meant he must oppose him. Doing the right thing was all the fuel he needed.

Brown gave little indication he was about to strike, so George had to hope he would repeat the same attack: head strike on his right. As soon as he sensed movement, George stepped forward, folding his right side inward as his left hand shot out.

Brown's blow blurred his vision for a second, but George had moved fast enough to connect his own. By the time the greyness faded, Brown was crashing to his knees, and George knew he'd managed the liver shot.

Keeping his right side clenched to stem the pain, George landed a second punch to the jaw. Brown toppled all the way to the floor.

Swaying, George started towards the door, but the thought of Dashkova made him pause. He ought to check her. Then he changed his mind and went back to unbolting the door. The two physicians would be able to treat the princess better than he could, and if George got to her first, he might be the one who had to tell the physicians she was dead.

"George?" Black was the first to step through the door. His eyes swept over George, noting his crooked stance, then across to the prone bodies of Dashkova and Brown.

He grabbed George's left forearm and appraised him. "Is

your vision clear? Can you walk unsupported?" Cullen ignored them and made his way to the bodies.

"Yes..." George managed, hoping that if he pressed down hard enough, the pain in his side could be forced out.

"Good work," said Black, touching his forearm briefly and then turning to Cullen.

Cullen looked up from Dashkova's side. He nodded once.

Relief washed into the cracks of George's body still free from pain. Dashkova's blow hadn't been fatal.

Cullen turned his face away, so George couldn't observe his expression. Cullen got to his feet very slowly, keeping his back to the others, until he stood over Brown.

Black was already across the room before George realised what Cullen intended to do.

"William!"

Black reached out and tugged Cullen's robe, trying to break his focus. George dragged himself across the room in a pitiful manner, angry that pain was making him lightheaded. Cullen didn't seem to notice either of them; his gaze remained fixed on Brown. George saw his fists start to work.

"William, look at me," Black was saying, trying to get between Cullen and Brown. "William!"

There wasn't much resistance Black could offer, George remembered, since he too was nursing fractured ribs. He hesitated a metre from his two professors.

"I need you to look at me, William. Concentrate." Cullen's back was still turned on George, so he couldn't see what Black saw in his friend's eyes. Black's tone was blending from urgency into panic.

"The man's caused enough damage, Joe," Cullen muttered, shaking Black off.

"And we don't need to be implicated in his murder," Black retorted. He was still trying to separate his former teacher and his quarry but didn't have the strength. "His patron is still at loose in the city, we've stopped his terrible plan…" Here Black paused to catch his breath. "We can afford to leave it there, instead of acting in anger and being unable to take our actions back."

"Damn it, Joe, we're ending this tonight!" Cullen's hands were glowing white.

It was terrifying to behold, Black and Cullen both tensing to strike. Neither one wanted to hurt the other, but they were desperate and furious enough to stop each other from acting using whatever means remained.

"He'll destroy himself anyway!" George cried out.

The novelty of hearing George raise his voice was enough to halt both professors.

"Everyone will find out what happened here today," George continued, thinking as fast as he could. "His students were defeated. His magic system was tested and it didn't over-come us. They all know about the dead students." He had to stop to take in several wretched gasps of airs, hoping both men would wait to hear him finish. "They know about the dead students and now they've seen their system isn't worth anything against ours." Neither Black nor Cullen responded, so George pushed on. "Time will do the rest."

George wished he had no doubts as he said all this. Who was to say Brown wouldn't rally? That he wouldn't try a new approach? But George knew his fellow medical students. They were attracted to demonstrations of power, compelled like insects to honey. Brown had gained power through adoration by his adherents. Then more students were drawn to that power. He'd lost supporters and respect today—it would take a long time for him to recover.

Black released his grip on Cullen's coat and tried to take his hand.

"Come on, William. The man's unconscious, for God's sake. We can let the city authorities deal with him, or return if he's not learned his lesson. But I'm not letting you act against Brown when he can't defend himself."

Cullen smacked Black's hand away.

"The thing I hate most about you, Joe, is that you're always so damn right about these things." He stormed out.

Black watched him leave, then turned back to George with a shade of his usual coolness.

"We better complete our task and then get Princess Dashkova to safety."

"Is...?"

"Dr Cullen will be fine. Just give him time." Black sighed, but he sounded a lot less furious towards his colleague than George felt. He'd put all his righteousness into those final two punches, and seeing how pitiful Brown looked—little more than a pile of clothes on the ground—took most of his self-sustaining ardour out of him. Enacting revenge on him in this helpless state wouldn't feel earned.

The two men moved as quickly as they could. Black dragged himself from desk to cabinet, stuffing papers under one arm and into his pockets. George did the same, though his attention kept flipping to Brown and any movement he thought he was making.

"We'll burn this when we get home." George supposed Black would inspect the experimental notes before then to see what information the grimoire contained.

Once satisfied they'd gathered everything, George attempted to pick up Dashkova. He nearly dropped her twice, and had to prop the princess against a table before managing to get her over his shoulder and support her without pain consuming him. Black's arms were now full, and the weight of the paper and books was obviously taxing him too.

George didn't wait for confirmation Black was following. He pushed through the door and began the long trek to sanctuary.

29

"There's a problem," Black admitted.

They'd all made it back to Cullen's house. When they arrived, Cullen refused to say anything, locking himself in his study. But Black knew that if Cullen really didn't want them there, he'd demand they leave.

Dashkova was resting on the sofa, a damp cloth over her face. She'd roused of her own accord halfway there and showed no symptoms of stupor. From her description of the pain and the visible bruising, Black hypothesised she'd been hit behind the ear.

To Black, it was detestable that Brown would strike a woman, though he knew that of all the knockout punches Brown could land, one targeted like this was the least likely to cause permanent damage. Right now, Dashkova only complained of incessant tinnitus.

Over by the window, George quaked and gulped. Black scolded himself: he shouldn't distress the poor boy with vague statements.

"What I mean," he explained, "is all these letters and handwritten, bound books are recent copies. Fresh ink, little damage to the paper."

Dashkova groaned and swore.

"We're still missing the original," Black added when George continued to stare at him.

Dashkova muttered something under her face cloth, but it wasn't intelligible.

"We might have to search Brown's property, but I suspect the grimoire remains with its original owner, who wouldn't turn over something so precious to a man like Brown."

Mrs Cullen deftly made her way to Dashkova, hovering at the princess' feet. It was a ridiculous hour of the night, but she'd been lighting candles in the parlour for them when they arrived. She made no reference to her husband's ill temper.

"Your Highness, can I persuade you to take a drink of something? A herbal tonic for your discomfort?"

"Brandy," was Dashkova's muffled response, "would be very efficacious, please."

Anna Cullen paused, then sighed as quietly as she could.

"Yes, Your Highness. I'll bring that at once."

Perhaps listening in, Cullen took this moment to enter the parlour with the pretence of searching for a book or piece of correspondence on his shelves. Black knew his friend was balancing his anger—directionless since he'd been thwarted from inflicting it on Brown—with concern about his injured friends. It was why Mrs Cullen had spent the past few hours serving them generous quantities of tea, soup and sweetmeats. Black was infuriated at Cullen for sulking while he was left to parse through the Brunonians' papers: he had a brutal headache and the pain had settled over most of his body. But Black had to act strong, for it allowed Dashkova and George the security to be weak.

Cullen approached Black in a sideways fashion, as if he were stumbling across the Brunonians' papers by chance. He picked up a few sheets Black had set aside to examine a final time and grunted.

Black continued, "There's someone I think can point us in the right direction. I overlooked them, as I overlooked many things, but a comment Brown made alerted me to their incidental involvement."

"Not another fucking salon," Dashkova growled from the sofa.

Cullen finally spoke. "No, Your Highness. I think we know who has the grimoire." He looked at Black, conveying a knowing expression.

Despite his simmering annoyance, Black's headache and chest pains unspooled. Cullen wasn't good at apologising: the best he'd get was a flip from sulking to pretending he'd never been sulking at all. In a month or two, Cullen should give Black a sincere apology and admit he was at fault, and that would hopefully be the end of it.

It was why Black remained friends with Cullen after numerous quarrels, while Brown became a sworn enemy after one. Black had the patience to wait for Cullen's full apology, and the sanguinity to accept that whatever his first move towards recrimination resembled, it wouldn't contain much contrition.

"It is a suspicion that needs confirmation before we act upon it," Black reminded him. "We have a little bit of time: I suspect Brown will want to lick his wounds before admitting to his patron what transpired."

That was the other reason Cullen and Brown had fallen to irreconcilable enmity: they were too alike in temperament.

Cullen hovered beside the table where Black sat, saying little, fingering the pile of papers. Black thought for a moment.

"There's too many papers to stuff in the fireplace. It's a

calm night—maybe you and Mr Stephens can burn these in the close."

"You're finished with them?" Cullen said. He didn't ask to read them.

"Yes."

Cullen shrugged. "Alright, lad, you can manage to get yourself downstairs?"

The boy nodded and shuffled over to the table, scooping up what papers he could. Cullen carefully piled the bound books. The two disappeared.

Dashkova pulled the cloth off her face and reached for her almost empty glass of brandy.

When Alice entered the room to offer more liquids, Dashkova touched her arm, causing the housekeeper to jump. Dashkova only whispered a few words before sinking back into the sofa. Alice lowered her eyes and tried not to look too pleased at whatever was said.

Black worked himself out of his chair and over to the window. By now he was bone-tired, and he was about to head to the Cullens' guest bed, not bothering to wait until his host was back indoors. In the close he couldn't see much apart from the ruby glow of phlogiston tearing through paper. They probably could have destroyed the material inside, but he thought launching some fireballs into the night would help Cullen release his anger.

* * *

The rest helped. Several days later Black was still in a lot of pain, but being old meant that he always had one pain or another to manage. Ignoring the needling complaints in his side, he descended the stairs to the old anatomy theatre.

He'd stayed at home since the raid on the Brunonians, doing little more than reading to exert himself. When the university and town delegation called, he convinced them his bruised eye socket was a result of bumping a cellar door when he dropped a candle, and that the explosion in the anatomy theatre was easily explainable by simple chemical principles. The Town Guard captain who accompanied the Council chairman scowled because he had no understanding of simple chemical principles—but didn't question Black further, afraid of exposing his own ignorance. The apprehended Brunonians evidently kept their mouths sealed.

He supported himself against the staircase walls, but was able to move at something close to his usual speed.

It was too soon to say what the final outcome would be, but the Brunonians appeared cowed. According to his contacts, Brown hadn't resurfaced. His Masonic and boxing associates hadn't regrouped in his absence, and in his chemistry lectures the Brunonians seemed docile. Duncan sent Black a congratulatory note that morning, claiming he'd delivered three lectures in a row without a Brunonian argument.

Monro, of course, was less effusive. After avoiding Black for several days, he had finally told him—well, he'd told Dr Young to tell Black—that they should speak privately on Wednesday before his anatomy class. Cullen's student Edward had led the clean-up of the new anatomy theatre after Black escaped and Brown's cronies dispersed, anxiously telling Cullen there was no way they could deal with the bullet hole in the ceiling. Today's confrontation was not going to be about that, though.

Black reached the bottom of the stairwell. The door to Monro's theatre was closed, but he knew the anatomy professor spent most of his mornings here and would be inside. Black didn't pause. His footsteps had echoed down the stone stairs; Monro would already know he was standing outside.

Black hauled the door open.

He collided with a wall of putrefaction. Ammonia stung his eyes. Unable to stop himself, Black stumbled against the doorway and retched.

He could hear Monro chuckle somewhere in the darkness.

Black fought the urge to retrieve his handkerchief to cover his mouth. The more weakness he showed Monro, the harder this would be. Instead, he took a few shaky steps into the miasma, letting his watering eyes adjust to the candlelight.

"Now I understand why you did your best to delay this encounter, Alexander."

"You must forgive me seeking what little advantages I can, Joseph. My father was a sombre man—you know that, obviously—but his reminisces of the otherwise unshakeable Joseph Black fainting onto the dissection table at the sight of his first half-opened corpse were one of the rare things that brought him to laughter."

Black heard the dais creak under him. Monro loomed at the centre of the room, next to a corpse covered with a brown sheet.

"The Prestonpans murderer?" He'd thought the man was to hang next week.

"Until three days ago, yes, he was," Monro said. "This is the last day I'll get anything useful out of him; the body is almost too far gone to be illustrative. The flesh is turning blue-green and its texture is entirely too slippery."

Another gagging fit wracked Black. In preparation for this morning's contentious rendezvous, he'd filled up with plenty of bread and milk, which of course played right into Monro's trap.

"There's a bowl on the table to your left if you need to vomit," Monro commented.

Curse Monro and the power of suggestion. Black immediately spun around to find it. Oh well, he couldn't win the confrontation if all his energy went into trying not to throw up.

Monro kept an amused eye on him. "It's nice to be reminded you're a fallible mortal like the rest of us, Joseph."

Black stepped down from the dais, wiping his mouth. His broken ribs ached with the heaving. He was now a few metres away from his colleague.

"I envy the famous Monro stomach. You know why I'm here." It wasn't like Black could back out of this conversation now.

Monro set down his scalpel. "The boy James would have died within the day, no matter who treated him. I don't think you or William dispute that."

"From a moral perspective, I don't think the affair reflects well on you, Alexander." Black did his best to only breathe through his mouth.

"Nothing about Brown reflects well on any of us, you included."

Black snapped his fingers. Every single candle in the room was extinguished.

In the darkness a small voice piped up. "Papa, why did all the candles go out?"

Black swore under his breath.

"They'll be relit in a minute," Monro called back. "Just stay where you are, Alex."

There was a little bit of uneasiness in his voice.

Good.

Black raised a finger. He drew a fiery circle in the air, with a single line cut across its middle. The symbol hung there for just a few seconds, then its glow faded. Black snapped his fingers again and the candles all spluttered back to life.

Monro was leaning with both hands on the table.

"You'll have to teach me that, Joseph. I've not seen it before."

"You saw the symbol I drew. It's the simple fire affinity symbol. But I suspect you've seen its more complex, darker version in recent times."

"Lord Ross," Monro replied without pause.

Black blinked. He hadn't expected Monro to cough up a name so readily.

"He approached me a couple of years ago, asking about dark chymistry symbols. Think he heard rumours about my father. I told him the symbols were dangerous—that was the first thing I said. More to the point, I didn't have knowledge to share. Always knew to keep away from the dark chymistry. Ross knew very little—that was clear in our brief discussion—but he drew something close to the correct dark fire symbol, which made me wonder if he had access to texts."

"Close to correct?"

Monro laughed. *"Well, I'd recognise a true dark symbol by what it did to its surroundings. The fire symbol he drew just sat on the paper, so it can't have been correct."*

Black nodded. *"You've had no further business with Lord Ross?"*

Monro rubbed his temples. Black suspected the extended proculopathy was giving him a headache, even if he wasn't going to admit weakness.

"I'm not the coward you and William like to think I am, Joseph. I wasn't going to help him, and he knew it. I imagine his interest in your chemistry course was his attempt to teach himself."

"Not that it would have given him more insight than he could find in a textbook," Black said, granting Monro the mercy of a normal conversation. "I'll take my questioning directly to him. I appreciate your candour, and doing what you could to dissuade Ross."

Monro nodded. At last his hands were no longer within

grabbing distance of his surgical blades. Black bowed and turned to leave, but he saw Monro had more on his mind.

"I just have one request, Joseph..."

"Yes, Alexander?"

"The boy, George Stephens. Don't you and William steal up too much of his time. It's a rare treat to find a student with a fine surgical head already attached."

Although he said nothing in response, a smile played about Black's face as he headed for the door.

30

"You have no right to be here!" exclaimed Lord Ross, absorbing who was entering his study. "Who let you in?"

"We let ourselves," replied Dashkova, resting a hand on her sword hilt. "Your servants agreed to stay downstairs until we were done." Tonight Dashkova was again dressed in men's attire, but this time her coat and breeches were black. George wasn't surprised at the fact she'd shown up in such an outfit for this mission; that she apparently owned multiple sets of tailored male clothing required more getting used to.

Lord Ross owned a freshly constructed townhouse in St James Square. It was a miserable night for trekking into the New Town: a lashing, cold rain had begun at two o'clock in the afternoon and persisted after sunset. George was grateful the princess permitted his use of her carriage.

Despite trepidation that the night's mission would turn ugly, George watched the servants melt away of their own accord into the downstairs quarters and side rooms. Loyalty to their master proved ephemeral when they caught sight of the visitors' faces.

George kept his hands away from his weapons for now. He

didn't want to spook Ross or make him too aggressive. Though at the moment the man ignored him as a nonentity.

"This is most undignified—Princess Dashkova acting no better than a jack whore! No wonder the Empress tired of you in Saint Petersburg."

"Good evening, Lord Ross." Cullen stepped around George into sight. "I can assure you our business here with you tonight will be as brief as you allow it to be."

Ross may have been taken aback by Dashkova bursting into his private quarters, but the presence of Cullen didn't add to his surprise.

"I'm not so foolish I don't recognise a threat when I hear it, Dr Cullen." Ross remained seated as his desk, affecting calm.

This study was a far more spacious room than residents of the old High Street could enjoy. Bookshelves lined three of the walls. Ross had positioned his desk opposite the roaring hearth.

"Dr Black sends his apologies. He couldn't join us this evening, as he needed to recuperate. Which is unfortunate, really, because he's the most rational of us." Cullen made a leisurely circuit of the study. It was about the size of Black's dining room.

"I don't understand what this is about, sir." Having dismissed Dashkova and George as beneath his regard, Ross focussed on Cullen.

"Of course you do!" snapped Cullen. "This is about the resurgence of dark chymistry!"

"I'm not..."

Cullen was moving away from Ross towards the fire. Dashkova stood in the middle of the room, arms folded and looking sceptical. George slipped right. Ross didn't notice him draw closer.

"You sought Brown's help unlocking the grimoires,"

Cullen insisted. "All he needed to hear was that you intended to make me pay. Brown didn't care how many students fell sick and died in pursuit of that twisted goal."

"If you..." Ross' face began to turn red. He didn't appear flustered or scared in the face of these allegations so much as angry at the disturbance.

"He cared about creating phlogiston vessels more than the other things—that was his way to make the rest of the medical establishment look foolish. You no doubt were interested in the more alluring tricks."

"Will you shut up and let me speak!" Ross demanded with the full force of his aristocratic bearing.

For a moment Cullen was taken aback, perhaps unsure if cutting off Lord Ross was a rudeness too far.

"Thank you," Ross said sarcastically. "Gentlemen, I don't know what your business is with me, and frankly I don't have the patience to find out. Leave now and we'll speak no more of this."

"You deny you have a grimoire in your possession, that you shared with Brown?"

Contempt smeared across Ross' features. "You forget not all of us live in your world of fanciful academic allusions. Speak in a language the real world can understand."

"God damn it, sir!" George roared. "Don't play games with us." An instant later his dagger was at Ross' throat. George turned the blade slightly, enough to cut the skin under his jawline. Ross had been startled by his exclamation, and hadn't the quickness to react.

George's heart pounded, but he wasn't going to check for Cullen's approval.

Ross didn't attempt to resist. If he'd noticed George sneaking closer, he'd presumed he wouldn't dare lay a finger on him. He didn't flinch from the knife still at his throat, but this close, George saw how fast he was breathing. His hands twitched. A single rivulet of blood pooled in his collarbone.

"As I was saying," Cullen continued, "we want to know where your grimoire came from. The one that contains instructions for creating sigils of power, if my meaning wasn't clear before."

"Family possession," was all Ross said. George kept his eye on him—not daring to look away for a second.

"Your late uncle was with the dark chymists, if I recall. Though not a major player." Footfalls suggested Cullen was moving further away from the pair. "I don't imagine you knew about the grimoire's existence until recently."

Ross remained silent. Thanks to Dashkova's prying, George and the others knew Ross' uncle died almost four years ago, and Ross helped settle the estate. They didn't know if the grimoire was bequeathed to Ross or he stumbled upon it, but George supposed it didn't matter.

Cullen's footsteps came closer.

An unnatural expression played across Ross' face. Unblinking, George applied the slightest force to his knife in warning. Ross twitched.

"Brown was a useful fool," Ross said, eyes on the middle distance. "Though 'fool' suggests a likeable or entertaining quality to offset his low intelligence. I loathed that hick. He smelled vile."

"It wasn't clear why a fine gentleman such as yourself would ally with Bruno, and not talk him out of his violent plans. You can't see him as the future of medicine he claimed to be."

"Oh, how I wish he was!" Ross' lip rose in disdain. "With him in possession of that worthless chair, the reputation of Edinburgh's school would be ruined within months. I knew precisely how it would look to everyone else. With any luck the worthless lot of you would be tarnished enough that you couldn't spread your phlogiston doctrines lower into the underclasses than it's seeped already. And if you managed to best him, why, that discredits the Brunonian approach and is fine by me too."

"Yes, Joe reckoned that's what this was about," Cullen said, his voice as bright as if he were matching wits at Dashkova's salon. "I was foolish enough to believe the dark chymists gave up imagining they could hoard knowledge. But the thought of Dr Black teaching you aristocrats the same chemistry he teaches farming boys barely an hour later still rankles you."

George wondered if Lord Ross knew what he was, that he was the kind of dirty wretch learning things only a gentleman should learn. What do I smell like to him? he wondered.

Brown had probably thought Lord Ross would usher the Brunonian doctrines into wider acceptance. Given the contempt with which he spoke of the man, George knew Brown would be bitterly disappointed.

"You know, Dr Cullen, I made the acquaintance of a friend of yours several years ago in Paris, a man of the cloth." George was aware Cullen's footsteps had stopped. Out of the corner of his eye he saw Dashkova frown. "He first recommended John Brown to me; he remembered him as a theology student." Ross' eyes took on a gleeful tint. He was making some kind of threat towards Cullen, and from his appearance George guessed the threat had landed. "Your friend conveyed the warmest wishes towards you, Dr Cullen. Told me he hoped to return to Edinburgh soon."

"I imagine he does," Cullen coldly replied. "Joe and I will be waiting for him."

Cullen's footfalls resumed. George saw his shadow begin to cross Ross' face.

"Hand over the grimoire, my lord, and our business here will be over."

"And if I no longer hold the item in question?" Ross quietly asked.

"Well," remarked Cullen, "we'll burn down your library. Just to remove any future doubt."

The flames in Ross' hearth took on an unnatural bloody hue. Growing in ferocity, they began clawing out of the fireplace up the marble hearth. There wasn't anything on the mantelpiece that could ignite, but the flames were three inches from a painting.

"The thing about phlogistonic fire," Cullen continued in a conversational tone, "is that it's rather hard to control once it's outside the body. Of course, phlogiston's tendency to disperse of its own accord is what makes it safer in the hands of man than bound through sigils...unless it encounters a ready fuel source."

Ross swallowed. One of his hands dropped from the desk onto his knee. George almost missed it. He held his breath until he saw Ross' hand dip into the half-open desk drawer.

"Argh!"

George slammed the drawer shut on Ross' fingers. While the lawyer was swearing and shaking, George pulled it back open and retrieved a pistol.

"Really, Elliot?" Cullen asked, shaking his head as if he were chiding a wayward pupil instead of a man attempting to shoot him.

The pistol was loaded. George took a step back and raised it.

"You might want to move further away, Professor. You'd be surprised how far the contents of a man's head can fly." Not that George wanted to relive the feel of splattered gore on his clothes and face, or how the smell came back to his nostrils like a vengeful phantom when he least expected it. Cullen and Dashkova could probably sense his false bravado, but when

Cullen retreated, it seemed to register with Ross that his life was in peril. He hunched over his injured hand and panted.

"The grimoire, Lord Ross." Dashkova tapped her foot. "Where is it?"

His nearest library shelves were a few metres from the fireplace. Following his gaze, Dashkova walked over to them. She turned to face Ross.

"Third shelf, on the right," Ross managed. "Next to the green-bound volume."

Dashkova reached for it. Neither Cullen's nor George's eyes left Ross.

Ross' red and distorted fingers twitched on the desk. Despite the excruciating pain that accompanied broken fingers, he looked like he wanted to strike out at George or Cullen but was conflicted as to how, or what the consequences would be.

Dashkova flipped through the pages.

"This is it," she confirmed.

Slamming the book shut, Dashkova pressed it between her glowing palms. After a moment's pause, she dropped it into the hearth. The book was already smouldering when it landed, and with a lick of flame it too started to burn.

"And now on to our remaining orders of business," Cullen continued once satisfied the grimoire was consumed. "Which should take up far less of your time. Withdrawing your opposition to Dr Black's laboratory proposal hardly needs mentioning, as you gain nothing from its continued obstruction."

Ross glared and fidgeted, but said nothing. Cullen gave a satisfied grunt.

"If you wish to cooperate further, might I suggest you use your Masonic lodge connections? Bruno is a man of self-importance, pageantry and ceremony. Let him play around in the brotherhood, where he can't endanger students. Consider this a favour towards someone I treated unfairly."

There was only the smallest nod from Ross indicating acquiescence. His pale skin gleamed with sweat.

"Yes? Then we're agreed," Cullen said sweetly. "Very good, Elliot." Behind him, the fire receded back into the confines of the chimney, returning the room to a warm yellow glow.

EPILOGUE

Only a few weeks ago, George knew he would have hesitated at such a task, if he was brave enough to try at all. But now he didn't fear rejection or scorn in quite the same way.

He knocked on Edward's door.

"Oh." Edward was sitting at his table, in a room George noted was more nicely furnished than his own. Or at least, all the furniture's wood and styles matched. Edward looked surprised to see him in his doorway.

"I don't mean to intrude," George began hastily, but forced himself to slow down. "But on Saturday I planned to head over to Duddingston with Prince Dashkov and Thomas, among others"—as if a Russian prince wouldn't be enticing enough company for a man like Edward—"and I—err, we—wondered if you cared to join us?"

Edward stared. George tried desperately not to ramble into the silence.

"We can dine in the village, and I hear Thomas has found a billiards place nearer to us than Leith—"

Finally Edward held up his hand. With some relief, George stuttered to a stop.

"You're asking about my Saturday plans…on a Wednesday morning?"

"Well yes, since I know your plans are shored up on Fridays, usually during clinical rotations," George replied. "I wanted to make sure there was some chance you'd agree."

"Very much so," Edward said, grinning as he turned back to his lecture notes. "This might be the first time this year someone's decided my weekend entertainment for me. Saturday it will be."

* * *

Following the incidents with John Brown, George found the days kept passing and the city plunged deeper into winter. Now it was only a few weeks before classes adjourned for the Christmas holidays. Getting back to normal was a slow process, but every evening he retired to bed with no calamity or peril befalling him meant another spool of tension unwound from him by morning.

As the first anatomy class of December was dismissed, Monro beckoned George to the dissecting table.

"That was a perceptive question you asked about the mandible structure," he said gruffly. "Glad to see your thinking has sharpened."

"Thank you, Professor." Monro had been acting almost as stiff as his cadavers around George the past few weeks, but here was a glimpse of a thawing. George's confidence had shot up the day he worked up the nerve to ask a question in class. Instead of mockery, the other students gazed at him with gratitude, and he realised the question he feared stupid was one they too desired an answer on.

* * *

"There were some matters I wished to raise with you," Black said, gesturing for George to sit with him at the dining table. "One of my esteemed friends approached me for assistance with a rather fascinating chemical project. However, after elucidating further information, I thought you might be better suited for several aspects of the work."

"You're sure, sir?" George had agreed to meet the two professors this evening at Cullen's, before receiving a note from Black insisting George call upon him first.

George noticed three teacups were arrayed next to the pot, suggesting he wouldn't be alone with Black much longer.

"But of course," Black said. "It is not onerous work, or glamorous if truth be told, but for a capable man it might be an opportunity to get his talents noticed by the right people, sharpen his knowledge of practical chemistry and facilitate his involvement in what promises to be a worthy industrial venture."

George was scared to agree too enthusiastically. But from what he knew of Black, the professor had a decent instinct for business.

"If you think the venture worthwhile, I'd be glad to assist. Thank you, sir."

Black began to pour the tea, filling all three cups.

"I advised my friend to wait until summer to begin the project, so it won't interfere with your studies, and maybe"— here Black sighed—"I will have the time to give the chemistry project the attention it deserves."

George assumed the matter was settled and Black knew he was willing to assist. It would save him from thanking the man too effusively.

"The gentleman in question was adamant you receive compensation for the work; the sum I suggested matches your course fees for the winter term." Black was trying not to look too pleased with himself, and George wondered what the private joke at the centre of all this was.

Footsteps behind him told George someone had entered the room. Before he had time to turn and greet the guest, he felt a familiar arm collide with his shoulders.

"Well, well, well," the Earl of Hopetoun said. "I hear from my friends that the incomparable Mr Stephens comes from sturdy country stock. All the better to take in fresh air on the Hopetoun estates surveying rock formations, one would imagine..."

* * *

George and Black stood in a sheltered corner of South Gray's Close. Night was falling and the intensity of the wind was rising, driving most of the close's residents indoors and forcing those out on casual business to lower their gaze and hurry. In less than an hour the rain would begin. No one would see them there.

"I know you understand what proculopathy feels like," Black was telling him, "so we'll start with a basic discharge of phlogiston, which uses a very similar mechanism."

George shivered and unfolded his arms. He swayed back and forth on his feet a few times, surveying the almost empty yard. Cullen would be joining them in a few minutes, he'd promised them. Mrs Cullen had set herself to prepare a beef and barley broth for when the gentlemen elected to come back inside.

"*Is there anything you're uncertain about?*" Black asked gently.

George found his arms had refolded themselves. Black knew he was stalling.

"You're sure it's safe?" George asked, raising his voice slightly over the howl of the wind. He remembered his nausea in the college library, but the thought of repeating that was less scary than the memory of James laid out in Black's dining room.

"While I'm here, nothing is going to go wrong," Black assured him. He raised one arm and held his palm a few inches from George's shoulder. *"I will draw out any excess phlogiston you raise so as not to cause injury."*

George suspected Black didn't need to hover a hand over him and that he could protect him just as easily from several yards away with both hands behind his back. But he appreciated the gesture. He raised his left hand, palm pushed outward into the close.

"Like I said," Black continued, *"just take it slowly to begin with. One, two..."*

* * *

It was much later that night. Rain tapped and tickled the window of Cullen's study, where the two professors sat nursing their drinks. Black with his glass of milk, Cullen sipping wine. George had departed for home hours ago.

"Brown is unlikely to return as a threat, but I fear his backers are casting around for the next pawn," Cullen remarked.

"I imagine they are. They always feared our philosophies would bring about destruction of the natural order of things." Black swirled his milk. "I'm not inclined to wait around for them, though."

"Then what's your recommendation for defeating the all-powerful of this city, Dr Black?" Cullen prodded his friend good-naturedly.

Black gave a thin smile.

"We commence the destruction."

HISTORICAL NOTE

Some of this actually happened. No, seriously.

The personal and ideological conflict between John Brown and William Cullen was very real—though arguably it never got as bad as depicted in my story! The trajectory of their friendship and the events that catalysed its rupture happened much the way I portrayed them here, though the timeline of said events has been massaged slightly in the interest of plot. The eminently readable biography by Guenter B Risse, *Explaining Brunonianism: A Biography of Edinburgh's Master of Conviviality* (2020) brings together the sometimes-contradictory accounts of John Brown's life.

Robert Anderson is the foremost expert on Joseph Black, and his edited *Correspondence of Joseph Black* contains illuminating footnotes and contextualisation to his letters. The appendix contains Black's household accounts, informing me which teas he kept in stock. Today Black is celebrated as a chemist, but in his own time he may have been seen more as a physician. He certainly kept a small but active practice throughout his life. Many of Black's letters are kept at the

University of Edinburgh Centre for Research Collections—they are written in this luscious dark ink.

The Cullen Project is an effort led by the University of Glasgow to digitise Cullen's voluminous medical correspondence. *William Cullen and the eighteenth century world* (1990) also shines a light on Cullen's teaching and medical research.

Andrew Duncan Senior: Physician of the Enlightenment (2010) examines the principled career of Duncan, and casually pointed out that he was a long-time participant in the Beggar's Benison. To the best of my knowledge, the Beggars didn't conduct secret orgies on Tuesday nights...but with a few internet searches you can see for yourself what they got up to in their regular meetings! Just don't use your work computer. *The Beggar's Benison* (2001) by David Stevenson does a good job of separating fact from salacious fiction.

For a scholarly overview of the Georgian era, Penelope Corfield's *The Georgians* (2022) proved helpful. Her 2017 paper *From Hat Honor to the Handshake: Changing Styles of Communication in the Eighteenth Century* delved into the thorny issue of handshakes versus bowing versus hat tipping.

Digging into the details of Georgian life involved *A New and Easy Method of Cookery* (1755) by Elizabeth Cleland, which was more vegetarian-friendly than I expected, and *A Classical Dictionary of the Vulgar Tongue* (1788) for some insults that deserve to return to popular usage.

Social Change in the Age of Enlightenment: Edinburgh 1660–1760 (1994) by RA Houston summarises the political and social forces at work during the decades Edinburgh transformed from squalid medieval town...to squalid capital of the Enlightenment.

The history of the University of Edinburgh and the 'Tounis College' can be found in *Building knowledge: An architectural history of the University of Edinburgh* (2017).

Descriptions of Monro's old and new anatomy theatre layouts were found in the article *The Academy of St Luke, Edinburgh - at work c.1737* by Joe Rock. By 1779, Black was running out of space to hold his classes and forced to share space with other professors while his new laboratory was being built. However, Monro had almost certainly moved out of his old basement anatomy theatre by this point to the new extension. You have to admit, it makes a good setting, though.

A Guide for Gentlemen studying at the University of Edinburgh (1792) tells us what courses students took, and the recommended order of classes. *The Diaries of Sylas Neville* (1950) and letters of Samuel Bard (available online), give us insight into daily lives of medical students and their relationships with Cullen, Black, Monro, Brown and Duncan. Neville was rather shocked when Black sang at a medical society dinner.

Although much of Doctrines of Fire is based on historical research, my goal is to tell an entertaining story, with interesting characters. The Doctrines shouldn't be taken as an accurate depiction of events and real historical figures, and I hope experts of the period will forgive any errors—stylistic or careless—contained herein.

AFTERWORD

Thank you so much for reading *The Doctrines of Fire*. With so many awesome books out there, I'm grateful you chose to pick up mine.

If you enjoyed reading this story, please consider leaving a review on Amazon or Goodreads, even if it's just a sentence. Reviews and ratings are the lifeblood of independent authors such as myself, as they help other readers find the book.

The professors will return in book 2 of The Edinburgh Doctrines series, *A Treatise of Air*.

George Stephens will return in book 3, *The Chronicles of Earth*.

ACKNOWLEDGEMENTS

Early chapters of this manuscript were critiqued by many members of Edinburgh Creative Writers Club. Thank you for your detailed and thoughtful responses to my work—I'm surprised how many of you want to sit next to Andrew Duncan at parties!

The staff at various research institutions have been uniformly helpful with my enquiries and made my long archival forays much more pleasant. These include the National Library of Scotland, the University of Edinburgh's Centre for Research Collections, and the Othmer Library in Philadelphia.

Chunks of this story were written during Writers HQ online retreats, which gave me the structure I desperately needed to bulk out this story to novel length.

John, Jon, Mitko and Andy provided invaluable feedback on early drafts of the manuscript, strengthening *Doctrines* in a multitude of ways.

Thanks to my copyeditor Toby for going through this manuscript with a fine-tooth comb and gently pointing out my deviations from British English. Any remaining grammatical mistakes are my responsibility alone.

My cat Snapdragon has provided stellar leg-warming services and been the perfect writing companion.

I'm lucky to have a family who has supported my writing and asked all sorts of polite questions about my archival research findings and writing progress. Thank you all.

Last of all I must thank my readers, fellow authors and online buddies. I love being part of this 'indie writing community' and enjoy every minute I spend here. I hope you do too.

ABOUT THE AUTHOR

CL Jarvis holds a PhD in chemistry and worked as a science journalist, healthcare copywriter, and medical writer before sitting down to write her first novel. She's held together by cat hair and double espressos, and lives in Edinburgh, Scotland.

To learn more, sign up to her newsletter, or contact her: www.clairejarvis.com.

facebook.com/cljarvisauthor
instagram.com/cljarvisauthor
goodreads.com/clairejarvis
tiktok.com/@cljarvisauthor